Zabor

or The Psalms

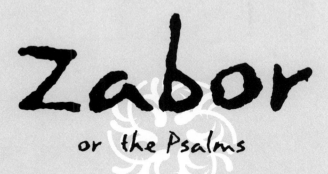

Zabor
or the Psalms

Kamel Daoud

TRANSLATED FROM THE FRENCH BY
EMMA RAMADAN

Other Press
NEW YORK

Production editor: Yvonne E. Cárdenas
Text designer: Jennifer Daddio / Bookmark Design & Media Inc.
This book was set in Centaur MT and Lettres Eclatees
by Alpha Design & Composition of Pittsfield, NH

1 3 5 7 9 10 8 6 4 2

Library of Congress Cataloging-in-Publication Data
Names: Daoud, Kamel, author. | Ramadan, Emma, translator.
Title: Zabor, or the psalms : a novel / Kamel Daoud ; translated from
the French by Emma Ramadan.
Other titles: Zabor ou les psaumes. English
Description: New York : Other Press, [2021]
Identifiers: LCCN 2020030700 (print) | LCCN 2020030701 (ebook) |
ISBN 9781635420142 (trade paperback) | ISBN 9781635420159 (ebook)
Classification: LCC PQ3989.3.D365 Z2313 2021 (print) | LCC PQ3989.3.D365 (ebook) |
DDC 843/.92—dc23
LC record available at https://lccn.loc.gov/2020030700
LC ebook record available at https://lccn.loc.gov/2020030701

TO MY FATHER

Hamidou

WHO BEQUEATHED HIS ALPHABET TO ME

HE DIED WITH SUCH DIGNITY,

THAT HE CONQUERED HIS DEATH.

You write what you see and what you hear with tiny letters squeezed together, squeezed together like ants, which go from your heart to your honorable right side.

The Arabs, they have letters that lie down, get on their knees and rise up completely straight, like spears: it's a writing that coils and unfurls like the mirage, which is clever as time and proud as combat.

And their writing travels from their honorable right side to their left, because everything ends there: at the heart.

Our own writing, in the Ahaggar, is a writing of nomads, because it is all made up of dashes which are the legs of all the herds. Legs of men, legs of meharis, of zebus, of gazelles, everything that traverses the desert.

And then the crosses determine whether you go to the right or to the left, and the periods, you see, there are a lot of periods. They are the stars that steer us through the night, because we, the Saharans, we don't know the way, the way that is guided, in turns, by the sun and then the stars.

And we set out from our heart, and we make bigger and bigger circles around it, to enlace the other hearts in a circle of life, like the horizon around your herd and around yourself.

DASSINE OULT YEMMA,
Tuareg musician and poet,
early twentieth century

ONE

The Body

1

(Outside, the moon is a howling dog, writhing in pain. The night is at its darkest, imposing large swaths of the unknown onto the small village. Someone violently rattles the latch of the old door and more dogs respond. I don't know what to do or whether to stop. The old man's belabored breathing makes it seem as though the walls are closing in, and gloom spreads over the surroundings. I attempt to distract myself by looking around me. On the walls of the bedroom, between the closet and the photo of Mecca, the old chipped paint forms continents, dried-up and perforated seas. Dried-up wadis seen from above. "Nūn! By the pen and what they write," says the Holy Book in my head. But it doesn't help. The old man has no more body, only a piece of clothing. He will die because he has no more pages to read in the book of his life.)

Writing is the only effective ruse against death. People have tried prayer, medicine, magic, reciting verses on a loop, inactivity, but I think I'm the only one to have found the solution: writing. But that means always writing, nonstop, with hardly any time to eat or relieve myself, to chew fully or scratch my aunt's back while very loosely translating the dialogue of foreign films that rekindle the memories of lives she's never lived. Poor woman, she deserves a book of her own that would let her live to be a hundred.

Strictly speaking, I should never again look up from the page, but stay here, hunched and hard at work, focused on my profound motivations like a martyr, scribbling like an epileptic and moaning about the unruliness of words and their tendency to multiply. A question of life and death, of many deaths, to tell the truth, and of all of life. All, young and old, bound to the speed of my writing, to the screeching of my calligraphy on the page, and to that vital precision I refine by touching on just the right word, the nuance that will save them from the abyss, or the synonym that can postpone the end of the world. A form of madness. The many notebooks I must cover in ink. Blank pages, 120 or more, preferably unlined, with a cover, rigid as rock but nimble and with an oily, warm texture so as not to irritate the side of my palm.

(A small cough. Positive sign. The light returns to the room and the body of the dying man appears less gray. A stream of shimmering saliva trickles from his mouth, disfigured by dentures, and rests on his chin.)

I bought so many notebooks, calculating how many to buy based on the number of people I knew or had heard about who were already dying from disease, old age, or an accident: two a day, sometimes ten or more; one time, I bought seventy-eight notebooks at once, after attending a neighbor's opulent wedding (sitting alone on the ground with a horrible plate of meat that I left untouched, indifferent to the wailing music, my body noiseless, ignored by everyone except the groom who wore a ridiculous suit and came by to quickly shake my hand) and staring unabashedly at the many people I had become responsible for, the secret guardian of their longevity. For I was the rower and they the passengers, O my Lord!

The nearest "bookstore"—what they call, where I'm from, those places that sell cigarettes, envelopes, stamps, notebooks, and newspapers—knew me and never questioned my purchases: in the village of Aboukir *(center of the world, situated between my navel and my heart, a few miles from the sea, which is a word that doesn't need conjugations to be infinite)*, they called me the butcher's son, "the one who never stopped reading," and they knew I'd been scrawling in notebooks like someone possessed since I was a child. My father's wealth had to have a consequence and it was me, with my long, hunched body, my eyes like lakes and my ridiculous voice, as though destiny were mocking my father's fortune. The kindest in the village sent me old books found in warehouses, the worn yellowed pages dating back to the time of the colonizers, torn-up magazines, user's manuals for machines that no longer exist or perhaps never did, and, most importantly, those enthralling novels with no author and no beginning because both had been ripped out (bindings maimed, stories skewed with incoherence, orphans I always collect). This chaos was the cornerstone of my universe, and the rest was recorded in notebooks. I was silent and brilliant in school, in the early years. I had neat, meticulous handwriting that served as the veins under the skin of appearance. It certainly helped to circulate a kind of blood.

(Now, I'm at the heart of the ritual. Completely absorbed and devoted to the struggle. I believe in it deeply. Without it, what is my life worth in this place and what are these lives around me? The universe is either a mockery or an enigma. What time is it? Voices. A hand set down a cup of coffee. And water. The face of a drowned person coming back to the surface. The mouth fascinates me. The collapse of the chin, as if death accentuated gravity. The old man is nothing more than a head, skinny shoulders over the sheet that hides him. The rest of his body

6

is nothing more than a blanket with tiger stripes subjected to outrageous contortions—"Everything okay?" I don't respond. The day will soon arrive because the lights curve like sheets of paper in the fire.)

The truth is that they hoped to do me a favor by anticipating my needs, especially when the rumor of my gift spread, covertly. Some, of course, mocked me discreetly and pitied my family for the implausible defect in our tribe's tree; I was a knot in the wood. In truth, they didn't know whether to ignore me or celebrate me. I wrote in a foreign language that healed the dying and preserved the prestige of the former colonizers. Doctors used it for their prescriptions, but so did the men in power, the new masters of the country, and the immortal films. Could it be sacred, descended from on high? No one had an answer, they shook their heads as if faced with an old marble idol or as when they passed near the French cemetery, to the east. The village was not big and its conversations were rarely secret.

I liked that label, "the one who was reading" or "the one who read." A definitive formula, getting at the essential, which is to say the Holy Book or Knowledge. They said it with gravity, contrition, they respected the power. In our country, reading was conflated with domination, not the deciphering of the world, it meant at once knowledge, law, and possession. The first word of the Holy

Book is "Read!"—but no one asks about the last word, the devil's exhausted voice whispered to me. One day I had to decipher that enigma: the last word of God, the one he had chosen to initiate his spectacular indifference. The exegeses never mentioned it. We were always hung up on the Last Judgment, not on the final word. I also wondered why the injunction was made to the reader, and not to the writer. Why the first word of the angel wasn't "Write!" It was a mystery: What is there to read when the book has not yet been written? Are we meant to read a book that's already before our eyes? Which one? I'm getting sidetracked.

So I bought the notebooks as I counted again, eyes closed, body calm under the gnarled vine of our courtyard, at the hour of the siesta, all the people I had met the day before in our village, which I mapped like an island. One by one, meticulously, like coins. Arranging them on the shelves in my head with numbers and letters and features and names and their tribe. Without letting myself get distracted by the clouds, or by the season's gentle heat that was transforming the blood under my skin to sugar, or by the few planes that emphasized the silence of the sky. I liked this exercise, preceded by stretching, lengthening both my body and the entire firmament with my arms. Unfurling the wings of Poll, perched on his coconut trees. Because, at certain inspired hours, I imagined myself in the form of Poll the parrot, responsible for a sumptuous racket in the tropics, a bird with an exceptional, civilizing destiny on an unknown island. I had stolen this name from a book written in the eighteenth century that tells of a shipwreck, an encounter with a supposed cannibal, and the history of solitude. *(Memory of summers I spent in a delicious convalescence with my permanently mute grandfather. Rediscovering things, desires, after a series of horrific migraines. A quick glance to gauge the return of life in the pebble of his body. His face still vacant, mouth open, but I glimpsed a tear. He's not crying. It's the automatic response of the eye combating dryness. I've always loved the word "retina" because it looks like a melting pot, the site of all possible sunrises.)* But it was slightly painful to always have a number associated with a face. It was difficult for my memory, at the beginning. Sometimes the faces of familiar people flattened new ones or stole features from them, their hair, the shape of their eyes. Rendering the inventory danger- ous and my gift a bit myopic. And when I tried to fix a face and immobilize it like a bird in my hands, it would deform maliciously. For nothing is more anonymous than a face we've stared at for too long. Even those of the people closest to us. But over the years, I've become agile: I've replayed the film in my head, scrutinized the details, recited the names to put an end to the scramble and firmly reorganize the genealogies, the filiations and kinships. Like the strict leader of a scattered tribe. Then I invented stories to perpetuate their lives, chosen from a long list of books I would have liked to read at one time or another in my adolescence. This was my method. The only one I had found to overcome the rarity of books in the village, and my boredom, and also to give solemnity to my notebooks. Why did I do it? Because if I forgot someone, they would die the next day. Simple as that.

I verified it countless times. It's my mute malediction. The law of my life that no one knows. I'll say (write) it: When I forget, death remembers. Confusedly, but abruptly. I can't explain it, but I feel bound to the Reaper, its memory and my own are connected like two vases: when one empties, the other fills. Well, that's not quite right. Rather: when my memory empties or wavers, death proves firm, recovers its sight like a raptor, it nose-dives and depopulates the village before my eyes. A matter of equilibrium but also, perhaps, the enactment of a law I have not fully deciphered. Similarly, when I remember lucidly and use the right words, death is blinded once more and turns back around in the sky, grows distant. Then it kills an animal in the village, attacks a tree to the bone, or gathers insects in the surrounding fields, to the east, to munch on while it waits to regain its sight. I love describing death thus disoriented. Confirming both my gift and its usefulness.

It's not about magic in the ancient sense of the term, but the discovery of a law, a sort of revived correspondence. Writing was invented to stabilize memory, that's the premise of my gift: we don't want to forget because we don't want to die or see others around us die. Writing came into the world so universally because it was a powerful way to counter death, and not just an accounting tool in Mesopotamia. Writing is the original rebellion, the real fire stolen and shrouded in ink to keep us from burning ourselves.

What happens when I sleep? Perhaps God keeps watch as a referee in this game. It's death's dead time, in a way. All I know is that I have to count the people I meet during the day or at night, buy notebooks according to their number, and then write before I sleep, or at dawn or even the next day, write their stories full of names and follies, or obsessively describe every place in the village—pebbles, rusty iron, roofs...Writing, simply, is in itself a method of healing those around me, a form of preservation. Another detail: between my forgetfulness and the last breath of someone near, I have a grace period of three days; I like to believe in it to maintain my discipline. I can delay writing about a person by three days, never more.

It's been like this for years, and now I understand the rules of the game, I've established rituals and ruses and reached the formidable conclusion that my mastery of the language, this language I've fabricated, is not only an adventure but above all an ethical obligation. Nailing me down to the village, forbidding me to leave the territory. Does this make me sad? Of course not! There's a form of martyrdom in my practice, to be sure, but also a sliver of silent satisfaction. Of all my family, I am the only one to have glimpsed the possibility of salvation through writing. The only one to have found the way to endure the absolute futility of places and the local history, the only possible restorer, the commissioner of our exhibition before the eyes of God or the sun. All my cousins, kin, and neighbors unknowingly run in circles, sink into despair as they grow older, and end up marrying young and bingeing until they're sick. The only consolation in their fate is somnolence, or the paradise after death that they populate with their dreams by repeating the verses that describe it as verdant and licentious. I am the only one to have discovered a crack in the wall of our beliefs. I am proud of it, I have to say, vigilant about the vanity that threatens me, confident faced with the winds. Searching for the right words, writing until I force objects to become consistent and lives to have meaning, it's a gentle magic, the culmination of my tenderness.

I am nearly thirty years old, I am single and still a virgin, but I have triumphed over the fate that awaits us all in these pitiful places. The only escapee. Of course, I've loved two or three young girls, including Djemila the mute, whom I still await and to whom I speak with scarce words that she doesn't understand, but my sexuality has slowly shifted to a greater need than procreation. Because of my body or my reputation, I've never been able to satisfy my desires in this tiny village, and my need to be embraced surpassed my yearning to bounce around in another body a long time ago. It no longer needs a pretext or a cannibalistic prop for its kiss. A true romantic, I flourish in the immense expression of compassion, beyond the few seconds of oblivion that orgasm typically offers. I think this accurately sums up my fate. At nearly thirty years old, I don't devour my children, as people claim, I save lives, I prolong them until they reach universal relief. I'm not sterile, but solitary orgasm has allowed me to attain a sort of freedom, it's opened my eyes. I know it's illusory to think you can possess the other, and in this need there lurks a deception of the gods. I sense above all that the body of another is a diversion. I've loved and desired, but books have opened other doors for me. The devil, Iblīs, is not the one who provokes desire, I think, but the one who cheats it by offering subterfuges. The true orgasm is a threat to him, I'm sure of it, it amounts to his defeat. I'm getting off topic.

Today, here, at this very moment, I lift my eyes to the walls, then beyond the window to the entire property, my own, of the world. The hill up top, where the old dying man lies, perhaps a woman who placed her head on my shoulder. Touching the warm earth, when I walk through the fields, provokes a sensual chaos in me. I swear. I know the mechanics of orgasm, but dispassionately, as when one visits a museum alone, at night, after the doors close. Years ago, I came to vigorously possess each angle, each shadow that works the hands of the clock under the steps of passersby. Even the vast night obeys one or two words that can enclose it within my sumptuous definition. I can write the word "starry" and all the ink of the sky stains my hand, climbs up to my shoulder and my eyes. The night sky is a glittering fleece. God gave me immense power. Or perhaps I stole some of his, lying in wait in this little village he doesn't know exists. Well, I only wanted to say that when I write, death recedes a few feet, like a timid dog baring its teeth, the village remains in good health with its few hundred-year-olds (thanks to me), and we don't have to dig any tombs on the western side of our hamlet, as long as I attend to synonymy and metaphor. *(Exhumation.)* It's a miracle that's been happening for a long time, since my tormented and ridiculous childhood, but I've kept it secret. Not out of modesty or fear, but because telling the story might interrupt the writing and provoke death. And I would be responsible.

I knew I had to keep quiet about the details of this struggle between me and decay or degrading illness and gather my strength in a sort of invisible abnegation for my aunt Hadjer, for my father, and for the rest of the village inhabitants running in circles around the siphon of our cemetery in Bounouila, to the west. But I also didn't want to attract the anger or jealousy that all gifts provoke. *(I'm hungry, but it's indecent to eat next to a dying person, right? And here, I know, they'll only serve me meat that's still moaning.)* The village gendarmes might be receptive to accusations of heresy or sorcery that have become commonplace in this day and age. I had to write, not talk. Fast and well. Firmly, like a guide. In the village, few knew how to read despite the State's efforts. There were numerous schools but the schoolchildren were still young compared to the older generation born before Independence. The secret was safe up to a certain limit. In one or two generations, they would surely grasp the meaning of my betrayal and hunt me down. Or idolize me. The ones I had to fear were the imams, the reciters of the Book, and the fervently religious who essentially lived in the mosque in the center of Aboukir. In fact, what was it that God said?

> As for the poets, they are followed by the lost.
> Do you not see that they wander aimlessly through every valley...
> and say what they themselves do not do?

The concern is that I wasn't sufficiently versed in that language to defend myself against attacks, I was neither a doctor, nor a former schoolboy of France, nor an engineer from Bridges and Roads. I was something of an anomaly, with a gift from God, who spoke in a language other than the sacred language. What could they do with me? They ignored me or greeted me with their heads down. My father was too rich for them to exile me, but my story was too troublesome—not interpretable through any verse—for them to declare me blessed and useful. I wasn't stupid, only discreet, envied and cast aside. Anyway.

A man who says he writes to save lives must be somewhat crazy, megalomaniacal, or so distraught by his own futility that he tries to counter it with idle chatter. I'll never be able to prove it, but I can at least recount how I came to be convinced. (*Exhume. It's obvious to the naked eye: scraps, handfuls of night fall at the bottom of the bed, in shovelfuls or in the form of cockchafers. The tombstone turns back into a pillow. All the weeds retract into printed cloth, the fabric of the slippery blanket with its tiger stripes that have turned to scribbles. At the bottom of the hole, the old man has the body of a child with withered legs. My hand moves faster over the notebook and it's a way of removing even more dirt, of pushing aside the pebbles. The paper is almost wet, with sweat or leftover rain. It smells like peat. Why do I feel nothing in this man's presence when I've been talking to him for years in my head, every night? Why?*) I know that I'm responsible for the increase in the number of hundred-year-olds in our village, it's not because of the food that's become available since Independence. I know I delayed their deaths by describing, at length, the powerful eucalyptus trees and the patient nesting of storks on our minarets, or even the walls; I know that my notebooks are discreet counterweights and that I am connected to the work of God. We can pray to him while looking him in the eyes and not only while bending our spines. Enigma of my own life, born to conjure and repel the most ancient power in the dark workshop of my head. What more is there to say? My real name, perhaps (*I should have started with that, the story of my name*): Zabor. Not the name my father gave me, suggested flippantly, I'm sure, while he was sharpening knives or butchering his hundredth sheep of the week, but my real name, born of the sound of my poor child's head thumping on a stone floor when I was violently pushed by my half brother, behind our house at the top of the hill, before he lost his balance in turn and toppled into a dry well. Later he claimed that I had deliberately fallen to kill him, and this lie changed my life. I was four years old and I still have the long scar, from my right eyebrow to the top of my skull, the memory of the sky turning into a white hole, my screams, the rope my aunt Hadjer threw to me to pull me up while crying all the tears in her dry body. My secret name reverberated for a long time like metal, echoed and then dissolved into a repetition of two syllables: "Za-boooooor," while the blood was dripping into my eyes and nose. When I wrote it for the first time, at about five years old, I discovered the bond between the sound and the ink, the incredible kinship I dreamed about later, inventorying everything in our village. I didn't know the phrase "table of contents," but I think that's the primary essence of language: to keep a record of the possible. A strange mirror, my own name, it was like discovering my spirit animal or hanging from the branch of a very high tree. Like an ancient coin

I was turning over in my hand. Even so it took me years to arrive at two critical moments of my life: discovering the Law of Necessity and writing my own name, alone, without anyone's help, hand trembling over the turns of the vowels, squeaking into the dry snow of the notebook. When that was done, I remained silent in the universe of my pink room, stupefied by the immense viewpoint now offered to me.

I knew from that moment on that I could leave my aunt's side to go to the bathroom without fear, at night or during the day, wash myself without dissolving into the siphon, stare for a long time at a stranger or an animal without the rush of vertigo. My fear of cockroaches waned and I stopped shamefully wetting my bed. "Zabor" was my first word, it put an end to a wailing in my head, and from that moment on I started to look at the objects around me with the idea of inventorying them. That illumination exploded the boundaries, it promised to attenuate the sensation of powerlessness I felt at all times. It inspired me to reflect on memory and the ways we can summon and master the invisible and the shadows. My second discovery would come later, when I shifted from the idea of the possibility of writing everything to the idea that it was a secret mission, a duty. But, as a child, this was all intuition, I didn't yet understand my destiny, its cost and its reward. I said "Zabor" in my head and I was a center again, a fascinating distinction. I could name myself and, abruptly, I was revealed to myself, in the immense mirror of my family's blathering. I don't know how to describe the joy I felt, along with a painful sensuality.

No one in our house knew how to read or write, not my grandfather who was now relegated to torpor and mastication, nor my aunt Hadjer with the brown skin who raised me like her own son, and it was impossible to explain to them the importance of my discovery. I was the first of the blood universe of our tribe to be bestowed with an incredible, exalting gift. I remember, even in my first weeks of school, I welcomed writing, with the first letters of my secret name and the Arabic alphabet, as a perfect opportunity for concealment and reveries.

But, at five years old, my chest was too tight for the sensation and I collided with the limits of language: I had just discovered something vital, and paradoxically I couldn't tell it to others! It stopped me short in front of my aunt Hadjer, who was napping in the other room, lying on the tiles to cool off at the end of that infinite summer, around September in my memory. Hadjer *(kept alive by a story: a woman who, after watching so many romantic films, can now speak all the languages without understanding a single* word of them and who saw it as a curse. *She ends up losing her own words, her language, and becomes the silent film she once saw years ago. Voiceless before her fate. Several notebooks with a single stolen title:* The Changed Face. *My aunt is small and dark, lively, on the alert, as if hunted. I've never seen her sick, pensive, or made up—except for one time. Yet she is the one who awakened my senses, discreetly, with her long and abundant black hair, which she combed the way one crosses a river, and her sweaty summer armpits. All the bodies of women in books had stolen some of her, or imitated her body in a game of mirrors that embarrassed and disturbed me. She is the youngest of my aunts, they called her "la petite," I think. She likes soccer matches, oddly, big-budget films and Bollywood, land of songs, of star-crossed lovers, of wild buses and dancing for no reason)* was still, her dress hiked up over her bare thighs, sleeping as she squeezed imaginary pebbles in her palms, so angry did she appear, even as she napped.

When, shaking a loose sheet of paper with the clumsy writing of my name, I tried to wake her up to show her my new skill, the vague possibility of not dying, she grunted and turned toward the wall. And I remained there, in the middle of our hallway, at the door to her bedroom, watching her body shunned by suitors, lying half on the ground and half on a sheepskin, worn out from household chores and from caring for her mute and impotent father. In the house, everything was the same as before and simultaneously everything was suddenly prone to chaos if I didn't get to work. I had just realized that writing a name is like a window, but that it doesn't make the wall disappear. Now I'm going too fast. (*The old man's breathing accelerates and he might die because of me. I like to sense the night and its cadences behind the walls, but tonight it's spoiled by morbid murmurs. The whole family must be there, acting as a screen between me and the cold stars. The smell of couscous, which for me is the smell of death, infiltrates and mixes with the smell of acidic agony, medications, and fetid flocks of sheep.*)

The truth is that my father saddled me with a thousand ridiculous names to mock me and distance me from his affection. He called me "the crippled freak" because of my knee and my gait, "the cripple," often "the puppet" because of my fainting spells, and so on. A thousand names that I could ward off, as a child, by reciting in my head the only valid name, my own, whenever he addressed me, stared at me for a long time, or wanted to show his friends that he expected nothing from me and that I was more of a defect than an heir. Zabor! (*Someone breaks a plate, I think, in the courtyard. A woman cries or coughs. It's one of his daughters, tied up in gold jewelry since her childhood.*) Years later, old and musty (*I'm twenty-eight years old, to be exact, with no children, only the name of a neighbor to address my discourses on love to*), it led me to that critical, extreme moment, to the summit with rarefied air where I write *(perched in a coco-nut tree, while a storm threatens the entire island and its methodical language, its indexed forms, its patient tools squandered by an English shipwreck)*, head bent over my notebook, barely looking at the dying man sprawled to my right. It took me years to get here, seated, silent, surrounded by the wary respect of the old man's sons and wives, all piled up behind the door, waiting for me to finish bringing their elder back to them like a swimmer. All there, on the beach of fake sand, skeptics and believers mixed and gathered through fear of death, hoping against all vanity that I would be able to repeat the rumored miracle. Even the eldest son, Abdel, brought up to hate me as a rival, who has controlled the old man's flocks since his childhood. A triumph of virtuosity, Zabor attentive to the words that come, passionately scribbling to strengthen his breath and save it from the temptation of dying to escape the pain. Yes.

(It's almost three in the morning, the night is hot and blows on the necks of the dripping black eucalyptus trees. A rumbling makes the earth pitch like sensual hips, unleashes its powerful perfumes, and clinks the fruit together, but I remain disciplined and serious.) There were twelve notebooks with black covers left, each 120 pages, piled up in a secret order, to my left, near my black bag. Pens too, to stave off death. I had plenty of titles for

these notebooks. *(For the first I choose* In Dubious Battle. *It's fitting. It has the sculpted form of a man strangling a lion on a hill. It's flared and muscular, sweating and severe. The lion knows it will die but that death renders it eternal. Where did I see that? I also have the title* Starship Troopers, *or* Castle to Castle—*the biography of a pedestrian.)* The notebooks? The people of the village bring them to me from all over, preparing pens for me *(fine point, black ink)* to save their kin when, desperate, let down by medication, the reciters of the Holy Book, and the doctors who barely speak to them—out of spite, or overwhelmed, or for lack of a common language—they turn to me, begrudgingly. It's never easy, in their universe, to believe that I could save a life and banish death by writing something other than their verses and the ninety-nine names of God.

What to believe, if life was not a trial imposed by a god who spoke only our language, but instead the conjugation of a foreign verb, come from the sea, that managed, in the hands of the village idiot with a goat's voice, to restore breath to the wounded, to the sick children in the grip of fevers, and to the hundred-year-olds roaming the village streets in great numbers, with the blissful smiles of newborns? What to think of God, if he expressed himself in a foreign language? Or a Holy Book that was no longer the only one? I could feel and

unfurl their contradictory sentiments, toned down out
of fear of contradicting me or making me run back to
my room that I rarely came out of, only at night, to
walk, sometimes smoke and sit under the streetlights
and make strange calculations with my fingers. What to
conclude then, in that universe where faith and hope were
rivals, each with its own idiom and its own calligraphy?
I needed patience and discretion if I wanted to triumph
here, in this very room, seated on this wooden bench, in
this contrite posture, leaning over this notebook turned
gray as a cloud, cottony and filamentous, with its beautiful title stolen from a book I had never been able to find.
I had been feverishly spinning the same gray and white
yarn, slightly dry and with its habitually musty odor. For
years. In the end, it would give rise to a notebook, not a
rug. But with the same underlying pattern.

2

They summoned me after the Isha prayer, knocking on our door. The night was still young, scattering the first stars over the trees that had only barely cooled with a deceptive flippancy. Car engines could be heard in the distance, along with the voices of neighbors. The eldest of the old man's sons, Abdel, the favorite born of an ill-formed love, was there, lowered head balanced uncertainly on his dry body, wrapped up in a djellaba. I know him better than he thinks: he draws all his strength from a permanent anger against the world of the village down below. Why such anger? Perhaps because he knows he's guilty, a usurper, a thief of something whose name he's forgotten. *(I digress.)* Perhaps because of what his mother has repeated to him about me since his birth. Abdel has had to guard the flocks all his life. He knew it from his earliest years, mandated by his mother who feared losing control over the fortune, and driven by his desire to be the old man's only son. I don't think he had a childhood, really, especially when compared to my indolence that lasted nearly twenty years. He turned serious at an early age, keeping accounts of everything, fastidious, angular and incapable of smiling because he was in constant fear of the sheep falling ill, storms, or calculation errors. Strangely, his face sort of resembled mine—same age, same skin—but it was pierced by an intense, black stare. He was the shepherd of many of the old man's flocks and knew the village's surroundings and pastures, the grasses and the far reaches, better than anyone else. But that's another story. (*I keep him alive unbeknownst to him, writing his story in my notebooks. His bears a title I've thought about for a long time, found at the end of a novel, on one of those "forthcoming" pages that have always fascinated me. His notebook is called* The Magic Skin. *He is a traveler obsessed with his own shoes who sees nothing of the rest of the world.*) We share a father and an old story that tells of how I almost killed him by pushing him down a well. A false and scandalous story, according to Hadjer, who remembers my head wound: he's the one who said it, incited by his mother, and that was why I was banished from Hadj Brahim's house for the second and final time in my life. My stepmother, cheeks scratched and voice hysterical, threatened the worst if I stayed, and my father's solution was to buy a colonial house down in the village. He used it to hide his spinster sister, his own father who'd turned into a dead branch, and his undesirable son with the goat voice, who could be slaughtered by an insistent gaze. A simple solution. I didn't push him. Hadjer swore it to me so many times that now I believe it. I remember only Abdel's snickering and his facility with the sheep who obeyed him even though he was only four years old. Like me. No, I never pushed him into a dry well. God didn't punish me. There was blood on his face and on a rock. Birds taunted from up in the eucalyptus trees and it was beautiful out.

I knew that, out of false modesty and real spite, he would never come knock on our door except on the day of the end of the world. And even then, he would settle, as he did earlier tonight, for shouting our family name. In the traditional way. So this was my moment! The moment of destiny. "Which is worth a thousand years to a human," says the Holy Book. The night when a god descends from the sky that is the most accessible to the voice and prayer, the only one we can see before death, and sometimes responds. I had replayed that scene so many times in my head that its imminence made me dizzy, canceled out gravity. Abdel and his brothers must have been in dire straits to ask for me after so many years of jeering laughter and gobs of spit at the mere mention of my name. In my room I was reading an old book about the meaning of the patterns of our ancient rugs when suddenly I felt a weight in the hollow of my chest and then palpitations after I heard my name repeated on the other side of the wall like a bark. It wasn't the first time I'd been called in the middle of the night *(evil has always been nocturnal, the night is an ogress that eats her children and tells them tales)*, but this time it was the voice of adversity and the moment was so important I had to gather all my strength. I'd been waiting for this for years. Yes. "Write!" thundered the Angel in my pink room.

My aunt Hadjer played ignorant, hidden behind the panel of the door. "Who? Who are you asking for? Why are you here so late at night?" she yelled, perfidious. She had rehearsed the devious rituals of her vengeance: make the client wait, make him think I was not going to answer his solicitations, force him to beg, to promise two sheep, eleven geese, honey, ask forgiveness or flaunt his despair to the point of humiliation. The village is two-faced, they didn't want her hand but now they ask for my writing. Hadjer never learned to read, but very early on she sided with my gift against my father, my half brothers, and their slander. Out of vengeance, yes, but also out of calculation, which turned to tenderness, then love. I suspect her motivations, but I love her. She decided years ago, wrapping her scarf around her head and rolling up her sleeves, that there was a link between her fate and my slobbering fits, and that bound me to her. I think her loyalty stems from a childish desire, the solidarity of the marginalized, solitude, and, I realized later, a desire for emancipation that she thought could be satisfied through my madness for reading and writing. She could never speak French but she enjoyed learning the few words that she rolled like rocks in her mouth when she wanted to imitate me, mocking, mischievous. Her love for Hindi films had a lot to do with it, because I translated entire scenes of dense and sometimes indecent dialogue for her. The saraband of actors' bodies was enough for her general comprehension but she wanted details about their conversations, their declarations, their secrets.

Hadjer then opened the door suddenly and stared, with evil eyes, at the beggar in the darkness. She examined him from head to toe before deciding to call for me. I rarely leave my room, and I always lock the door behind me. Hadjer would never let a stranger enter, but it's safer this way. The end of the world for me would be the day they steal my notebooks and scatter them in the streets, in the wind, as when school lets out for the summer. Names made public, genealogies reduced to pebbles, slow and powerful descriptions of the world turned to sprigs of tea in the fields, clinging to bushes. A dispersed encyclopedia, a universal cataclysm. I dread that potential dislocation of my language, which would reintroduce epidemics of death and threaten the lives of all the villagers. Arrogance? Of course not! It's a simple fact.

At a certain point in my life, sure of my gift, I almost didn't read anymore. I reread or I got hung up on collecting the titles of forthcoming books. A register I presided over as secretary and guardian. When I wanted to, I held the entire village like a translucent marble, backlit between my index finger and my thumb. Pen in hand, I could make miracles and heal illness with the titles of books I had never written. *(At night, the village is empty and its walls squeeze around the electrical lines as around a cold fire. Everything is yellow, with swarms of impassioned insects and tousled trees that try to flee into the finally open sky, abandoned to intrusions. The air is a little cold despite the season. It must come from behind the hill, from the north, like the storks, the trucks, and the names of other cities and villages. Dogs mark the borders with their barking, to the east, and harass the early risers. It's the season of swollen, dusty bunches of grapes. To the west, the cemetery cloisters the world with its stones and its verses.)*

I left with my death-defying supplies and I walked behind Abdel without saying a word. Hadjer followed me with her eyes, lingering on the doorstep for a long time, immobile. I understood that she was hesitating over whether or not to accompany me: she feared for me, but there was no one to watch over our house and our meager possessions in her absence. Perhaps she thought that her intrusion into the brotherhood risked ruining my chances to finally be admitted. There was bitterness in the air but also agitation, fear. At night, the storefronts of closed shops made the village look as if its eyes were shut. There are no more houses, the storefronts and the windows turn to eyelids. I walked blindly. The sky, hazy and diaphanous, like an open palm over shiny stones. "Then, look again and yet again: your look will come back to you humiliated and weary," says the Holy Book.

They were all there, in the end, the half brothers. At the top of the narrow street, lying in wait like cattle thieves, mixed together by the shadows of angles. In the night, I smelled the odor of animal skin and the flock. The fragrance of money for our people, a sign of riches and roots. I didn't greet them, only a nod of the head, for behind me Djemila's window was open onto the dark interior of an old colonial house. Because of the heat, surely. Or insomnia. My agitating voice has a reputation and I wanted to spare myself the ancient grimace of my tribe. I know each face, I've noted their features in my notebooks, their habits and their tics. They followed me, walking behind me as if to signal their wariness, hoping to make it clear that they weren't involved in my business. Abdel at the head, fiery and nervous, playing the leader as his mother taught him. I guessed his thoughts: this night could be my vengeance, but there's an even greater possibility that it will be my final humiliation. He doesn't know how to read or write but has the mean instinct of those who feel deficient because of it.

"How are your children?" he snarled without looking at me as we walked down the last side street toward the hill. He knows I don't have any. His brothers didn't react to the jibe. I saved their lives, all of them, one by one, years ago, and they have no idea. *(Forgive them, O Lord, for they know not! Their notebook is called* History of the Thirteen. *Because of their brooding band, like a conspiracy at a medieval inn. It takes place during a cease-fire, a man recounts. Each of the twelve brothers bears the name of a planet that spins around the village.)* Idlers who, when they sit in a circle at the end of the day, near the central mosque, give the unfortunate impression that the universe serves no purpose, that it's nothing but a game of marbles and names.

We had crossed the main street of the village before heading toward the hill, passing behind the central mosque, where the imam and the reciters live. There, the slope becomes abrupt. The red-tiled houses silently followed us. On the sidewalks, empty packs of milk and wrappers. No moon, though the sky was waiting for it like a medallion. At one moment, an ancient breeze tried to stir the branches and the trash but it gave up; it fell back down into the dead, dry leaves. The walls stayed there, accompanying us, leaning against each other. Higher up, colonial houses are rare and the village scatters like a flock. I was running out of breath, halfway up the slope, because I'm frail with small lungs. I started to sweat. We were "like the damned following each other to the precipice," murmured my inner dog *(O faithful companion hated by our religion that doesn't know what to do with dogs, celebrate them as guardians or banish them because they chase away the angels, inspiration for my writing, my private animal, the first drawing of my childhood and the invisible toy of my earliest boredom. I've devoted three full notebooks to it under the stolen titles of* A Many-Splendoured Thing, Tropic of Capricorn, Five Weeks in a Balloon. *Nearly all of the Tradition and the Prophet's Hadiths were written by a single man, Abu Hurairah, the*

man who raised a kitten. I imagine him sitting, caressing the sweet
animal for forty years, using it to stay connected to the world. My
own cat is a dog and my tradition is new). Even in these rather
inauspicious moments, the dog chatters away in my head,
inspired by each detail, reciting entire passages of books
I've read, proposing various titles and indecent passages.
After the last public streetlight, the road transforms into
a path, marking the territory of the douar dogs and the
pebbles that try to bite with their single canine. I turned
around, I saw the houses shrink in the darkness and turn
their backs to us, ebbing toward the bottom of the hill.
They're unpainted, unfinished, not like the houses occupied by the colonizers. The brothers behind me could
have thrown me into a ravine, no one would have accused
them because there were no witnesses at that hour. In the
Holy Book, the story of the jealous brothers ends well for
their victim, but in life things are different. Sometimes
God lacks inspiration…

3

The old man's sickness had been known for months, but it had taken him an incredible amount of time to bend his knee to the ground. Out of pride, because he couldn't accept it, he who had survived the colonizers, hunger, and exile. He was a man who told everyone that, in a dream, God had promised him fortune and countless flocks. A man terrorized by the void, who tried to ward it off through abundance. I didn't want to feel affection or remorse. Especially not now. The ink must be cold and somber to better describe and scribe. The old man's hour had come knocking and his leaf would soon fall (*"for the cosmos is a tree, souls are birds* and lives are leaves, fruits are stars and time is a painstaking autumn," says the dog in my head). Yes.

But it wasn't easy for me. I had been waiting for this moment for so long that I enriched it with too many details and lines, too many quips and pauses. The most important novel of my life, turned extravagant like false sorrow. And now it was sagging like a trestle stage. Hurrying with the dying man's sons, I felt nothing more than the physical effort of the climb, and the indecent desire to caress the old walls or sit down to survey the fire coming with the dawn, to the east, behind the French cemetery. The faces of my half brothers were hidden, indecipherable. Rolling tombstones. What did they feel? To whom would the defeated grumbler grant his blessing and his inheritance? The old man had twelve reasons to die before dawn. Thirteen, counting me. What were they? Bitterness, impatience. Perhaps, but not only. I longed for his death so I could finally breathe fully, feel the vertigo of freedom. We walked like a flock, the muffled sound of our boots in the sand. Someone coughed, a smoker, no doubt. There was nothing left of the village except the distant, feeble tree trunks. We were in a rush to eat our father. I started to think of the winds I've always hated *(the Prophet tells us not to insult the wind, for it's a sign of the spirit)*, it's my first memory of the house where Hadj Brahim abandoned us, me and my mother, far to the south of Aboukir. Behind the imaginary Sahara (I called it Sarah when I was a child, so I'm told by Hadjer, who has invented an intelligent and marvelous childhood for me). With each wind that kicks up, I worry the roofs and the walls will fly off and leave us exposed to the bites and the bushes electrified by hidden snakes. The gusts carry grains of sand and dust into the houses, slip the desert under the door, destroy the thresholds and the border between the vague and the intimate. The sand then covers the tar of the streets, the crockery, the greenery, and forces the inhabitants to hole up. I hate the wind because it's the symbol of the precarious, of the nomad. I remember now, as the night spreads everywhere, soothing and intact, reversing gravity. I like walls and I'm afraid when there aren't many around me multiplying the labyrinth against enemies and winds. What did Hadj Brahim think on the way back, when he left us on the doorstep of a nearly empty house, the wind wailing? Did he feel light, at peace with his god? Did he perform ablutions to wash away the crime?

I didn't want to miss this occasion. I had to prove to him that I could save him, but first I had to find the motivation in me to do it. Hadjer had an explanation for everything about my childhood: the glasses that fell from my hands, the curve of the moon, my sickness, the aging or the return of the storks, the mark on my arm, which made me different from the other children when they stripped me bare; but she kept quiet when I asked why my father had abandoned my mother when I was a newborn. She stayed silent, then acted as though she had suddenly remembered she had something urgent to attend to. The story is nothing spectacular, she diminishes my exceptional destiny to the whim of one of my father's moods. It's a banal story of jealousy between spouses, my mother and my stepmother. The patriarch decided on a rapid renouncement, accompanied by thirty sheep offered to my mother's tribe, and abandoned us, with neither bread nor spring, in the jaws of the Sahara, which I had never seen. How could he? He had slit the throats of thousands of sheep but I was the first sacrifice on his list, the offering in exchange for the blessing of a troubled god, led astray by his fantasies. I was born when I understood that I was an orphan and had to start all over again, alone. Before the whole history of the entire world *("the secret motive of writers," claims the dog of my inspiration, an immense German shepherd, soft, furry, with wise eyes).*

We were still climbing, each of us absorbed in our own calculations. That's how it is, when a father dies, we share his body and his features, we draw from his cadaver, who will get his possessions, who will get his words, his mannerisms, his shoes. With age, your father invades you like a shadow, inhabits your blood and climbs under your face, as if leaning out a window. Little by little, you take on his voice, his habits, and you find yourself enacting his law on your children. I didn't want that. I decided not to have children, to break the cycle.

There was no sound except for our muffled footsteps on the ground. We were scaling a whale washed up under the scattered stars. Nothing but our pack's breathing on our way to the house up top. The village, for my people, was divided in two: the top, the midwife hill of our line, inhabited by a distant ancestor of whom all that remained was a name stuck to a newborn, the Arab douar at the time of the colonizers; and the house down below, recuperated after the War of Liberation, constructed in the heart of the village by a Frenchman who had left behind his furniture and his future when he fled upon Independence. More comfortable, but too big for our trio: my grandfather, until his death, Hadjer turned hard as stone in the hand of a mountain, and me, the Arab Robinson Crusoe of an island with no language, master of the parrot and of the word. Between the two, there was the mosque, the weekly market, and the main street bordered by trees with their dresses hiked up on the single leg of their trunk.

Suddenly, the eucalyptus trees spread out, and, in the night, I could see brightness and lamps behind windows and hear the voices of worried children. Silent dogs ran to meet us, which frightened me. The eldest son chased them off with a murmur and turned toward me: "You have three hours. Be quick and then get out!" No one protested. An owl hooted behind me in the hollow sky which had receded. My heart jumped when, suddenly, I felt a brusque exaltation. A nasty jubilation mixed with fear. As if I were living a waking dream or a sacred moment, weightless. A father's death is outside of time, like a parallel scene that plays out endlessly, resumed and enriched or ignored. It wanes for a long time in several forms, omens, dreams, or rages, and we spend our lives preparing the details. Like that day when I threw stones and laughed, mockingly, at Hadj Brahim because he couldn't run as fast as me to catch and spank me. Or when I stole his money after he'd dozed off at our place, in the house down below, and then denied it while matching his prying gaze. Or when I gave myself another family name in his presence, to humiliate him in front of his friends, who were fawning over him because of his butcher's fortune.

I kept walking, almost by feel. As though I were living inside another's story. It was strange. I finally found the entrance to Hadj Brahim's house and I hesitated, despite my severe and superior demeanor. It smelled like cooking, fatty animals, and promiscuity. He lived there as a patriarch, with women, sheep, great-grandchildren, and hundred-year-old vines. A tribe between walls. I didn't like this place where, in the dim light, my shadow became a knot or a sock, where people had the angry and nervous silence of an audience that hasn't found the exit so they can disband. I was surely the most odious recourse for this family. A puny guy who's afraid of blood but not of the dying, to whom God gave the gift of writing to repel death, whom everyone has always tried to avoid, and who now makes a glorious return. Abdel, still curt, made a brusque gesture with his hand, shoved me aside to precede me, pushed open the panel of the door and yelled for the women to hide and disappear like embarrassments.

I entered, feigning disorientation, but the truth is that I knew the way all too well. My heart was racing as I inhaled the stale air. It had the musty smell of upturned old rocks. There were insects, frozen, naked, surprised, agitated by the new disorder, caught in their intimacy. Under the night lamps, I noticed the different paint, the

new whitewash on the prehistoric walls, and the smell
of couscous, greasy and heavy. It's always prepared at the
same time as a casket or a wedding. The lack of light had
destroyed the night, now in tatters. I felt a pang of regret
for the generous opacity of the stars that had stopped behind me, forbidden. An amusing illusion to find oneself
on the edge, where geography ends and the tale begins.
It was perfect to complete the oneiric illusion, the mean
enchantment. My heart was a ball of paper. I imagined a
heavy, hairy butterfly, with wings like talismans, crashing
into walls. The cold ran through me. I shivered. I pushed
open the front door and the night stayed outside, hesitant, while I stepped into the feeble light of the courtyard. A child stared at me, mute like a judge, before an
invisible hand pulled him out of the meager brightness.
I lowered my head so as not to meet their gazes and thus
spare myself the responsibility of their lives. It had been
years, after all, since I'd last come here, and I recognized
the rocks by their wrinkles, the chipped tiles, the water
basin to the right, and the vine, now wild, that wrapped
around the walls and then itself, as if desperate. I was
walking on the soft ground of a nightmare. Returned
but undesirable, rejected. I walked quickly and the feeble
stench slowed me before I could touch the handle of
the door to the sovereign bedroom opening onto the

courtyard. The old man was in his usual room, thrown onto the bed like an old jacket that was no longer useful against the cold, nor fashionable. *(Where does this idea come from, one I've had for years? Cemeteries have never convinced me. They're like a coatrack or a wardrobe to my suspicious eyes. How am I to believe in the corpse or the grave when I know that death is nothing but a broken glass? Laughable, the customs of visitors to tombs, those sobs over heaps of marble and bones bound with verses. I have to keep quiet and get to work. Cemeteries are nothing but thrift stores. A storeroom of clothes. Of badly stitched eternity. Anger.)*

The old man is there, like an excavation. I still feel hatred and guilt when I'm in the vicinity of his knives. Trembling slightly, like every time I'm too near him. My gift is to preserve life, his was to sow doubt within me. Hadj Brahim the ridiculer, for whom the greatest thrill was answering the bleating of creation by evoking the name of God before slitting the throat of the sacrificial beast and spreading out a large handkerchief of blood, a mournful cloth. I lingered there for a few minutes, but I knew they were waiting for me on the other side, at the end of the test. According to legend, I had already saved dozens of dying people, but legend also said that I was an insidious monster hiding in the body of a eunuch. O Ibrahim, turning into Abraham, it's my turn to hold the smiling blade to your throat and decide whether to save the sheep or your old age. I felt heavy, as if I was suffocating. *(I can leave, flee. But what will become of my gift then, denied at the most critical hour? A verse about the prophet Yunus, whom others call Jonah, drowned in a white whale as big as indecision, comes to my mind, imperfectly. He possessed both the name of a whale and that of the inkwell of the night, according to the commentators of the Holy Book disfigured by a strange laugh: "When he flees for the full boat, he takes part in the random draw that selects him to be thrown [into the sea]. The fish swallowed him and he was to blame.")* The eldest son burst through the scramble of brothers who followed him, comical in their clump, but he remained standing, imperious, and his mouth hung open for a few seconds before he started yelling. I knew what he was going to tell me.

4

I chose to keep my eyes down and probe my true desires. I had three hours of reprieve, three coffees, and no excuse. My first reflex, leave the long narrative of my own life at the door, the monologue opposite the mirror that impedes the story's flow. Not confuse the hour of destiny with my mental clock. Clear out so that the dog or the god are forced to speak. Necessity has rules: you have to refine the style, force words to be exact. The author? He's the navel, not the stomach or the pregnancy. The law on the tablet: if you hope to vanquish death, begin by not believing in it, not believing what it whispers.

I told myself then that perhaps I had to kiss the old man's head, a gesture of ancient and weary respect. But it felt absurd and dishonest on my part. Abdel fixed me one last time with his hateful, cold gaze, then left me with his father, my father. I opened my first notebook slowly and took up my pen. What to do? What end should I grab to strip the cloth and reverse his mummification? I always experience a moment of emptiness and willingness just before inspiration strikes. The beginnings of books I've read and loved come back to me. Scraps of phrases. But I wait for something better. I had a hard time not looking at the dying man, his heap. I suppressed a ridiculous sob that became a cough, then a throat clearing, then nothing. I took another minute or two and then gave in: I wanted to scrutinize him from the perspective of his death, alone and shut away, finally vanquished. Without his thousands of sheep raised in the mountains of the south, without his fake-toothed smile, his burnoose, his words that slit my throat at every possible occasion. A long, long story reduced to a cotton thread that I will pull and cut and retie between his breath and my desire. Spinner, carder, and weaver all at once. Three Greek goddesses in the body of an imbecile. With a click of the tongue, I called the dog in my head and sent him to collect the waning stars and the luminous objects from the fields. And I proclaimed. *(Writing is the only effective ruse against death. People have tried prayer, medicine, magic, reciting verses on a loop, inactivity, but I think I'm the only one to have found the solution.*) And I started to write, resolute and strict, spurred by the firm decision to prove my gift and to leave triumphant, like every time they called me to counter the last page of a life with the first page written by my hand. But it didn't last long. I had sensed it upon entering: there was a bad equilibrium in the air that night. At a certain point, they broke the silence and the possibility of a miracle. The door was violently rattled by an impatient hand and insults were unleashed... I thought I would have at least two hours of reprieve. I was wrong. Hardly one hour to guarantee my miracle and, suddenly, I felt the hateful wave seep under the door, like a draft. A group of his relatives and descendants were still trying to impose me as a solution, another group was already rearing its head like a devil to stir up outrage, demand an imam or a doctor and chase me out like an ungrateful son, a bad spirit of cemeteries and dead languages. Cries and tussles interrupted my momentum and suddenly the door gave way...

5

(Worshipers come back from the mosque and some stare at me, unsurprised. I'm the village phantom, I haven't prayed for years, nor fasted, and I don't recite any invocation when I sneeze or trip. The call of the muezzin doesn't concern me because I wake the dead, not the sleeping, in my own way. Dawn begins on the skin of my forearms because I left without my jacket, forgotten in the scramble. The day emerges with a gentle coldness, a rush of air, starting in the distant foliage before reaching the epidermis. It's as if someone is burning a large page of a notebook behind the distant mountain. A fine incandescence still consumes the blackened line climbing toward the hand that holds the page. The indirect fire touches the shells of frozen snails, revealing moisture and trails. In the Holy Book, I liked the descriptions of comets, of dawn, of stars and the moon cut in two. No one describes sunrise better than the nomad or the shepherd. I'm sitting here, at the entrance to the village, facing the fields where the douar farmers come with their barrows each morning. I can make out the poplars of the Christian cemetery that shelter the drinkers and the children playing hide-and-seek. To my right, the last big trees seem to return to the ground, restored by darkness, leaning dangerously, giant or indifferent. It's on this vague terrain, between the side of the hill and the fields, that they normally set up the Friday market. Everything is sold there: nuts and bolts, crops, dangerous sweets, cars, sheep, mats. I used to go sometimes, as a child, to look for coins fallen on the ground after the vendors left.

On the walls of the houses bordering the village, the night's retreat reveals the wear and tear, the paint regains its age, the inventory is reconstituted before my eyes. The stones return from the shadows and are arranged into ancient houses and facades. Then colors are recomposed and objects take back their exteriors, their names, or their faces. The dogs have lost the moon again, they go quiet, far at the end of the road of eucalyptus trees that runs through the Christian cemetery. In order: first the mountain to the east obscures and turns back into the night itself, in contrast to the sky, already pale. Then the darkness leaves the sky, the grass, the trees, the stones, and my narrow streets. Defeat reaches the main street of the village where I'm sitting, fists tightened around my notebooks, in front of the closed store of Ammi Mahmoud, the former school principal who's now our milk seller. Everyone is asleep, used to the regular return of the universe. Confident as lambs.

The village is a beach that slowly unfurls under the dry retreating wave. The central square, the orange of the gas station and the mosque, tall, formerly a church, crowned by the nest of three storks. I feel my bleeding gums with the tip of my tongue. Coming back down the hill that chased me away like an evil spirit, I hesitated to wake Hadjer and knock on the door of our house down below. I didn't want to provoke another incident, she would have reacted recklessly had she seen my bleeding nose and the scratches on my neck. I stayed outside, busy watching the waking day and cataloguing its routine. Attentive as if the sun were an insect under my magnifying glass. I wanted to attempt a sort of report on its nuances. In my mouth, the taste of blood dissolved. My cheek was burning. The east breathed suddenly and I shivered, then the paper of the sky caught fire. There was a moment of equilibrium between the number of stars to the west, a sort of transparent moon in the process of disappearing, and the intense brightness to the east. The temperature finally conquered the infinite. The great curtain took on the color of incandescence, the night turned to cinders, then there were only two or three stars remaining, the last embers to the west.

I turned my head, my neck was hurting. The path snaked under the eucalyptus trees which were becoming more visible, like foam in the night. It blanched under the tall hills to the east. It was over there, at the foot of the first slope, that I fainted three times when I tried to flee to find my mother's grave years ago. That's one of the limits imposed on me by my gift. Sometimes I transform my fate into a substantial story and I describe myself living in a palace, limping, forced every night to recount a story before dawn to save a life. Tried and true formula, except that toward the end the palace overflows with hundred-year-olds who slow down time, overpopulate the numerous hallways and the bedrooms, insidiously impede births, and exhaust the possibly of encounters and desire. I really like the hundred-year-olds, and the honeyed, toothless childhood they reincarnate when they sit on the square near the mosque after the siesta. It amuses me to imagine they're waiting for storks to carry them off somewhere to resuscitate them.

I pace in circles. I have to go back. My cheek is hot and there must still be a trace of the slap on my face, as well as scratches on my neck. The blood in my mouth has the familiar taste of metal. The sound of an engine puts an end to the metaphor. A shopkeeper abruptly draws the curtain of his store, far behind me. Garbage collectors pass and glance at me with a smile. Nearly all of them recognize me. Greet me. Four, plus the tractor driver. I have to save them, too. I have a title in my head. A book I've read this time but whose title seemed to surpass the number of pages: Season of Migration to the North.

Images of storks, of course, but also of the awakening of sex, of rituals that serve as an intermediary between eternity and the calendars. "You've seen Djemila's face, but you must find the rest of her body," whispers my secret animal. Oh, that story has no solution yet. Djemila is an unresolved case stuck between my father who refuses her *and my aunt who hesitates. A silent pack of dogs approached me and then opted for sniffing the empty trash cans. Numerous, their leader in a hurry. They turned their heads toward me in unison and yelled, mockingly, "Zabor on larboard, Zabor on starboard!" I was angry, I wanted to cry and yell. At myself and at the absurdity of my situation. The sun rose all at once, leaping, striped with clouds like a pheasant.)*

6

(The day turns brutally bright, lays bare every corner, cuts the angles, unveils the barks and stones until they're vibrating. There's nowhere to hide anymore. "Except in the heart of prayer," says my dog.) The Law of Necessity is sometimes obscure, even for me. A woman can be stupid, ugly, mean, or pretty as the proof of paradise, she will never be able to explain pregnancy. *(The smell of my aunt's morning coffee. The kitchen reeks of vegetables that are already rotting. Hadjer has the sharp eyes of a woman on the alert, worried, but she only makes small talk. I want to ask her questions, find out if there's any news about the request for marriage I made to Djemila's family now that Brahim is awaiting death and can no longer oppose it or take offense. I feel guilty and pace in circles. What did I do that I shouldn't have done? I return to my bedroom*

and touch the books, flip through them rapidly, but I'm not in the mood to read. The Confessions of Saint Augustine? No. I hate the way he moans and betrays his body. He's the Judas of our flesh. I start to get sleepy. My hours have been reversed for years already, I sleep when the sun rises and wake when it wanes. Maybe I'll write to her, Djemila, and ask her to be patient. One day I'll find your entire body and give it back to you, O decapitated neighbor.) The surrogate mother knows the cause, the pain, or the weight, the embrace or the name of the man who moaned over her, but not the mystery that rounds her out like an earth. Becoming pregnant is like listening to music, perhaps, but above all it means being subjected to a major law. That's my metaphor for explaining my situation, in a way. (Hadjer's face is sealed. She touches my eyelashes, examines my cheek as if it were her own skin. She turns serious and launches into a harsh, angry grumbling at the ceiling, and the sky above it, and the god that ballasts them. Everything trembles in her, even the walls of the kitchen. A sandstorm seems to dry her out before my eyes. "Why? Why, O my God?" she repeats, taking off my torn shirt stained with blood, calling as witness my grandfather, who's been dead for years, her imaginary ancestors and her own mother. Wringing the cloth, because she can't find the right words in her emotional state. I'm ashamed to have provoked this anger that disrupts our routine.) I understood this law intuitively. Years ago.

I was fifteen years old, it was four in the afternoon, a winter without rain, I was standing at the intersection of two narrow streets struck with glacial, creeping winds. They had sent me to buy bread at the bakery, which was accosted by mobs of people anxious about the flour shortages, at the end of the reign of socialism. I was standing there, contemplating two cockroaches that were stirring slowly, immobilized by the cold of the gutter. People were yelling and arguing with their empty baskets under the dirty gray sky, at the entrance of the bakery under attack. The pack was ferocious; everyone had a number on their basket but the line had degenerated into a stampede. We had been a free country for two decades already, but the memory of hunger is a fear tattooed inside us. I had just finished reading a novel about a group that found themselves shipwrecked. They had eaten each other, spurred by hunger and the delirium of the saltwater. Then I had daydreamed about the titles of the "forthcoming" books. I particularly liked *The Mutineers of the Bounty*. It made me think of fire and flames, this brief, united plural, this place that was the "Bounty," the name of a land, a prison, or a city perhaps, where they were trying to break the locks. I knew, suddenly, that there was a clear and precise purpose behind the apparent futility of the village of Aboukir and its idleness. The village's vanity was absolute, its inanity was so obvious that it had to be the doing of someone who had wanted to skip the essential, the engine of the fire, the will to create.

I went back home and curled up as my grandfather used to, head between my knees, hands on the back of my neck like a prisoner. And my fear morphed into anger, because I didn't want to endure his fate, lose my words. The Law of Necessity flowed from the spring of that first vision, between the end of childhood and puberty. The proof of a mechanism that would push me to reflect on how to escape from the prison of my family, from their way of living and turning a blind eye to the facts, from their tricks.

At certain times in my adolescence, I couldn't tolerate a single word that came from the mouths of my relatives, their sighs, the story of their pilgrimage, their orgasms, their salaries paid by the State. Everything was odious, small, and provoked my scorn. I mocked them out of spite. And nothing escaped my laughter, not even Hadjer's face, hard and protective. I felt I was looking at my universe through a magnifying glass that heightened its ugliness. An infinitesimal and severe prophet. A small world destined for the slaughterhouse and ridicule, arrogant in its way of explaining the world, deprived of stories capable of saving it except for its Holy Book, recited on a loop to exorcise anguish. Even more humiliating was the idea of eternal paradise *(Everyone was always describing it, planting trees in it and going into detail about its pleasures and rivers, nodding their heads with gravity and patience. They all told me that God gave life here on earth to the Westerners and reserved the beyond for us, who had been cheated by an insane and idiotic wager)* that emptied our universe and transformed it into a waiting room, a nomadic encampment. To my young eyes, it was suddenly nothing but sandstorms we tried to fight with verses and genuflections. Memories of crude voices, as though slowed down by the lowing, by the daily frustrations, because I didn't eat meat, by fermenting jealousies between women and rotten teeth in the mouths of men. If God loved beauty, how could there be so much ugliness before my eyes? If life was impurity, why were we subject to it? The worst was that feeling of insufficiency, that hollow in the stomach that obsessed me like hunger before my penis was alert enough to fill the void. I don't know how I managed to survive, frankly, to arrive at the port of this language. Perhaps through an intuition about a salvation different from that of my relatives, through fear, or through cowardice.

Of course I tried faith, but it wasn't enough. There was something stubborn in me, and, according to my readings of the Tradition, the son of a prophet was never the best believer. Look at the son of Nuh, Noah in the other Book, whom I adored, sitting on his mountain, drowned and dignified, refusing the ark or the plains. "I will go take refuge on a mountain that will protect me from the waves," says the Holy Book. Why did God need my faith to believe in himself? And what was this business that demanded the defeat of my body in exchange for paradise? Jealous of my clay? Incapable of eating without passing through my mouth? He had invented paradise while forgetting that he had no body with which to taste the fruit, so he decided to ask for mine back. Through verses, through extortion, through threat or through seduction. At the summit of the mountain of my catalogue of resentment, Hadj Brahim, with his wart, his nose hair, and his brown burnoose, his eyes injected with the blood of slaughtered sheep, yelled over my open throat. O God! O God, it was so long, this calvary. Which didn't stop until I understood that the world was a book, any book, all possible books, already written or to be written. Then my fainting spells spaced out, I began to eat again in front of my relatives, and I started to recover. Yes, any book could restore order to the world, no matter the story, the important thing was the proven existence of the order of language, the possibility of words and of an inventory. That was the most urgent thing.

(I drag myself to bed, determined to redo the count. There are twenty this time. The brothers that I can eliminate from the inventory, the three nameless wives I passed in the courtyard when I entered the house up top, the five garbage collectors. I noted everything, the descriptions of their faces, their expressions, the condition of their teeth. I have three days. A door slams in the entryway, I recognize the sound of its heavy wood. Hadjer on a crusade against infanticide, I tell myself. Or on a mission to test the waters with the neighbors. The house falls into this delicious silence that strips me even of my body, if I remain immobile. Rare moments when the world rejuvenates without saying a word. What title should I start with? My Mother's Castle. *Or* Robinson Crusoe, *that disconcerting moment when he finds an impossible footprint on a barely outlined island, still untouched and unknown. A moment of short-lived panic on my bed. I also love the moment when, in* The Mysterious Island, *Smith discovers the cave and his inner architect emerges. I'll go to sleep pondering this today.)*

I have to explain this famous Law of Necessity. The pearl of my ocean, the proof of my gift. The mechanics that have allowed me to counter my death and the deaths of others. For all laws are cogs. I began with the smallest.

7

In the summer, I like to sleep almost the entire day, relishing the excess like a drug. Ditch the sun, the village, its customs, and the potential visitors who might show up at our house down below. Spared from earning my keep like everyone else, with no wife or children, I sleep at odds with the darkness: the whole day inert on my bed, at night watching over other people breathing, inventorying vines, faces, and synonyms. At dusk, I often get up with a sort of vertigo, a distance between me and the objects that perturb the ritual of time. I savor that sensation of weightlessness that comes from the disorientation *(decomposing time is the first step toward ecstasy, according to shamans, necessary before you can break out of the enclosure).* When everyone else is already dozing, tired, I study the night at its flared birth, attentive to its rituals that restore the infinite to the hollow of the sky. And I can keep vigil for a long time, reading or rereading my books, as the night advances and everyone is asleep on the back of a slow, universal whale. My aunt knows my routines since I no longer go to school or to the reciters to memorize the Holy Book. This is also the time when I feed my notebooks, arranged like slates, opened onto the white of their broad throats, pulsing like headaches or organs. I wash my face, I have my afternoon coffee, I talk to my aunt about my family, my half brothers, and my dreams. *(This time, she keeps quiet. She wasn't at the neighbors' house to speak to Djemila's parents. I ask for an update on the old man's health. She responds that his sons will kill me, that they eagerly await his death but they'll be disappointed. I translate: he's still breathing. A blank spreads in the middle of the conversation and both of us know what I'm waiting for. "It's not the right time," she answers my silent question, then adds, "She has two children. What will you do with them?" I don't answer, because I don't know. Fatherhood gives me as much anxiety as the sight of blood. The responsibility I have to keep my people alive condemns me to virginity and self-sacrifice. I'm lying to myself, too, because the truth is that I want to save that woman, restore her body, and I've never thought about her children. But there are other obstacles: her status as a divorced woman, my father, and my intimate*

secret, which is to say my naked flesh, different from others. My aunt
knows it, but we haven't spoken about it since my childhood. I'm not
circumcised, distinct from others in body and mind. By accident or out
of fear, I refused the pact of flesh, in a way. Hadjer fears scandal, dis-
grace, dishonor, and the hallali of the malicious if word were to get out,
which could happen if a woman were in my virginal bed. Do I feel
humiliated? No, only undecided about my future: something awakens
in me when I think of that woman's face, but perhaps it's nothing but
temptation on my sanctified path.

I leave Hadjer to watch television. The black-and-white world
that has nothing to do with me. An animal documentary plays after
the reading of verses from the Holy Book. Today, according to my
personal calendar, the world is a wrinkled page. Better not to read
it. In the kitchen, Hadjer is speaking to someone, probably a relative
asking for news of the death in our family.) I was still ashamed of
what had happened the night before. I should have been
more courageous. Because of the thousands of stories
running through my head, I kept any real emotion at
bay. I live as though off-center, outside of the village, in
its black heart. I almost went into the courtyard, under
the shed, to watch the stars appear in the sky, but I had
more urgent things to do, faced with the ceiling. I had to
understand why my gift had proven incapable of reviv-
ing Hadj Brahim, even though I had a clear view of his
agony, even though I knew thousands of details capable

of resuscitating him, of reconstructing his story. Was it hatred? Perhaps. Vengeance? Perhaps that too. If I'm honest, certainly. Then I went back to my room.

When she watched over me during my former illness, Hadjer had, through her long soliloquies, embedded an entire imaginary map in my head: the village of Aboukir, indistinct in the rurality of my native country, had its own geography, according to her. Interwoven with my story, mixing names and trees, legends and the three marabouts. The navel of the world was nestled between hills masquerading as the beginnings of mountains to the east, the Bounouila cemetery to the west, where all the eucalyptus trees came from, crossing our paths before continuing on their own. To the north, the city was enclosed by the hill. The hill of my ancestors who had witnessed the arrival of the first colonizers in 1848 and had erected their exiled communard tents. The elevation separated us from the big city and the sea, which I had never seen except on television, gray and exiled. As for the south, that's where my great-grandmother was from, a rug weaver and the owner of her tribe's last horses, before the first wave of famine at the beginning of the nineteenth century. Depending on the geography, the south was strewn with other villages like ours, up to the high plateaus. then to the Sahara with its assaults of sandstorms at the end of every summer. But, so the story goes, the voyage came to a sudden end when they took a wrong turn that brought all the travelers back home, unbeknownst to them. According to Hadjer, when the night was long and my fear atrocious (*my hair anointed with oil and my temples compressed by a coarse scarf*), the cartography of the beyond was simple: a contemptuous city, to the north, that watched over the sea (*"Your grandfather Hbib would go there barefoot, put on new espadrilles when he arrived, go about his business, and then take off his shoes when he started back on the road to Aboukir,"* she said. *"That's how he kept the same pair for a decade,"* she added, proud to teach me frugality), the hill (*"They don't even come up to your ankle, your half brothers, they envy your beauty and your gift of interpreting dreams in books; and you never pushed Abdel into the ravine to kill him. Never"*), and the big thorny circle of a forest of Barbary fig trees that surrounded us infinitely, protecting us but keeping us from leaving, from abandoning our mothers or from traveling. (*"Your uncle Chaabane managed to cross it at twenty years old, but once in France, his mind turned slow, stupid. It was a way of protecting himself from sadness. When he returned, for the summers, he would bring us bananas, apples, and francs."*)

And where was my mother's village? We reached it leaving her skin among the thorns. "That's what killed her." How did I get back to the village? "An uncle brought you back and left you at the doorstep of the house up top, then he disappeared, leaving a bit of money and a red wool balaclava, the cosmonaut cap." But how had he survived the journey? "He knew how to gather the Barbary figs, as our people do": by using a long pole made from a reed, split at the tip. He knew how to grab the fruit with the beak, turn it downward delicately *("it's all in the wrist, I'm telling you!" Hadjer says)* to pick it, collect it in a pail, and hold it tight between the thumb and index finger to skin it. You can't eat a lot of them because it'll fill your stomach with a tombstone and you'll die of constipation trying to give birth to a mountain. And the Sarah full of sand? That would be like trying to grasp the infinite, and Hadjer didn't know how. So the desert became a sort of stranger whose footsteps we heard when we pressed our ears to the tiles. A wind-borne monster that liked to drink all the water and eat all the roots and lost travelers. A sandstorm in the inflamed red sky, where the world loses the trace of itself, asking where it comes from. I imagined it like a handmade rug, chaotic and changing according to the gusts of wind. I felt afraid when I looked to the south, because the Sahara had ninety-nine names, too, and it was also invisible and enraged. Perhaps because of the only memory I had of my mother (a scream and a sound of falling), tied to the wind in the house where

Hadj Brahim had abandoned us, it represented the void, death, or the accomplice erasing the traces of my fleeing father. Now you know the geography.

I've been telling this story for hours already. That day, opposite the bakery, in the scramble of the shortages of the time, I cried. Out of compassion for my people: my other aunt and her endless migraines; my grandfather and his silent life; our neighbors, one by one; Taibia the old woman; the one-legged Aadjal, who collapsed one morning and was found in the fields at noon; Hakim, my cousin, who was born without a mind and waited for it for thirty years until he died foolishly; my uncle, who crossed the sea and left half of his body there. I cried over the lack of food, the greed it brought to their eyes, the scarcity of flour and the sadness of the television, which we could only turn on at dusk to watch black-and-white series. Everything was futile and hopeless like the life of a slave unaware of his fate.

There's nothing else to say: the real meaning of the world was in books, and that language *(this very one, before my eyes and fingers, still able to save a life at the top of the hill, the tool of my talent and the fruit of my autodidactic learning, filling my umpteenth notebook)* offered me the essential. Everyone had to be included. Everything had to be indexed, inventoried, classified, designated, named to keep from sinking into the weeds of the island my village symbolized. Poll, the enigmatic parrot in *Robinson Crusoe*, this third character to whom no one pays any attention, possessed the colors of a beautiful secret language that I enriched patiently, like a miniaturist. A little voice was already saying to me: Who remembers the ancestors today? And who must save this world from oblivion? Surely not the person who recites the Holy Book without understanding it, but rather the one who writes without stopping except to take care of his needs, eat, or gather his strength with rest. I was the only one capable.

Hadjer understood: "I'll have my revenge on every last one of them. I don't care who's dead or dying. No one touches my son," she yelled at the neighbor. I said nothing, out of laziness. In truth, it's my fault: I could barely write even one or two pages. It illuminated a distant candle in the fighting body but it wasn't enough to vanquish the gnawing of death. I swore, shouting at the horde of half brothers, that the old man had turned his head toward me, that he had looked at me with a thousand words in his eyes, that he had even shed a tear, but they found no trace of it on his face and the scene of the miracle was vandalized by the stamping and insults that sullied everything. After that night of doubt about my gift, chased out of the dying Hadj Brahim's house, I slept poorly, silent, blood in my nose, body aching as though I'd been wrestling. I suddenly remembered the dream from that summer day I spent sleeping, agitated: a monkey sat on my chest, bit me when I tried to push it off, suffocated me while laughing in its spasmodic language.

8

Another two nights including this one. A starry reprieve. It's always like this, guided by a rhythm that might stem from superstition. Like how I always step into the bathroom with my left foot, or put on my right shoe first, or gather all the keys found on the ground during my nightly inspections of the village, never shake anyone's hand, study the calligraphy in dry tree branches, and such things. I had been chased out by my half brothers, kicked, brutalized by their anger, their spite, and there's very little chance I'll be summoned again, or be able to return to Hadj Brahim's bedside. The whole tribe will now block my efforts. And yet I have to find a way to sit next to him, watch over him, wake him *(cloaked in a sheepskin to escape the giant, disguised as a beggar, hidden in a jar like the thirty-ninth thief, concealed by a woman's veil, invisible by the force of an invocation or crying with regret and anger in front of my half brothers, on a flying carpet woven into a pilot's scarf? "Choose," says my inner dog).*

According to my law, I had a reprieve of three full days between the moment when I met a dying person or a passerby and the moment of their death if I didn't write about them, even something made up, even with the title of a book I hadn't yet read, even with a single powerful metaphor, delaying degradation, reducing time like an equation or an embrace. So I have to go back, as quickly as possible. With Hadjer this time. It's the only solution. She'll know how to create the opportunity and distract my rivals. I wrote a single phrase in the last few hours and contemplated it: "Language is the impetuous slope of silence." Then I opened a book on Persian myths, read it until morning, and finished by writing another letter to Djemila, who doesn't know how to read or write, to communicate my ardor and my notion of salvation. In vain. Do I love her? Yes. I feel guilty when I evoke her fate and I know that, for her, writing will never be enough to wrest her from death and give her back a whole body. At twenty-four years old, she's divorced (spurned perhaps) with two little girls, and thus condemned to go through life decapitated, only showing her head out the window. I will save her not by writing but by telling her a story that will heal her decapitation and help her regain the use of her hands and her senses. The idea is hazy, fragile, still insincere. But her fate is somehow linked to mine. I think more and more that, in her case, the story I have to imagine must use even my body. Perhaps love is nothing but solidarity, a form of waiting together.

Then I slept like a storyteller who goes back home with his own ashes to revive at the next vigil. The dawn muezzin had given me the signal.

9

At dusk on the second day, that sentence took on its full meaning in the orange light: to write is to illuminate. So I tried to understand what had happened. *(What title should I use for this notebook?* The Rosy Crucifix-ion, *perhaps. Sometimes I like writing when I wake up, on an empty stomach, before my body impedes my weightlessness. I cultivate this vertigo like a premise in my world of inversed hours.)* Why did this gift, which has saved hundreds of people, which keeps watch over the faces, names, and angles of the village, cede to panic and stampede? I can't remember a similar occurrence, except maybe at the beginning, when I was knocking on doors to offer care for the ill. But there, up on the hill, I proved to be an inadequate healer even though it was the moment I had always secretly dreamed of. I had imagined my father's death so many times that I had rendered him immortal. But it was the chance to repair everything, his death and the malaise within me, my body, my voice, my fainting spells at the sight of blood. I didn't know how to resist my fear that he wasn't truly dying, that he might start talking again to mock me and my gift, grab his cane to beat me.

Hadj Brahim had a bad reputation in the village, and he was only shown respect because of his fortune. Or maybe because of his surprising capacity to guess the true nature of his customers: delinquent payers, sly smirkers, liars about the wool and weight of the animal, wily shepherds, thieving breeders, hustlers and go-betweens. With a simple glance, he could gauge an animal, its flesh, its weight without wool, its taste, he could guess what pasture it came from as soon as he bit into the steaming meat. A real mystery, for our ancestors didn't know the butcher's trade, he had learned it on his own, "in one of God's dreams while everyone was resting on their laurels after Independence." That kinship with the executioner granted him a few supplementary gifts: dogs quieted at his approach, he wasn't afraid to go into the cemeteries or other supposedly haunted places at night, he knew how to help animals give birth, he gathered honey without

74

being stung, and he walked barefoot until Independence, as he liked to say. The legendary Hadj Brahim, shrewd as suspicion and false as a film.

So that night, I wrote the first line and I saw the true shiver, known since antiquity, like a wave under rock. The old man fell back down from the sky as I began. *(The real cemeteries are not tombs but photographs. I have a few in my bedroom. Of famous or unknown people. There's a photo of my grandfather staring angrily at the person stealing his soul, which is to say the photographer. I like to look at the faces flattened on the impossible window that separates us, me the living, them the dead dazed by the void or striking hollow poses. Ruined from thinking about them endlessly. From proving that we can be the entire universe, its convex navel, then be nothing more than an accident, a juncture between futility and flamboyance. At once both the center of the world and its perfect negligence. The proclamation of an eternity and its clean denial. I pay particular attention to the eyes in the photos, those chatty mouths even though the tongue has already died with the rest of the body, invisible in the portraits. The grain of the skin, impossible to degrade, then I imagine the back of the neck, which is proof that there is a life behind the face. That we can turn around, like a mountain or a low hill, a dense monument. I have several of those black-and-white photos. When I stare at one for a few minutes, I panic. As if I were staring into a hole. Or at people who don't know that their neck is between the jaws of an animal that grunts and finishes them off like a meal while they go on believing they're happy and fertile.)* He was indeed dying, he looked like a kite spread foolishly on his bed. I knew his demise was imminent because of the insect noise emanating from him. I recognized all the signs of that strange toppling of life into death that has no eyes or mouth and yet swallows the whole world, and half of my thoughts, and much of the land to the west of the village, in the Bounouila cemetery.

I had the capacity to save him or return him to life, brand-new down to his teeth *(simple mechanics: you just have to give death a bone to chew on, trick it with a very long story that exhausts it, distances it)*, or perhaps already destroyed by his struggle against darkness, barely capable of uttering intelligible words, but that would not excuse my renunciation. Behind the door (which had to be closed so the soul wouldn't escape), I heard the rustling of people in the little courtyard waiting for the end of the session, the sounds of dishes, of children they were trying to keep quiet who were asking for their mothers, the creaking of the front door that opened from time to time onto a group of neighbors who had come to offer compassion or help rolling the couscous.

They knew, in the village, that I was not to be disturbed while I kept death at bay by barking more loudly, but in its mute language. Even those who mocked my talents in cafés or outside the mosque ended up asking for me sooner or later, heads lowered. Death makes us stupid and submissive, I know from experience, and before coming to find me, my detractors submit to fear like cattle. Why me, and not the reciters of the Holy Book or the imam? Maybe because I had access to the right alphabet, new and revived by my savage dictionary? Maybe because I seemed innocent? Or because I had already saved old and sick people who were now walking through the streets of Aboukir like sweet monstrosities? I knew they hesitated for a long time before coming to knock on the door of our house down below, even though there were many reciters and medicine was free in our country.

My dying man was there, hardly a body around bones. Barely recognizable despite the furrowed brow that encapsulated his authority, stupefied with fear, bewildered by the idea of losing the reality of his world, the eternity that had never been denied him until then. I knew him, of course, but I didn't want to go any further. The rule is that I had to disregard him to find him again. Resuscitate the image of the breath, give him back a pulsing jugular, rough skin, wrest him from the darkness by unraveling the bandages. A heavy task, but a sweet revenge on that man, that man specifically among the hundreds of others I'd saved, among the trees I keep green and charming, the waterways, the Barbary figs, and the walls I support, the entire village, stone by stone, down to the dogs and chicks. *(Third page of the notebook: reverse the course of mummification. The title?* The Hollow Needle. *An ancient history of astronomy.)* Sweet revenge. Unfurl the words, reinject the brain fluid through the nostrils, the humors, the liquids that unite blood and nourishment, restore all the water and then the organs one by one like cornerstones, then wash the body to pull it out of the invisible Nile and restore its name, its breath, its heartbeat, the dark vein that brings rhythm to the immobile. A whole process. With nothing but words, a long story intertwining with another, and so on until the final awakening, the grateful smile.

Then they rattled the door, unfortunately. Someone intervened and shouts followed. I felt hatred. *(My father worked hard. He would say so ostentatiously when, early on, he would come at the end of the day to have coffee with us, down below. An old obsession making his lips move in his beard. A story that lasted seventy-six years, dried my skin, killed dozens of trees, penetrated deep down to the ancestors' tombs and the springs, spread all over and ravaged the beauty of the crops, the sky that washed its hands of it, the entire world that was the village. His incredibly long story exhausted me, nearly killed me. I survived thanks to the books in my head that formed a barrier, shielded me from guilt and kept me from gouging my*

eyes out. I'll get back to that later, around dawn. I still have a few
hours left, which rouses my predilection for digressions.)

My first fall. It was long. It lasted days, the bottom of the
well was so far down. I was pushed into the hole while
I slept and woke up still falling, dislocated. Not panicked, just stunned by the novelty, touching the sides of
the walls with my fingers, the roots of things, the bulges
slicing vertically through the ground. When I lifted
my head, I saw the world grow distant as I fell, feeling
almost relieved. It was nearly four in the afternoon that
summer day when they threw me to the bottom of the
well. I didn't fall all at once like a rock. No! I floated
slowly, spinning in the blackness like a feather wearing
shoes: I didn't understand my fate very clearly, I was four
years old, but I enjoyed the sensation. And because I had
lost my mother two years earlier in the village of Ammi
Moussa, far behind the mountains, between the fig trees
and the desert, I liked dark places with narrow walls and
hot breezes. I associated tenderness with burial. Or death
with weightlessness. Or dreams with conclusions.

I landed in the house down below, gently, like sprigs
of tea at the bottom of a cup. There was nothing on the
ground of that abyss, only tiles with frivolous designs,

a few white stones in the courtyard, a miniature but intensely fragrant lemon tree. I think it deserves a name, like a puppy. At high altitude I had guessed the places I was losing: the rectangular courtyard, a shed, the large gate, a pool of dead water. I had just touched ground, scatterbrained, and found myself so close to all things, in one soft piece. Water was flowing behind me. I saw a faucet in the right corner of the pit, the pool made from verdigris cement, the entrance to the kitchen on my right. A large window of my pink room gripped the bars that sequestered it with both hands, a wooden face crushed behind its prison. And, at the very top of the well, the sky, as through a hole, blue, inaccessible, barely concerned with my fate and the weight of things on earth. Gaggles of birds passed by like verses of the Holy Book.

I felt like I might fall in the opposite direction this time, toward the top, faint if I persisted, head raised, forehead exposed. I was four years old and it was my first day in the house down below where they had decided to exile us. Hadjer, already a spinster by then, was at the stove making coffee. My father had repaired the water inlet, glanced at the dry courtyard with no grass, observed me for a moment while I was playing with my white stones, even opened his mouth to say something...but then turned around—for twenty or thirty years, in fact. He had decided it was better to focus on taking care of the property rather than his family and announced that he would redo the tiles, the bathroom, and the paint. My aunt was smart enough to suppress her emotion, as if to force me to grow up a bit and leave behind the sniveling childhood of the abandoned.

It was the end of the day, yellow dust softly slipped into things, there was the silence of a dry desert, all rocks and stumblings. A lizard trembled on a wall. It tried to mimic the outline of an Arabic letter, then vanished. I was suddenly cold and tempted to cry just to feel my body, find my face again. But I was, I think, too tired, worn out from my harsh confrontation with my step-mother and her son Abdel who was bleeding from the nose and forehead. The events had shunted me back and forth too quickly and I felt like an orphan, because of the overly large house more than because of the loss of my mother. They had brought me back to my maternal tribe in Ammi Moussa, on the other side of the fig tree forests, to the south, one week after the burial, and I ended up here, sitting cross-legged, because my father's second wife claimed I had pushed her son into an empty well.

The world then became a series of nervous reloca-tions, dreams, and demonstrations of tenderness that were too emphatic to be real. I was given new shoes, and another red wool balaclava that I wore for a long time, refusing to take it off even when it was hot. I don't remember feeling sorrow, only a strong desire to sleep on a gigantic sheepskin. Which I did, in that new house, in the dark room with a chimney. The room was blue, then black, and weighed down my legs and eyelids. When I woke up in the middle of the night, Hadjer caressed my hair and argued for a long time with her brother who wasn't there, lying next to me, body warm and mind burning in her imaginary duel. Then she decided to serve me soup and bread in the kitchen. Through the window, I saw the stars outside, above the walls. So numerous that they seemed about to spill onto the earth.

My grandfather arrived the next day, also falling from the sky, pushed by his descendants. My stepmother got rid of him under the pretext that it wasn't right to leave a child and a spinster alone in a village that was so quick to malign. He was very old, but could still serve as an alibi for the family's honor. Despite the risk of the curse, my father ceded to the whim of his wife and decided that his father would meet his end discreetly, far from the brouhaha and the bleating of his fortune. He bought him a nice burnoose and brought him to us without saying a word. My grandfather was nothing but a phantom with an incoherent language that became more impoverished with each day because of his strange illness. He remained silent for a long time, then decided to inhabit the place in his own way. He would walk into the courtyard, touch the walls and the objects calling them by the wrong names. He would despair as we watched him search for precise terms, stumble, snivel, fall back into his torrent of disfigured words, a brutal chaos. I think at that time he was still aware of the world and of himself: it was visible in his gray eyes, in his way of designating things with his fingers rather than with language. But that didn't last. His illness became ferocious, tore up his memory, devoured it, then attacked the core: names. My grandfather became a stupefied corpse, vanquished by oblivion, and it was Hadjer, his youngest daughter, who took care of him, even when he didn't recognize her anymore. He died years later, in my arms, when I didn't yet know how to counter decapitation with stories.

Why do I mention that fall into the house down below? Because, from that moment on, my father became chatty, loquacious, talking himself dizzy, inexhaustibly going on about the time before the sheep and Independence. He started talking for two, himself and his father, then for all of us. He invented a legend meant to cut off the words of the entire world. A king forsaken by his own *Thousand and One Nights*. But how long and boring his story was!

My father's first story, the real one, is about his misfortune before Independence. At that time, poverty was so tenacious that the women of the douar walked around crazed, thighs squeezed together, trying to thwart violent men but also children, who were desperate to crawl back into their stomachs to shirk hunger. Eat the mothers from the inside, for lack of potatoes or bread. People sucked on bones, stole the roots from the trees. Hair fell out from typhus, leaving lice exposed and disoriented on skulls. The world was narrow, the eucalyptus trees had no purpose in the sky, the douar was a place of silence situated in the nape of creation and there were a lot of names without children, their carriers dead of exhaustion in their sleep. To find work with the colonizers, you had to get up early, cross nearly an entire continent, be the first to arrive at the homes of the farm owners to the east of the village and hope they chose you to take care of the horses or gather the crops in the frost. So, to ensure they didn't miss their chance, some spent the night in the stables. "We had to hang onto the necks of the beasts to keep from falling asleep, or sleep standing up so we would be awake when the call came," my father recounted. And then he would look at me unkindly, as if it were I who had forced him to undergo this torture, before I was even born. "Today, you have tile floors, white bread, electricity, sodas, meat. Yes, today," he insisted. And he would slip into an easy anger because his childhood had been stolen and I was the thief. At the time, he would still come to see us, down below. Hadjer served him coffee and he would launch, like a swimmer in a pool of old water, into the story of his misfortune that blamed all the children born after him. I was left feeling dirty and traitorous, nauseous and dizzy, always. As if I owed him all the money I might earn until I was a hundred years old. Ah, the butcher! He used honeyed insinuations, fine as knives, a master of ridicule like an evil wind, and he knew where to strike my meager chest.

The story was long like the climb up a mountain: he, verbose and megalomaniacal, me, behind him, knocked out and tied by the horns. Climbing toward the summit of morbid hallucinations, reciting my verses. And it always ended with the same con as in the Holy Book, the same swap: he came back to earth, set down his cup of cold coffee, and smiled at the imaginary sheep of his fortune as the oldest butcher in Aboukir. Sheep had started to fall from the sky like cotton balls on legs at

the very moment when he'd decided to abandon me with
his sister: as soon as they threw me down below, in the
home of the spinster they hid behind the walls, God had
given him an entire herd that had launched his reputation
as a butcher. His fortune had multiplied in his hands like
froth on the seashore. Blood had flowed, and money and
honor along with it. Behind the scenes, I was sure, the
mysterious and noble beast had let out a sad bleat and
offered his throat to save me from my father's influence.
He could have kept me as one of his own and I would
have ended up like Abdel and the others, a meager shrub
in his vicinity. No. The celestial sheep had raised its
eyes with a poignant sweetness, interrupted its eternity
and scattered into a thousand beasts destined to keep
Hadj Brahim's eye away from me. To spare me, the sheep
had surrendered to my father and given me the power
of a writer able to counter death. That's how the gift
was slowly able to infiltrate our village, sending me on
a journey through repudiation and maternal mourning.
It saddled me with an illusory body, a voice evoking the
memory of the sacrifice, and an anguish that heralded
my calligraphy. In truth, the old ram saved all the village
inhabitants, one by one. Perhaps all of humanity.

A mute being, an animal that was once a constellation, chose to sacrifice itself in my place, and I adopted

its bleating voice, its dry and clumsy body, its immense eyes. Today, after reading nearly seven thousand books—a figure infinite as the seven heavens—and just as many imaginary books, I have come to some big realizations: my life and all lives are linked to a bigger, essential tragedy, at the origin of time and separation. What I live and what I give to save lives does not belong to me. I am only a pretext. *("Perhaps death is nothing but a being in love, searching for someone, scrutinizing us all, one by one, until the end of time, in search of them," says my dog. I ask him: "So how do I keep death away from my family?" "By making death forget its sorrow with stories," he answers.)*

A few more years of paying attention and I vaguely understood that Hadj Brahim hated children, and childhood in general, which translated to a sickly fear of dying, of being pushed overboard, from behind, by his offspring.

10

How many times have I healed strangers! (Kaddour the widower, Aïcha, a dignified and silent woman, my uncle Chaabane when he fell to his knees one summer, ill and disoriented by the changes in the village, Abdelkader, my father's friend who loved baths and vineyards, Badra who had inhaled carbon gas from cursed charcoal, et al.) If death finds your trail again, it's because you're on the edge of your path, because you don't believe in your story anymore, or you've scattered your listeners, dead and alive. My uncle Larbi, for example, my father's older brother, died when his tribe's attention switched to Hadj Brahim's fortune and sheep. His story fell into disuse and in the end he found himself carried off once

again by his indifference for even himself. I remember
the cold stare of that man, stranger to all things, whom
we found lying in a vineyard to the east of the village.
He died in good health, but emptied. A story is a shared
breath, a rediscovered body. A story can take your breath
away? Then it can also restore your breath when you're
dying. I'm talking about the mechanics of it, but the
mystery remains intact. My mission involves the metaphysical, and especially the Law of Necessity. I believe
in God, but I don't try to speak to him. To exist is a
greater tragedy than that one-on-one discussion, which
has grown tiring. The essential lies outside of prayer
or disobedience. It's in the imminence, delayed by each
person, of the end of the world. My prophecy doesn't
involve a holy book but rather a holy explanation of all
possible books.

That's what I've been trying to figure out for years.
The link between my writing and its culmination in
the body of the other. The enchanting consequence of
a word on the rhythm of a body. Reduce the phrases to
their bones, to their strict intimate figure, to demonstrate
that Necessity is a law that provokes a return to life, but
also a simple, firm link between the living and the written, precision and resurrection, or permanence through
memory. If I remember everyone, no one will die, but to

remember I need the power of a precise language, rich as a swarm, reconstituted by flesh and breath, rediscovered word by word with the patience of an investigator, pushed to the limit of exactitude. If creation were a book, I would have to rewrite it constantly. Or perhaps reread it, like the former mystics and alchemists. The Holy Book describes itself as a version descended from the sky, but which has remained preserved there, antecedent like motherhood. We speak in our country of the well-guarded Tablet, the Mother of the Book. The celestial version we find through prayer and meditation. The meaning we restore through asceticism and bodily sacrifice until we're dizzy. But all religions speak of a book as the world or the back world. They insist that the pilgrim is a distracted reader, the believer a blind reader, the contemplator a reader hesitant to turn the pages, and the writer a reader who reproduces. I don't believe in the theory of hidden meaning. I believe in the inventory and in the preeminence of memory over death. Things are held suspended in space and time because they are inventoried in a mind and because a language keeps them in permanent immediacy. It's a story of magical encounter: the present (and its universe) exists because a man remembers.

Is that it? I admit compassion. I remain indifferent to the announcement of my father's death, to his agony,

and every encounter irks me, but at night, when the
whole village sleeps and I keep watch, recounting my
encounters, I feel immense pity for my family's fate.
In mounting waves, up to the high tide of mercy. I feel
anger against this God who enriches the inhabitants
in cycles, makes them believe in pleasure, then crushes
them with illness and death. I position myself as an
intermediary, as a defender, the kind of man whose sense
of dignity and strength pushes him to provoke duels
with the fiercest highway bandits, just to turn their anger
on himself, gain time and help the weakest avoid their
fate. So there is a mechanical reason for my compassion
*(the more I write, the more the village resists, its people can live long
lives and the hundred-year-olds multiply like victories, exhilarated
by the endless present)*, another reason that comes from the
heart *(the world is a tragedy, a sacrificed ram, and I am its voice)*,
and a final reason, the basis of my belief *(I am responsible for the lives of the people I meet daily, and I can save them by
writing, all of them except for one woman whom I can only protect
by exchanging my body for hers and remedying her decapitation)*. It's
a complex system, like gears with interlocking teeth. My
gift's system is derived from meditation and asceticism.
Because of the Holy Book, because of my diligent religious years, my study of a foreign language that became
an instrument of life and death, I understood very early

on that there was a link between our capacity to speak and the objects we designate. Everything is written, nothing is silent, oh yes! The opposite of God is not Iblīs, but the inaudible. I'm sure of it.

The hundreds of books I've read prove to me that eternity exists and we can preserve it through transcription and deciphering. All we have to do is read endlessly and, for lack of an infinite library, write endlessly, but diligently: a number for each face, a title for several notebooks, signs and symbols where the word is no longer enough for embrace and possession. The titles are like pebbles. They help me to write, to bounce back and fill the void. *(Television introduced our country to a foreign language and unknown people who communicate their passion with grand gestures. Hadjer must be watching her film without me there to translate. I haven't done it for a few years now, for the sake of decency. I'll go out in an hour to inspect the village, note the details, register the names of the newlyweds or listen to the loud voices from under the windows. I can go all the way to the nocturnal fields. Where the dogs torment each other. Near the Christian cemetery. I visit it sometimes, because they decorate death differently than we do: lacework stones, vaults, French or Spanish names, verses from another holy book, cherubs. My dog tells me that it's paradoxical to sculpt angels into stone. The tombs are desecrated often, by kids. And, once night falls, I cross the silence disturbed by wine drinkers, seated, silent, in a group, like conspirators*

behind God's back. This place is a land of refuge for outcasts, lovers,
or alcohol peddlers. During the day, there is a magnificent, pure shade
from the cypress and poplar trees. No one has stepped foot there for a
long time, the vandalism is garish. "Dead two times," sighs my dog. I
don't agree: the tomb is a con, a scam. It's to fool the investigators who
stop after they've found the body. Like in crime novels. Rather than
going further to interrogate and understand all the metaphysics, the
visions, the books and legends. That's why I never come to write in the
Christian cemetery despite its beauty: it's like writing under a coat rack
and calling it a streetlight. But tonight I might go there to kill time. For
lack of any other idea.)

The first notebook I wrote was called *The Lord of the
Rings.* The title was so beautiful that I made it into a well,
with water at the bottom reflecting dozens of zealous,
passionate characters. And when, years later, I read the
real book with this title, I was a little disappointed: my
story was better, it was about a ring salesman who had
become immortal by showing off his merchandise from
city to city. And how his skill had led him to sell imaginary rings, because he described them so marvelously to
curious crowds. Before writing, hunched and coiled like
a mollusk, I always hear a music that sounds like water
approaching, or like sugar recounting its life. I'm getting
off topic, I know, but I can't make progress any other
way. To write is to listen to a sound, preserve it and turn

it over, endlessly, try to render its melody, get as close to it as possible to bring it from the ear to the mouth. The Prophet says that the revelation came to him like a timbre, the sound of a bell, and that the terrible Angel was a ringing sound before degrading into words. I liked that confession, which seemed sincere, about the profession of God's emissary. Those I meet during these sessions describe me as tense, angry, harsh, my gaze menacing. It's the shell of my trances, the outline of my circle.

The patient from the night before last is an old man I knew well who never considered my gift something important or real. For a long time he treated me with contempt or an affected indifference to make me feel ashamed the few times I crossed his path. I promised myself I'd wait, and now his hour has arrived, and he's here, sliding into my memory, known for its precision, like a blind man's sense of touch. Revived by my habitual insomnia, words and spit mixed inside of his lungs, he scrutinizes me valiantly, with curiosity, anger, then renunciation. As when someone, weary, entrusts his survival to a charlatan and sees the proof of his own cowardice, the sign of his abdication. At worst, I couldn't trigger his death; at best, I could perhaps slow it, he was surely saying to himself, lost in the multitude of family members who wanted to see how he would lose his body. The man I have to defend from the tomb is too old, skeptical, undone by his life, and it requires serious effort. Hadj Brahim, aged seventy-six, a wealthy butcher, doesn't help me. Because he doesn't believe in me. He's always said again and again that my notebooks are the skins of sheep that never existed. I don't care, I keep going: the speed of the writing is one of the conditions of inspiration: it imposes the humility of the porter on you. You become the sweat of the ink, not its inventor. The silent servant of a conversation that's beyond you.

It's only recently, in the village of Aboukir, that they've stopped thinking of me as being troubled by a spirit of dirty waters, or disoriented by a curse resulting from my father's fortune and bloody opulence. Some pity my father for his rotten luck with his first wife. I endured my fate like a gift that came with a duty, despite my sick body, the scandal of my fainting spells, and my refusal to eat meat. There are surely martyrs who have no need for paradise or God to devote themselves to the path of sacrifice. Perhaps the idea of compassion is enough. Or the secret ambition to supplant an idle god with his own eternity. The truth is that it's the confinement of the village that helped me to understand the link between my writing and longevity. I knew every corner of it, the colors of the curtains, the old windows, the chipped cartography of the walls, the slanting tree trunks, the habits of the elderly and the storks. When I wandered to perfect my inventory, list in hand, I provoked the laughter of the passersby who watched me examine the trivial details. Of course, order was often disturbed by the arrival of a stranger or a newborn, we don't live isolated from the world, only restricted, immobile out of laziness or satisfaction, somewhat fearful. And then I would have to redo my calculations.

Sometimes the strangeness severely tested the richness of my inner language and I struggled to find real words for lack of a good dictionary. But I always made up for it with signs, symbols, and drawings that were inexplicable to the layperson. There were also those hackneyed rumors about sex or curses cast by saints, jealousies enormous as fires, divorces, but all of that was meticulously inventoried in the memories of the inhabitants and in my notebooks. What I myself preserved was something else: the inventory of nuances, of faces, of greenery or rust, the order of eternity that I had to restore and the exactitude of presence in the world, the repaired coincidence between the living and their real stories. There you have it. What did I have to do with the story of the unknown donor who had enabled them to construct a very tall minaret for our mosque? Or the story of the Cuban doc-tor who had come to live in our country for a few years and married a thousand women? Or the recurring stories of old migrants in France who came back in coffins to spend one night, one alone, in the vast villa that they had constructed years ago, without ever living in it, at the top of the hill? No! Those stories were only important when they had a connection to a dying person or a child in the grip of fever or afflicted with abscesses.

The village was rather banal, from an outsider's per-spective. An architectural mix between the old colonial houses, occupied by us, and the cinder block extensions, signs of unfinished appropriation. The richest had re-painted, the others were content to sit on doorsteps and await the last prayer. The walls were shared, but not the genealogical trees. Each person recognized his tribe and held onto it as to a border of Barbary figs to ward off intruders and hide the women. We also had connections: the bus from the south, which passed through our village twice per day. At dawn, for those setting out on a quest or a long voyage, and at the end of the day, offering a brief spectacle to the loiterers sitting on the side of the road, near city hall and the gas station.

As a teenager, I had diligently charted that island en-clave. To the north, the hill, the pivotal hillock, place of origin of our family history, place of sacrifice for dozens of sheep per day. On the eastern side, the vineyards, the asphalt road that leads to the farms of the former colonizers then to the inaccessible mountain, the Christian cemetery, enclosed by a low white wall; to the west, the Bounouila cemetery, dug into a stony hillside, between the fragrant grass and where the sun dies. Arriving in Aboukir, you could see an evergreen forest to the right, where I'd discovered two or three old tombs engraved with French names, the market, and a school, my own. The village slumped to the south, connected to the road leading to the Sahara—which never reached us except by the sky—and joined that same road that came from the north, where the city and the sea eroded each other with rocks and salt. A completely blank ostracon, this village pierced with a minaret, engraved with all my childhood strolls. But, in my head, the map was drawn differently: the meager forest became suffocatingly tropical to the east, in response to the swampy lagoons of the south. And, deliberately dazed, I identified, on the big hill to the north, the gutted husk of my father's house, washed up on the reefs, the final imprint of my shipwreck. I could plant coconut trees all over, live in a cave with pink walls, and flee the billy goats that the celestial blessing multiplied around my father, or make a useless inventory of dead trees, walk on the sandy bay to revive an ancient story, and recount the adventure of language like a repopulation.

Poll is a parrot I had found in a book whose duty and name I sometimes assumed. A legendary bird who says a single phrase in *Robinson Crusoe*, but this phrase captures the perfect tragedy, the material limit, the infinite possibility. When I reread this book (often), I stumble upon this enigma, a sort of island within the island. *Zabor* is a book of a legendary and indispensable inventory, and I have to recount the story of my shipwreck. It will save someone, somewhere.

TWO

Language

11

What happened? When did my gift lose steam? I don't know.

I remember feeling a guilty pleasure when I saw my father follow me discreetly with his gaze for the few seconds he was awake on his bed, stirred by sweat, hollowed by agony. Incapable of speaking but screaming, with all his being, his wild hope and his anger at the indignity inflicted by the illness. I remember being struck by the size of his body, so minuscule—bones prominent under his scraggy skin—dislocated by his prolonged bed rest. He was so thin, so malnourished by his vanity! In the bedroom, the silence accentuated his isolation as if he had been quarantined by all of humanity. This diligent silence we create at the bedside of the sick: contrite but respectful, slightly wary of possible contagion. *("When the prey is bitten by the predator, the entire species or the group divides,"* explains the dog. *We say we want to let the dead rest in peace. Yeah, right! We abandon him so we can flee more quickly, or so we can avoid attracting the gaze of the dark wanderer.)* The bedside lamps in the corners tried unsuccessfully to add a sense of mystery: death is harsh, and has an artificial smell despite the sighs or perfumes. The old man *(I remember, there, seated in my pink cave, with my aunt's coffee, while she clumsily tries to keep from making noise)* was dull, blackened by a rage I thought I understood. He was angry at the entire world, not because he was dying but because he was suffering atrociously while others were there, outside, all over the vast universe, insolently showing off their health, unfairly thriving, scattered and vigorous. At one point, his face changed and the anger turned into disdain, perhaps for God. The old man didn't give up, the others didn't notice and believed he was at the end of his life, but I saw it. His face changed again, like a stretch of stagnant water, it drooped, his jaw unclenched and his pupils were eclipsed behind the gray horizon of his irises. That's all I could obtain that first time before being chased away like an outcast. So I had to write another story, as quickly as possible. Which one? I had several, some more powerful than others. *(The story of my uncle who immigrated to France who, each time he tried to come back to the village, lost the use of his legs, couldn't find his shoes, or missed his plane. Or the story of my great-grandmother who understood her death was imminent when she discovered a pair of new white shoes outside the room where she'd been sequestered. Or the story of my cousin who lost the ability to speak after watching too many Indian films, every Friday, in the Colisée movie theater in the big city.)* Then the old man sank into a sort of obtuse refusal, grimacing. I've seen that reaction before, watching over those who come back to life. I think he was questioning why he was the one being sacrificed this time, rather than someone else *(everyone thinks that life must be the spectacle of his own eternity, and death's stage, yes, but someone else's death, always!)*, he couldn't identify the throat-slitter, didn't really know the butcher *(fake laugh)*. That must be a devastating mystery, no longer being able to grasp things. To twitch without being able to hold or grip anything. To lose the sense of touch, of smell, the order of words and the meaning of gravity. I read in a book that the dead, just after passing away, must first crash into the inexplicable: they can't understand why, during the funeral, meals are served to everyone except them, and they feel neglected and humiliated by this oversight. They take offense like kids and see death as an affront.

I'm getting off topic. My gift is afraid. Too antici-
pated, it rebels and withdraws into the lair of my head.
Which didn't work. And neither did the idiotic ultima-
tum of the eldest of the twelve brothers when, last night,
in the shade of the eucalyptus trees (upright sperm whales
dripping in the dark), they pushed me to the old man's
bed. "Three hours, and then you get the fuck out of
here!" Abdel threatened, his gray plaster face completely
still. The same face as the day they pulled him out of the
well, at the top of the hill, when he claimed it was I who
had pushed him. Standing in a line at the bedroom door,
the brotherhood assented, approving the compromise, just
before withdrawing into the night and closing the door
on the father-son one-on-one. Things will get worse for
me if the old man dies, I tell myself. After having been
relegated to a well, I will surely be thrown on the street
with my notebooks and the dangerous legend of my gift.
I'll end up in a zawiya. In the mosque, as a rug duster.
Die of thirst in the forest of Barbary figs that encircles us
for miles in every direction. Impossible pedestrian of the
great Sahara, a perfect labyrinth with no walls or angles. I
can't even leave the village because I faint when I stray too
far from Hadjer and our house.

I remember that the old man, admirable in the revolt
of his heap of bones, stirred slightly at the thirty-ninth

page and almost moved his head. I swear. Still enraged, with his brow furrowed. To greet—even still!—the final hours of his life, he raised a rebellious flag and turned his head so as not to grant God the pleasure of meeting his gaze, which was begging for relief. I've met people like him in the village, angry at the hand that slowly empties their pockets, rifles through the bag of their body and scatters its shiny obsessions. Nothing can fight that, not even verses. (*Death? It inspires faith in spectators and steals it from the dying. I change position because my knees hurt, sitting like this. I leave in a half-hour. No later. Notebooks in hand, I will recount the houses, examine the footsteps, walk around the French cemetery. "Strange, these people who've become memories," concludes my friend the dog. "They are either tombs, or books. Great astronomers lying on their backs." Perhaps...*) The mummy's struggle to recognize the embalmer or catch his gaze. "What can the cadaver do in the hands of the corpse washer?" a proverb asks us.

The fighter in him had recognized me, I think. It ignited a fire in his eyes before he turned away, pretending to sleep under the stone of his face. Same old story. Bitter. I understood. They had of course tried everything to avoid summoning me. They wanted to deprive me of a victory. According to the rumors, the old man's head had been corrupted by chaos; and his long story of a man to whom God spoke in his dreams had transformed into stammering and confusion. Recently, the old man was uttering uncontrollable insanities directed at himself, which didn't help to preserve the memory of his prestige. They had even limited the visits from old friends and from imam Senoussi because, in a strange backlash, the dying man was vehemently ridding himself of all the curse words he had suppressed during all his years of piety and courtesy. Nothing, now, obliged him to keep quiet and conceal his bitterness. Sweet revenge for my grandfather, who had been condemned to silence and reclusion by this eldest son dying today, and who now came back, through the dying man's mouth, to announce to Aboukir what he thought of everyone. I was astonished, to be honest, caught off guard. I thought my grandfather Hbib was dead forever, after bequeathing to the world nothing but silence, a knife, an empty wallet, and a sewing kit he'd used since my grandmother died. And now he was talking again, but on the other side of an agony that was not his own. I suddenly missed his gray eyes. Perhaps he is the real secret of my gift, the convoluted reason for my anger at the gravedigger who had his fun before taking a bite of him. *(He died of tuberculosis, suffocated by his own lungs. The first cadaver I carried in my arms and on my back. When he died, we went through his things, my aunt and I: we found an old pencil, two knives, and a wallet with a photo*

of him inside, eyes wide open, wild, as if hunted by the light, as if he'd
come out of a legend to be exposed. Why? His story is written in a
notebook under the definitive title A Moveable Feast *for, as a child,*
I clearly saw an entire city in his eyes when I examined him. And he
recounted his fake voyage to France and the details of his imaginary
return so wonderfully . . .)

I looked around the room where they had placed
the dying man: plates with the scraps of sweets, proof
of old visits. A somber odor of goat: the reciters of the
Book, who always wear the same djellabas. They must
have been called as a last resort, just after the doctor (I
found evidence of him in the pile of medications pushed
hastily under the wooden bed) and my stepmother's first
ostentatious migraines. Other details? The outline of
a white rectangle on the wall. They had taken down a
pious photo, I'm sure. The kind I hate. The rolled-up
carpet behind the entryway, in a corner. A bottle of
water, probably water from Mecca, from the Zamzam
well that saved the lives of Ishmael and his mother when
Ibrahim reunited with Sara, his wife. Holy water. Except
that death is made of sand. The half brothers had set
the stage for my prestige, despite their manifest doubts,
before coming to knock on Hadjer the spinster's door
to solicit the moron who was always writing unreadable and yet powerful things in his notebooks. What

vengeance! But anyway, I have to set aside my jubilation and vanity.

Get back to the matter at hand.

Typically I ask the name of the dying person. In this case, of course, that wasn't necessary. I wrote the date at the top left, but with a far-fetched, impossible year, sometime between the strict Gregorian and the Hegira led astray by sandstorms, inaugurated by the name of Ishmael's mother and not by the flight of the first believers to Medina. The sons of Hadjer, the Mouhadjiroun, and not the "exiled" as the exegeses claim. My calendar's time is a rare time, between nativity and exile. The tree and the camel, in other words. And I start with three ellipses, almost as a rule, to exorcise fear. In fact, I still have the secret impression that I'm stealing the text from someone else and that reassures me, for paternity and speaking cause me terrible anguish. The paper is still cold under my hand like an empty skin and, when I start, I'm slow as a tattooer. Bad sign, I said to myself, rightly so.

In my notebook, I brood over that humiliating night. Again and again, as a tongue flicks back to the hollow left by a pulled tooth. Because there's something that escapes me and which is the hint of a refused truth. *(In a few hours, it will be dawn. I have to save this life, this specific life, before the muezzin calls and the horizon is ablaze. I lift my head to look at a piece of sky stolen from blind tiles. Behind the door, night must already be searching for a place to cool other parts of the earth. I return to the notebook but it's silent. Nothing happens. My mind is scattered and I don't feel the rush that always precedes my trances. Nothing. Just sweat, which is an inconvenience. It's because the old man worked his acid on my life. For years he's repeated the same story, mocked me and reduced me to a doubt, pushed me away, laughed at my differences, and he ended up inhibiting my capacity to save his life. Perhaps he didn't know he was annihilating his only chance at survival. This is my real vengeance: silence.)* He will only have had what he deserves. But I know that this is a ruse of my vanity. The truth is that I haven't managed to save him. Time goes quickly, embraces you like an ally and then suddenly betrays you, there, in front of everyone *("Time is the heart and its hand your blood that circles and circles, with your arms, your neck, and your thoughts").* It was perhaps the vengeance of books I never finished reading, the ones I dropped at the first page like abortions, disfigured by the tactlessness of their authors. Those stories that didn't manage to seduce me and stayed there, bitter, crouching like widowers, to now come steal my tongue from my mouth. Tiles have started to fall on my head. First one, then all the others like dominoes. I wanted to piss, and to flee. The walls were made of paper and would be ripped by enormous hands, the brothers' hands. Alif, Lâm, Mîm. Nothing came but the reddish, burnt wind of the Sahara...

I have to overcome this unprecedented breakdown of my gift. I write letters as though on quicksand. The old man, now a drooping fox, has always had this effect on me: as soon as he's in the vicinity, I feel as though I were laboriously writing my first words in school, stumbling on a new path in tight or too-new shoes. *(Then the night sky exploded with the thunder of powerful kicks and the door was knocked down. O Hadjer, protect me, they're hitting me, they're chasing me!)*

This is how I must finish this notebook that tells the story of the night when I failed to bring my father back to life.

12

Six months ago, a neighbor was sick. She was thirteen years old and her name was Nebbia. Which means "prophetess," funnily enough. I knew her, she was a staple in my notebooks, described in detail (*The Defense*, followed by *Doctor Brodie's Report*), which preserved her for a long time. A skinny, frenzied child, with big bony knees and a body like a reed, androgynous, sharp, and fast. Sometimes she brought me letters, so that I would read them to her, sent from France by her grandfather's family or by administrative offices and, at the beginning of the month, she agreed to deliver my missives to her mother (*Loose explanation of the word "ardent": link between love and temperatures. Short explanation of* The

Thousand and One Nights *and their three major equations—salvation is in the tale; the final celebration is a book; the book saves the palace, the king, and the storyteller. Strategic encounters for a couple in a village where it's impossible to hide anything. Messages written in a simple language, punctuated with drawings and symbols, hands stained with ink. So that her mother would understand).* Little Nebbia listened carefully as I read and then went back home, cautiously, as though she were carrying a goblet of precious water that she was afraid to spill, repeating my messages to herself. Her father had divorced her mother, and the young girl, with a sister who was still a baby and whom I sometimes heard crying, lived on our side street like a cat, with no schools or borders, near her grandparents who'd been wounded by the fate of their spurned daughter. Nebbia was my responsibility because she was somewhat similar to me, her childish spirit moved me, she was the echo of another reclusive woman whose childhood she was reliving. I was amused by her vivacity, which accentuated her emaciated face and her braided red hair, and I loved teasing her about her boy's games and her harsh manner with the male children who feared her.

They came to summon me when, seated on the doorstep of our house, I was staring attentively at blood of dusk spreading over the clouds *("The night demands a slaughtered sheep, each time, to come show its shiny stones," muses the dog in my head*). The call to the last prayer had just sounded and all the believers were busy absolving themselves. Nebbia's grandfather took me in his arms and murmured: "God sent you" ("God sent you packing!" corrected the little voice in my head). He was wearing a strange white fez, embroidered with a design depicting a miniature town, which wrapped around his skull and made him look like a giant transporting a city on his head. I followed him wordlessly, heart caught off guard, thinking it was for his wife, already old, on the verge of erasure. At the time, my glory was great but my reputation as a widower without a dead wife made some hesitate to bring me to their spouse or into their home without a witness. I thus accepted promptly, as if to refute the rumors. We climbed three steps, then the old man opened the door. Since childhood I had had a keen sense of smell, and I could identify evils by their odor. This time, a fragrance alerted me because, around here, women awaiting death envelop their bodies in fragrances that mitigate their captivity. I detected the scent of a spurned woman—their daughter, the little one's mother. Just an olfactive trace, a path on the sand of absence. The beginning of a tale: a decapitated woman. They explained that Nebbia had been ill for a week and they feared the worst. Her grandfather spoke like a powerless god, through verses and supplications.

In a little dark room, I sat down and started to write while the child was suffering, miserable, asphyxiated by a terrible fever. The same odor of sweat, an acidic sting, was floating in the air. The family had stayed behind the door. The voice of a young woman rang out, anxious, the shadow of a persistent perfume. I knew from my aunt that she was named Djemila. Why did that woman occupy my mind, even though my gift restricts me to asceticism, to a battle more consequential than the struggle against lust? I don't know. Because she was a spurned woman, without a body, a recluse? I myself lived half reclusively in the territory of women, with Hadjer, but that's likely how I learned that there exists an even greater, more terrible isolation. I was disconcerted: suddenly I felt an unfathomable compassion for this invisible body.

Just behind the door, the poor grandmother was moaning and wringing her hands. She called to God, even though he had already sent me. Strange sensation: I was a sort of necessary monster, born of a law, but also the caricature of a body, a third uncircumcised sex, between women and men. For example, I felt compassion for the other even though they were an abstraction, an absence inscribed in memory. But, confronted by the body and the pain of someone present, I became cold with indifference, distanced myself through the exercise of writing. Asceticism is an anesthesia to save one's people. Nebbia was like the other saved neighbors: she served my desire to contain a gigantic memory, tolerating not even the tiniest corner of shadow, absolute like a sun, coinciding with a perfect, complete language, stretched from east to west, each word designating something unique and immortal. Next to the little girl, seated and silent while the perfume outlined her mother and the etymology of her name, I was absorbed in this prodigious dream of the double martyr, of the sufferer and the writer linked by the same work. Every invocation is a book waiting to be written.

To save Nebbia, I wrote, soul cold and vigilant, a single paragraph, a sort of ferocious metaphor, wise, naked as an ancient vase. The single-sheet notebook was entitled *Musashi*, a title stolen from a samurai novel I had never read, and consisted of dialogue. Between the sedentary and the wanderer. Between death and eternity. The stone sharpens the sword, as does desire. But it breaks it too. As does death. Both are necessary. Simple as that. The little girl trembled and, in a murmur, asked for oranges because she was thirsty. I called for her family.

At eleven o'clock, the little girl opened her eyes for a moment, examined us one by one, then sank, finally confident, not into death but into a gentle fatigued slumber. They gave me eggs, honey, coffee. The grandfather didn't know what to say and declared once more that God had sent me. "In the face of death, we are all the same age," he said as if he were reciting a verse. "But Nebbia is still too young!" he groaned.

I thought of the source of the perfume because, since reading *The Thousand and One Nights*, I'd had a weakness for female prisoners. The town had disappeared from the skull of the old man with his fez, revealing a hill afflicted with baldness. His eyes watered, and I didn't know if it was because of his age or his gratitude. Leaving, I hesitated, I searched for a gaze, I could only distinguish a silhouette behind a curtain, slender, with large hips, then the curtain parted and I glimpsed a woman with long black hair, her face seemingly posed on an invisible shoulder, as if detached from her neck by a scarf. That woman's eyes were strange, fascinating like pits but extinguished, sad. She appeared to look at the world through her lowered lids. Nebbia's mother was there, but hidden, half incarnated, as though dead. I was struck because I had heard rumors about her, her inability to leave the house, to go to the baths or laugh at weddings. After divorce, a woman slowly immolates herself and becomes the target of a vigilance that dismembers her. She is nothing more than a fire to survey, cunning genitalia, potential shame. When she is spurned, her head is cut off, separated from her body, and she devotes herself to erasing it, to making it hazy and shapeless beneath the fabric, to empty it of its senses and its shivers. When she raised her eyes, I was destabilized by her soliciting, curious gaze. Should I confess? Yes. Suddenly, all my metaphysics were uncertain, susceptible to being refuted, insufficient to save lives. Salvation reclaimed my body. I'm embellishing, but in truth it made me stumble. I remained there examining this face, until the old man finally pushed me gently toward the exit; his thanks were sincere but circumspect.

In the street, the spurned woman was surveilled very closely, as much by her family as by the idling men. That woman didn't belong to anyone, she sharpened appetites and slander. She was an impasse through which everyone wanted to pass! Body trampled, open, discounted, useless for a wedding, only good for infidelity or hunting. Her fate was a pyre.

I left, I was a bit lost. Then, in my body and in my world, despite my years of writing and devotion, I felt the echo of a past, ignored life. Temptation that I believed impossible—unrealizable because of my choices—or sated by my readings that had brought me something more sophisticated than the desire to marry a woman. Did I want to, in that moment?

There you have it. When I save a life or attenuate the suffering of the sick, that's how it happens—on the best days. Other times, it can lead me to excruciating hesitations. People think bestowing time is easy. They're wrong! Sometimes the great question of Evil is evoked, and that of choice. What to do, in fact, when saving a life amounts to sparing a monster?

I once had to care for an unworthy son, a violent drunkard, who was beating his father and mother. I passed him at dawn, on his way back from a bender, while I was watching over the secret hues and breezes of the early hours. He never looked me in the eyes but nodded his head. He was my age, a face creased by a blind and somber rage. One day, one night, they called on me to save him. He was lying in bed, immobile, masked by bandages, eyes hard and dry searching around him for stones to throw. He had survived a bad motor-cycle accident. Two broken legs and more seriously a broken back. His father stared at him, distant, hateful, and overwhelmed. His mother was trembling with fear. She was awaiting the worst, since this outcast would now have to stay at home. Should I save him? I despised him. It was a question of conscience. I had the choice of a god: write or keep silent. Does evil exist? I don't think so. It's only a consequence. The effect of a cause. It was written that this son would live cursed and that I had to save him, but all that was to be rewritten. By me. Destiny is a notebook filled with mistakes that we can correct. No, the image is not perfect, I'll express it differently: we are the words of a great story, recorded somewhere, but we are in a way responsible for our conjugations.

Three new faces, since yesterday: Nebbia's aunt, who, six months later, came to thank me *(tattooed, enveloped in a haik, fat and benevolent)*; a tree-trimmer who knocked on our door to offer his services *(emaciated, one-eyed, bony as grief)*; an old aunt come from a distant douar to renew the rumors about Hadj Brahim and discreetly ask questions about my heritage. Three lives. *(Hadjer yells that the movie is about to start. I rush to sum up my definitions. My gift is that of a somber man seated at the back of a theater or cinema. It observes: we are all actors paid poorly by the gods, sent back as soon as they get bored or want to change the story and the cast—and then we collapse, fall into holes, die without compensation. Our only resort—ruse of the heavens—is pretending that the play is endless, that the actors and extras are eternal and that the whole universe is this stage, divided by a curtain between the beyond and the here on earth. Which is not true. Which is not TRUE, I shout. Hence the compassion of the somber spectator sitting in the theater that no one notices. Tall, skinny, face hard and handsome, bearing the name Zabor, writing psalms. Rebellious and indignant, he starts to write stories, he rekindles plots, to save the maximum number of actors and extras. He fashions replicas, breathes to mitigate the holes of memory, prolongs the rehearsals. He assigns names, adds text and postpones the end that is on the alert. He manipulates birth dates to perturb death dates. He is alone. He is me.)*

13

(A conjecture: read a book starting at the end. The story goes back in time instead of completing it, and at the same time the pages deteriorate, grow old, become fine, fragile. You turn them and they change, paper becomes papyrus, hemp, goatskin, shoulder blades, tree bark, water under your finger, constellations. You turn the pages and the writing itself turns back time: from typography to manuscript, from manuscript to the drop cap of the copyist, then the symbol, the stroke, the scar of cuneiform, the icon, the design, the rupestrian engraving before finishing—restarting—at the index finger of the hand denoting something, the outline of fur, the undulation of a reptile, the movement of eyes, the hoarsest of sighs, the syllable. Once you've arrived at the first page, you find yourself seated, poet or hunter, contemplating a forest that resembles a line of ink between the dawn sky and the still-dark earth.)

The bedroom window is wide open onto the sky and the lemon tree. Nothing moves in the sparkling dark blue of the afternoon. The surrounding walls block the horizon but the sky is so big that I fall in each time, hands behind my neck, I imagine the tiny planes with passengers watching us, reconstituting our lives in their dreams. I relish my weightlessness when I wake up at the end of the day. Since I can't be an astronaut, I make up metaphors. Earlier than normal, Hadjer turned on the television, finally immobile. The sound is imperceptible but enough to ballast me. Poor aunt who, for lack of a prince, married a magic screen that transports her each night. Hadjer's story is magnificent. Born brown and slender in a country that prefers white skin and women with large hips, she was disgraced from the beginning. Over the years, no one asked for her hand, despite her trips to the baths, her feverish dances at weddings, and the zealous efforts of various matchmakers. She had long hair, beautiful skin, and big eyes, but it wasn't enough to divert her fate. The youngest of my father's three sisters, she was nicknamed—and would be called for the rest of her life—"the little one," Esseghaïra. Now old and on the other side of the dried slope of virginity, she was designated as a "spinster" by the silence of all, refused by men of all ages despite her brother's fortune. That forged her character. She gained tenacity, willpower, independence. But also bitterness and anger, which diminished her. She came into conflict with all the women of the house up top and the affair was settled when my stepmother demanded that we leave—Hadjer, my grandfather, and me—after the incident with the well, even though I never pushed Abdel, my half brother, I swear. Hadj Brahim appeased his conscience by buying the house down below, which sheltered us somewhat from the sandstorms.

I could sum it up with three bizarre stories. Hbib, my grandfather, renounced speaking little by little, prisoner to his powerlessness, surprised by the amplitude of the silence that surreptitiously invaded him; he stopped drinking bagged milk, eating bread from the baker (which is to say bread not kneaded by his sister), commenting on the world or speaking of God and prayers. Ishmael, which is to say me, lost the use of his senses and started to experience strange panic attacks at dawn, which caused him to scream when faced with mirrors and the reflections he saw in them, and to write feverishly in chaotic languages in his notebooks—before he discovered his gift. As for Hadjer, my aunt, her solution was fabulous: one day, in her head, she married a tall man with a languorous gaze and long eyelashes, angry as a force, virile but gentle because he was an orphan. His name was Amitabh Bachchan, he was Indian (Hindu) and rebellious. Hadjer was secretly wild about him; I realized it because of her groaning when she saw him on the TV screen embarking on quests or hunting his parents' murderer, whom he'd recognized thanks to a gold bracelet. I was only ten years old and had to translate everything that man said in those films in his various roles, but also what he said to her, to her specifically, when he turned toward the camera and thus toward our village. A strange exercise that opened the door of digression through infidelity to words.

The films were in Hindi, subtitled in French, they unfurled to the wild rhythm of endless, tumultuous diatribes, actors who spoke rapidly, with emphasis and ample gestures, luminous dresses and burning stares. The subtitles came at an impossible speed, which left me too little time to translate, because at that point I knew only a few French words. I filled the holes or lacks with fantasies inspired in me by their facial expressions, grimaces, intonations and cries. In the end, I was translating directly from Hindi, without waiting for the subtitles, embarking on my first betrayal of language but also my first ruse, the fabulous malice of all idioms. Amitabh spoke to me and I transmitted his words to my aunt as we watched reruns of the film on our television *(at the time, we could watch broadcasts from dusk to ten o'clock at night, except on the weekend, with one feature film per week, in black and white).* Amitabh would come to our house with his frightening haircut and that sultry swaying of his hips, he was part of the family, he walked through the house, distraught, face melancholic or seductive, with his tall and sensual silhouette and his white pants clinging to his body, and Hadjer decided, slowly, that I would inherit his physique as I grew up. The landslide was irreversible. I was destined to end up as a vigilante desired by all, an acrobat, a wild conductor, a dancer, smiling in all circumstances, with strong arms capable of whipping up entire stories. Son and husband mixed secretly in a single body, which allowed her to satisfy her desire for revenge. *(As I write this, I cry over her fate. I was her son, but I wish I could have also been her husband, her lover, her father, the missing half of her body, the sweat of the white horse in promising tales, the Hindu actor, the kingdom streaked with omens, the gallop, the hand touching her and the mouth bringing her a new language. Her aging is the cruelest refutation of my gift's power.)*

Our movie nights extended into the next morning, blurring into images projected onto my future, my clothing, my way of walking and my destiny. Beyond this bleak and exciting game, I had another realization, more essential: translatability. After interpreting so many dialogues, I started to adapt them, then replace them, and finally invent them. As a child I discovered the rift between the word and its meaning, the arbitrariness of sound that reduced language to an attempt, not an essence. Amitabh put all his strength into his words, but he seemed trapped in an illusion, secluded behind a system of gutturals and yelps that claimed to say everything when all they did was summarize the conventions of another village in the world. I didn't understand it so clearly back then, but I had an intuition, even a certitude: language was a lid over the void. An abyss opened softly under my child's feet when an undeniable truth emerged: there had to be a comprehensive, immense language that summed up all the others, that served as the matrix of their possible translation from one to the other and with which one could recount every story without them getting lost or erased. A final and definitive writing in which all writings were united at their mouth, downstream. There you have it. The actor, handsome and immortal despite the car fires, gunshots, poisons, and perilous jumps, played a role, but I entrusted him with another part unbeknownst to him. Amitabh was in our home, but I could go over to his home and say things to my aunt that were difficult to express, forbidden or taboo.

She ceded to the illusion too, and there were nights when we almost spoke like lovers! Such disgrace, I say to myself today, recalling films like *Deewaar* or *Shollay*, and especially *Zanjeer*. But such fun, too.

From that vaguely sensual and troubling time, I remember most of all the first inkling of my task: I needed a perfect, powerful language, capable of replacing Hindi, of sating my aunt, of organizing the world, of offering a release for the excitement already making my body tremble, and finally of protecting me against my father and his stories. I was nearly eleven years old, I was speaking Arabic fluently in school and reading a bit of French. I needed a revelation. Amitabh stayed at our house in Aboukir for a long time, and one day I gave my aunt a photo of him. She was over forty by then. She looked at the photo with indifference but, at night, she cried, combing her long mane, her last remaining adornment. After that, the actor died from neglect; Hadjer opted instead for Egyptian films that she could understand sometimes without my help.

(Another two days of reprieve. If I don't write a long story at his bedside to repair his life, Brahim will die and cut off my own. And Djemila will die because she will travel alone backward through her labyrinth.)

14

How did Hadjer manage to bring me back to the house up top after what happened the day before yesterday? She shouted, threatened, promised to slash their cheeks, bellowing her scandal through all the villages of our valley, yelling curses until she went hoarse, her brother couldn't die without seeing his sister or his son *("half son," says the dog, mindful of true genealogies)*. And in a great spectacle of anger, she insinuated that, if her brother did die, she would be a pebble in the shoe of the surviving brothers and sons and would refuse to go to the notary. The eldest, Abdel, somber as the soot of his melancholy, conceded in the end, explaining that he was giving in to her caprice out of respect for his aunt, but that he refused to cross paths with me again. A neighboring family on the hill intervened in my favor, arguing that, even if I failed to revive the dead, I wasn't killing anyone with my notebooks. Two neighbors escorted me up—it was just yesterday, the day after my first visit. It wasn't at night, this second attempt: I had to break with my routine and follow Hadjer and my bodyguards at around one in the afternoon, under an odious sun that burned my neck and charred the ancestors in my head. I was sweating, nameless dogs followed us at our arrival, up to the threshold of the large portrait of the house up top.

In the brightness of the day, the house revealed great filth, scraps of meals eaten in the courtyard, intimate laundry lying about. The vine seemed small compared to the nocturnal tricks of the foliage the last time I'd seen it. No one dared cross my path, except for the children, whose gazes revealed what the adults thought of me and my aunt. In the room, the shade was cool but the odor still acidic. The old man had become a fistful of flesh in the rumpled hand of the sheet. The storks of death were there, in the large invisible nest of its tomb. I drank the coffee that was offered and Hadjer sat down on the doorstep, my guardian. She started speaking, to erect a sort of wall. She talked about everything: names, resentments, old stories, her mother's names, malformed verses. Her voice got louder and then died back down, became a murmur, a discreet hourglass. She had to keep going for as long as it took me to revive the old man.

I generally begin by searching for a connection between me and the client whose body is withering a little too quickly and whose breath I have to reignite as one relights a fire. The dying person responds with a slight quiver, sometimes lifts an eyelid heavy as a stone and, beyond the crowd of his ancestors, recognizes me or tries to recognize me. It's a troubling moment, my throat knots. And, at the end of the cycle, the dying person always responds with either odious gratitude or jealousy. I'm not an idiot, in this realm of mute truths they inevitably realize the singularity of my gift. Sometimes, gratitude morphs into hatred. Why? The debt to pay is immense. The man understands that the rest of his life, his breathing, and the hour of his death, depend on me, on my diligence and the consistency of my tense conjugations and the precision of my adverbs. All I'd have to do is stop writing and he'd die; as long as I'm hunched over my notebooks, he survives. Somewhat. Or entirely. He might even recover full health if I write faster, if I stop eating, drinking, if I turn the pages at the wild speed of my passion. Often illiterate, my patients start to

hope for endless notebooks, they evaluate them, counting the pages, and rush to procure me more notebooks,
even thicker, in the stores of the big city, along with ink
and pens. In the corner of my boxing ring, their family
members shoo away the flies around me, wipe my sweaty
forehead.

This time, the old man who died was not really a
stranger to me—or was absolutely. He knew, and I knew.
That made him angry like a shameful destitution. He
knew from his panicked memory that I could take my
vengeance for all those years he had tried to belittle me
with his bleak stories from before Independence and
crush me with the epic saga of the sheep that fell from
the sky to take my place in his heart. That was the risk
of the trade. That I might mix my affairs with my magic
herbs.

In the bedroom hung a musty odor, I could almost
smell the stench of decomposition flowing under his skin.
The fragrance of death is not as terrible as its cry, but
it is odious. My notebooks often responded to this by
exhaling an aroma of wet clay that only I could smell—a
phenomenon recalling the impossible disintegration of
the bodies of the three saints who gave their blessing to
our village. The Prophet, they say, experienced the same
miracle: his body remained unchanged and his death

was a perfume that moved to a new vial, from body to tomb. I often wondered, as a child, why no one went to dig him up, either to verify the legend or to boost that religion's miracle. At the time, I believed impiety should be vanquished like an electricity outage. But perhaps what was unchangeable was in fact the Holy Book, the body of work rather than the body, and perhaps we had to recount things in this way to set pilgrims on the path of reflection and miracle. Perhaps this prophet had written or heard a book so powerful that he could no longer decompose after death and would carry on endlessly, over the entire earth, made solid and immutable by the book's chains of transmission and the reciters' dissemination. I don't know. He had surely discovered this miracle long before anyone else, in his cave.

Protected by my care, my school notebooks were always chosen according to the number of pages but also the pattern of the lines, the texture of the paper—which had to be thick, rasping, almost coarse in order to better absorb the ink and consecrate the gesture of the hand moving over it. It was important to write well but also to elevate calligraphy like a lofty song, a preliminary drawing of the territory as a prerequisite to any resurrection.

Without discipline, the ink and the letters clouded again with birds, bushes, vermicelli between my aunt's fingers, snakes, palm trees, the Nile, beaks, horns. The alphabet collapsed, to my anguish, into the ancient bestiary it had come from: the *S* of Sîn was the snake, the *B* of Ba' was born of the hearth, the *A* of Alif with the silhouette of a vulture perched in a dead tree or the gaze of the piercing eye, the *T* of Ta' was the image of the cooking pot, and so on and so forth, provoking my panic. I had to fight endlessly against the temptation of the pictogram and be blind to the letter's ancestors or to its persistent ety-mology to keep nothing in my mind but its immediate usage and my concern for salvation. The ritual I practice is born of a desire for precision, because I had admired the manners of the reciters of the Holy Book with whom I spent my adolescent years *(O sidi Khloufi, our master of the Holy Book, who always regarded me with suspicion)*. I learned from this, despite myself, that the outline of the word is as important as its meaning, like the caress during a proclamation of love, or the contour of the lip to cali-brate a kiss.

In those idiotic, fervent years, I realized that the act of tirelessly rewriting verses on the tablet, the curve of the ink released in the upstroke, the care brought to the thickness of the symbol as it blooms, are already an apposition of hands on a body, the start of reparation through palpation. If writing comes from the hand, we can move from its outline to the palm and from the palm to the heart or the illness. It was the implicit law of this profession practiced by the talibs and the reciters of the Holy Book trying to wrest from oblivion the exact translation of the word of God as it had been revealed to the Prophet. Which is to say that I always experienced clumsy writing as a troubling stain, something like a betrayal or an epidemic.

In that room with the leprous walls, my hands trembled before I even grasped the first pen with black ink. I almost spilled the cup of cold coffee they had served me and I didn't dare meet the gaze of the old man who had destroyed my bones for so long. Yes, I had a desire for vengeance or murder, I admit it. So to tempt the devil, who is a rumor, I decided to do nothing, as he had wanted to do nothing for Djemila, or for my mother. I suspended my gesture and time. Behind the door that they had barely repaired, I could hear Hadjer's voice, indistinct but familiar like the old scarf she used to wrap around my head to soothe my migraines.

The truth is that I felt cold, indifferent, incapable of love or tenderness. The old man, his breathing painful, seemed to be climbing a slope. From time to time, his feet jolted abruptly as if he'd missed a step or tripped over a pebble. He was already half cadaver, his index finger pointed toward the sky. The other half was trying to extract itself from the tomb with the single hand and the fourth of a leg that were still alive. An insect on the bark of a eucalyptus tree. Gnawed by illness, his flesh no longer held any temptation for death, that ancient animal who so loves the aromas and cracks of bones nourished with greasy marrow.

In my first notebook, I described his limbs, so scrawny under the sheet, like branches covered with cloth. He had clearly been suffering for months, but that left me cold and distant like an asteroid. His cancer had been slow, patient in its devouring, and now it was sucking his bones, sated. On the altar of God, the debris of the ceremony that had gone on for months: a pile of useless medications, honey deemed miraculous by Tradition, a chamber pot of a dubious white, numerous bottles of mineral water, and the fruit that visitors kept bringing him when only his eyes could still bite into them. *("The fall is initiated by a fruit and the departure by a raven!" explains my dog.)* The old man would die in turmoil if I couldn't find a story to write.

I tried to focus on making an inventory of the objects in the room, as we do when we're invited into an unfamiliar home and the host excuses himself to serve the coffee. A horrid carpet, Koranic illustrations (replaced after my first visit), and the armoire from his wedding, the second one of course, when he married the spouse who was there, on the other side of the wall, worried about her fate or vaguely happy at the idea of being free. Vile plastic flowers and fabrics covering the orange and mauve mattresses intended for visitors. Not a composition of colors: a nausea. And the stench of a fermenting body that the earth would soon drink. In his solitude, the man sometimes opened an enormous eye that seemed to drift on its own above black water, then closed it again, vanquished. I looked at my hands. Strangely, they had an almost autonomous life: free to grab on to what didn't exist or to rifle through the tapestries of phantoms, they moved, gripped, crocheted, pointed at an invisible being or piled up denials with the same finger that had become a tiny god at the end of the prayer, establishing a fascinating dialogue between the appendix and the cloudy sky that I would be smart to translate into my awaiting notebooks.

Which chattering parliament would the sufferer have to face in the guise of a prerequisite to his final hour? I had convictions: death is a quarrel against memory. I speak from experience, and because my intuition is

ferocious as a tooth. I don't believe we die in solitude, as
is said in sad songs and books, but in the heap of dense
crowds, jostling our elbows to forge our path, as when
we try to find our shoes leaving the mosque. I'm sure that
death attracts a crowd: the living family members, the
dead who approach with curiosity. On one side, silence,
on the other, the hubbub of a hammam. Right? I imagined the beyond as a stampede where millions of people
with different beliefs pile up and cross paths. Sometimes,
after the hardship, people have asked me to remain at
their side so they can dictate their memoirs to me, for
"O, glory to Allah, I've finally understood!" But this
desire runs dry and at first their regained health brings
embarrassment (when the miracle survivor crosses me
again in the street), then to that bitter oblivion I've already mentioned. In the end, the man prefers the mosque
to shaking my hand. Those who have money leave for
Mecca to wash their bones of my memory. As for the
women, I never see them again, or only after they've lost
their last teeth.

This time, the man before my eyes was not yet in the
clear. What could I do? I had to scribble, faster, sur-
mounting the scattering of my mind and of the alphabet.
Outside, Hadjer was going up against a dozen women:
she was evoking her rights as the sister of the dying man,

her share of the inheritance, the glory of her father who
had become mute and then saintly before he wound
up a cadaver exuding the perfume of paradise; she was
patiently explaining that my refusal to eat meat and my
fainting at the sight of blood were proof of my purity
and not of my curse.

Then suddenly, I started to write. My salvation depended on it.

15

(In a few hours, my half brothers will return; time is their dog who searches for my footprints and barks at me. They agreed to leave me at Hadj Brahim's bedside for half the day, to give me—give him—a chance. Sounds of dishes remind me that I'm hungry and that the members of this stingy household haven't served me a thing. I slept very little and I'm not used to being awake during the day. It makes me nauseous. Too much noise. I feel like I'm in a train station or a hammam. I had forgotten just how glaring the sun was, after so many years of nocturnal vigils.)

We always start with ellipses, as if to signal that we are resuming an old story interrupted by dawn. Before starting the song or the recitation, the oracles and poets from before the Prophet let out a series of cries, noble

jabbering that turns into letters of the alphabet. Alif/
Lâm/Mîm. The famous Nūn. The mysterious Sâd and
the evocative Taha. That untamed abecedarium rattled
like a necklace of bones, intended to draw attention as
much as to show the cracks in language, the Holy Book
reveals this through its Meccan surahs, created when the
Prophet had to distinguish himself from poets and surpass their prestige in the eyes of the tribes of that time.
I thought it was a whim when I discovered this custom,
but I understood later that it was actually an invocation
to exorcise silence, or witness the very place of the birth
and the limit of language. The letters had been thrown
to the sky like dice, to break with routine and clear the
way for renovation. Through the god or the poet. They
were the verbose opposite slope of a great silence, indifferent and savage.

I use these three periods in my own way, like bread-
crumbs in the forest, white pebbles, another man's
footprints on my deserted island. I can multiply metaphors ad infinitum but I could never express the relief
they bring me each time, hooks in the heart of the night,
artifices to conjure fate, before writing takes me like a cadence. I was sharing breath with the dying man, finding
his story again within his defeat and restoring his need to
live. Amusing, right? It was a Friday when I read my first

book cover to cover. *("Faster!" whispers an annoyed shadow. A black face contrasts with the bright light of the outside through the half-open door. Hadjer has interrupted her story to speak to me for a moment. "Faster! They're going to get in, those bastards.")*

The village is surrounded by about twenty douars where endogenous marriages guarantee the same old name for all and assure that the first names of the dying are transmitted to newborns. The familial hill is the site of the shipwreck. That's where one of my ancestors set foot, the father of the first tribe that settled on this land, outside the village, at the time of the colonizers, and maintained the fear of descending the slope, the desire to live discreetly behind the world, and the perfunctory mannerisms of secondary characters. Our house down below, in the village, belonged to a Frenchman whose name I never knew. It's an old building with three rooms, a ceiling, a kitchen, and a "four-season" lemon tree with heavy, neglected fruit.

I go back there, to that house, at dawn. I sleep nearly all day, to avoid meeting people my age preparing for their weddings with smiles and lewd innuendos, seeking the best carpenter to make the nuptial bed and the wedding armoire. I don't work but, sometimes, families that have solicited me on an uncertain night for a dying loved one have brought us eggs, vegetables, leftover crops, or even coffee, sugar, sodas. Depending on their degree of gratitude. My aunt Hadjer hesitated at first, then she decided to accept these offerings that she came to consider a right, maybe even an homage spilling over onto her, a reparation for her family's scorn. In the courtyard, I would listen to the long debates between her and her rivals or imaginary neighbors; she would use reason and negotiate her good faith with invisible beings, as she plucked the chicken offering or washed the potatoes left by my father in a crate on the doorstep.

I remember my grandfather sitting in the sun, immobile, all covered up, his greenish eyes noting everything in a vast imaginary notebook—until he died drowned in the blood of his lungs. Hadjer's dark skin gleamed with the effort of cooking, exuded a sweat that made her desirable. Those were the best moments of the summer, the endless season in my narrative. The most beautiful part of her story was the list of supposed suitors who had asked for her hand and who, one after the other, had succumbed to a fatality. I loved when she described the nice car, the virtue of the handsome stranger, the illness that would later ravage him, and she would list parallels between him and her Indian actor. There were about thirty of them: distanced by a brother, led astray by a future stepmother, driven away by a bad-mouthing cousin, discouraged by the barriers of the Barbary figs, given the wrong address to our house by a malicious neighbor, etc. At thirty, she was already, in our universe, too old to seduce or bear children. So she stayed there, peeling potatoes, taking care of my grandfather and me and watching Indian films.

The poor woman, I understood early on, had no role, between the bride she was not yet, the old stepmother she would never be, the prostitute she couldn't imagine being, and the young spinster still waiting for someone to come knock on her door. We were alike, that's why she decided, I think, to keep me as one sharpens a knife, as one fashions a slingshot, or perhaps as one raises a son. I loved her and I made sure to populate her world by translating as many films as possible. When I was a child, she would hit me hard when she got angry; I knew it wasn't out of hate or a lack of love, but because she had been hurt by the village. Like me, she avoided the outside world, the bath at the end of the week, the weddings of others, the meetings between women, or the matchmakers who made fun of her and her withered hope. (*"Yes, that's my son. He was given to me by God, and not by an idiot with empty pants,"* yells my aunt, sitting in front of the dying man's *bedroom door.*) I was her son in the disorder of dead leaves fallen from the genealogical tree. She never ceded to the temptation of letting death in, except for the day when she waited for a suitor who never came.

I remember that day like a bad night: two of my aunts had been there since the morning, Hadjer had suffered through the ritual of the bath, the clay exfoliation, the waxing, her hair had been braided, and she'd tried on dresses. The house smelled like sugar, the vanilla of cakes, and we had dressed my grandfather in a lovely djellaba and placed him in a corner of the courtyard. The marriage proposal is a rite for women which is then validated by men. The first negotiations are among women. That day, the suitor's family had to come scrutinize my aunt's body, evaluate her health, examine the whiteness of her skin, and determine her real age. We had practiced everything, including my discretion. The novelty was exciting to me at first. But then, wandering through the courtyard, watching my grandfather and counting the leaves of the lemon tree, I vaguely understood that it posed a vital threat to me. Another of my aunts had been telling me since the day before that I shouldn't worry: at worst, I would go live with her in the douar, to the east of the village, and she would raise me as her son. I understood then that the crumbling of my universe was possible, perhaps even imminent. The memory of the wind came back to me and lifted the flaps of my grandfather's djellaba. Dust filled my mouth and worry coursed through me. I had been an idiot fooled by sweets. Who saved me? A beggar, perhaps. Or a cunning child who looked like me, who scattered the visitors telling them another address and watched them grow distant with their baskets. Or a rumor about Hadjer's age. In any event, my aunt and her sisters waited the entire afternoon, in vain. The most painful moment was when her sisters departed: they had to find a pretext to leave without trampling on Hadjer's adorned body. She said nothing that day, nor the next, nor the next. She stayed riveted to the television, didn't move even when there was nothing on the screen but wild agitated ants in black-and-white. She started eating raw lemons, excessively salting our dishes, and her skin dulled. It would take her years to forget that affront and she shut herself away even deeper inside our house, which became a body for the both of us.

She's the one who insisted that I go to school; she's the one who drove me down chaotic paths toward this gift she only half believed in, I think. When I was five years old, she dressed me in a black apron, combed my hair with a painful vigor, sprayed me with bland perfume and explained to me that I had to cut across seven side streets to the west, before crossing "the street for cars." On the first day, she was there, enveloped in her haik, eyes burning with pride and something like anger to dissuade slander. She took me by the hand until the eighth side street and remained planted there following me with her gaze while I thrust myself into a suffocating, dusty universe, swarming with commotion and the stamping of the other village children led as a group toward the free school. What did she feel? Fear, certainly. Time took my hand in her place, leaving a shadow and a rock in her stomach. I was the only man who had sought out her touch, sometimes, on stormy nights, I knew. I remember the gleaming golden buckle that decorated my new shoes and shone in cadence with my steps, in the light of the hot September day. I also have a distinct memory of the other kids' attitudes toward me, their curiosity and distance. I was the son of Hadj Brahim, a rich and respected butcher who sold the meat they were only allowed to eat once per week, on Friday, with the couscous. The illusion of esteem broke a few days later when I heard one of the children, the most brazen, imitate a bleating goat. That made the group laugh, and their violence was unleashed. Soon after, I concluded that school was not at all enjoyable.

I realized my difference there. I learned things quickly, with a facility that surprised even me and which, I think, was explained by my fear of being bored. My schoolmaster, Mr. Safi, half bald, alert and often skipping about despite his enormous stomach, was amused by my unenthusiastic intelligence, but he worried about my uncommunicative nature. I wasn't sad, just distant, indifferent. What might have passed at first glance for a sharp mind was soon revealed to his adult eyes to be a deception on my part to remain far, elsewhere, by refusing to join the group. Or the sign of a graver illness destroying my mind much more than my body. And on top of it was my nasally voice, the bleating that dissuaded him from asking me questions in public to avoid the other students bursting out laughing. My timbre was a stigma but also a nice excuse to consider my silence as a compromise agreed upon by everyone. No one seemed able to tolerate this tremolo that struck the heart like the bleating of a goat and transformed the beautiful words flitting around my head into painful croaks. *(Could Poll have rid himself of it, without jeopardizing his gift? There's nothing more horrible than the squawking of parrots, as we all know.)* They left me sitting alone at the table in the back and they granted me my silence as a right and a duty. A recluse, I was brilliant but with the nonchalance and indifference that neutralized the admiration of others and kept them distant, wary, or even disgusted. My distinction was seen as a handicap and the other schoolchildren sometimes opted for meanness, other times for quarantine. But what escaped my schoolmaster as well as the agitated kids of my generation was that it was a godsend for me: I learned more quickly and, although I was barely six years old, I was already stumbling over the unbelievable convention of writing and the major conceit of language!

It was October, I think the beginning of the afternoon. I remember a feeling of suffocating, of boredom, and a persistent desire to go back home to watch the lizards on the whitewashed wall of the courtyard. The shack that served as our classroom heated the air and made the teacher's head sweat. As he inspected our rows, I traced a vertical line in mauve ink, blotting paper under my hand. The wet tip of the quill squeaked against the paper then stopped. Above the tree, I drew a curve. We had to retrace the same stroke, over and over, until we could control it between the fine lines of the notebook. To draw what? At that age, I hadn't yet grasped the connection between the ink and the scattering of the world. How writing ropes everything together. I learned to write

through obedience, without accessing the forbidden.
Writing, the alphabet, remained limited to the frame-
work of repetitive exercise, Hadjer's universe stayed in its
corner, and I was there, mute, incapable of overcoming
my bleating voice. Through the classroom window, I
could see a distant fig tree that looked like an old man
trying to scale a wall and, closer, two eternally green
weeping willows, cascading. The wind kicked up dust in
the playground and I was missing a lot of words, including the ones that could have summoned my mother's face,
now hazy. It formed a knot in my throat that made me
cry. The teacher looked at me for a long time, hesitated,
then decided to send me home before the end of class. I
remember saying nothing to my aunt that day, I rewrote
the few letters I'd practiced relentlessly, entangling them
like twine, stretching them until they overflowed the
pages, linking them to ink stains. Savage once more in
the house, I saw a strange liberty in them, the possibilities of composition. Taha, or Alif/Lâm/Mîm. Those
were my first steps on the island. (*I turn the last page; I still
have three notebooks left of seven, it's like my hand is holding vibrating
reins and Hadjer is an ancient warrior.*)

A week later, I discovered, at the same time as my
schoolmaster, that I had learned to read long before the
other schoolchildren. Seamlessly, because each night I

devoted myself to the exercise, mingling the letters like jacks. A sudden order emerged, and my bleating voice stopped bleating, in my head, at the very moment when I learned to decipher the first words. A deceptive recovery for, as soon as I closed the textbook, I fell back under the sheep's sonorous reign. It was then that, in an almost sickly haste, I started to hunt for words and utensils, the smallest objects came alive, were revived, inventoried: I just had to know how to write them to bring them back to my attention. O inaugural miracle! I was looking at a dark new world, like the forest at the entrance to the village. I felt my new dignity as firmly as if they had bought me new clothes. My joy was nearly complete, but it was very quickly ruined by an unexpected and troubling result: compared to the language of school, Hadjer's language, which had been my language since birth, proved insufficient, meager, like a sick person whose hands couldn't grasp objects or point at faraway or dimly lit things without trembling. I realized this over the course of my education. When I understood, I felt surprise (especially because no one could explain it to me), then scorn, and finally anger. *("You ate my brother's sheep, and today you eat his body and his eyes!" yells my aunt, as a diversion I suppose, to draw their attention, like a lightning rod.)* I don't know what fallacious reasons I used to conclude that my illness and sadness, which had endured for so long, didn't stem from a character flaw, or from my mother's death, or from my bleating voice, but from a reclusive language, ignored by books and school, hidden and forbidden. Like my aunt. Abruptly illuminated by that revelation, the house down below seemed dirty, drab, vulgar. It was the island of desolation, the site of my shipwreck, bodies swollen on the sand, the beached boat of my memory, the darkness of the flora still silent behind the lines of writing. The discovery of the miserable gap between Hadjer's language, mixed and hybrid, and the language of school, evolved into bitterness against my own world, and I became a mean child at home, and cowardly outside.

16

Hadjer didn't understand my sulking in the days that followed, nor why I was striving more and more to imitate my grandfather, staring, seated at his side against the same wall. I remember the disappointment provoked by that betrayal: the words that my aunt had given me were somehow, inexplicably, the last echo of my mother's voice, whose face had been erased in my memory. In the end, the storm culminated in shame and I renounced, after two or three tries, writing the words of Hadjer and the village in the Arabic alphabet they had taught me at school. The words were stiff like the peasants who arrive in the city, stammering and clumsy, hesitating in front of stores. I was sad and irritated, but

also stubbornly in love, attentive to the interruption
of the other language, the Arabic of school, which was
slowly taking possession of the walls, enriching itself
with each new term, tattooing and snatching the various
objects of my universe. Oh, not an infinite language,
but already sovereign! I found it strange that the village
language didn't have a name, while the school language
had books, poems, songs. Hadjer's language was experienced and concealed like the body of a woman, or like
genitalia; as for the school language, we had to attach it
forcefully or carefully—like a protective cover—to each
pebble, tree, stork, or minaret. A difficult but fascinating
language, treating the village like a wild horse. With my
years of schooling, it started to speak in place of God
and the heroes of the War of Liberation, and I started to
notice the weakness of that powerless, deaf, and loquacious language: it had a lot of words for the dead, the
past, duties, and the forbidden, but few precise words for
our everyday life. Even though I was very young, I had
the feeling that it spoke only of the dead and not of my
village, which for me was big as the earth at that time,
nor of my body or my universe. Its way of describing the
world seemed to conceal a sickness, a secret shame, scorn.
To tell the truth, it closely resembled my father when he
approached me stinking of his burnoose and his sheep,

repeating his prayers at the mosque and his invocations, giving me grand lessons to flatter his own vanity. I mean to say that the language was missing the ability to tell nice stories for people my age. (*My back starts to hurt and I can't feel my right shoulder anymore. I pause to search for the best word, consider a few, then opt for the most vigorous. The old man sleeps as though he's been wrestling. The sugar at the bottom of my coffee cup induces a cold shiver.*)

In my first school notebooks, the alphabet was tempted by calligraphy, the pictogram, the strikeouts imitating fleeing animals. Letters reached for their supposed roots and revealed their ancient births. Ba', derived from *beit*, meaning house, the place we return to, where we take off our shoes. Or the inaugural Alif, the vulture with the sharp eye, the first gaze, perched on a tree in the form of the *hamza*, the domestic animal, the ox. Or Jîm, drawn like a rippling snake in the clay of a river, with its one eye. The series was long and made me think: Ta', meaning bread, the hearth with the fire, the cooking pot, *ettannour*. Kâf, derived from *kaff*, meaning palm, or Ya', come to the world to evoke the hand, *el yadd*. And especially Nūn, which I repeated tirelessly, evoking water, the inkwell, the horizon, dusk or dawn, the whale, the immense and slow fish that swallows the earth to turn it into a holy book. I was lost in reconstituting this dictionary, an inventory of animals or utensils of primitive times: the hearth, the fire, the house, the dusk, the ox, the grain. Each letter indicated an object at the end of its imprint, caressing an ancient presence. And I immobilized it like a hunter to catch the meaning in my notebook. I told myself that there had to be a meaning to the order of the alphabet. Perhaps Nuh had saved the animals in that order, which gave birth to the order of writing after the water ebbed. I wrote more and more quickly and marvelously well, the shepherd of my flock of wild animals, a happy and triumphant parrot (Poll, who became sovereign by multiplying words). It gave me a sort of aura that spared me from elbows and kicks during recess. The other schoolchildren also sometimes needed me to transcribe their lessons for them. Intrigued, Mr. Safi figured out, I think, this pathological pleasure, and sometimes worried about it as though it were a form of possession. His evidence was that my voracity didn't stem from intelligence alone, but also from panic. "Haste will cost you!" he repeated to me, powerless, before picking up his chalk. He must have been astonished by this chaotic gift that had emerged in the puny body of the butcher's son.

That happiness lasted a long time, intoxicated me for a while before petering out, faced with a physical boundary: the few books capable of making an inventory of all the things I could see and sense. The village didn't have collections, bookstores, old books, or a library. The Arabic language was omnipresent on the radio, at school, at the mosque, but seemed to possess, to my eyes, only two books: the schoolbook and the book of God. At the start of my second year, I grew tired of the textbooks and verses. *(What time is it? I have to be precise: my art is not a matter of simply sitting near a dying person to make them a centenarian or to spare a sick person from suffering and oblivion. Of course not! The world is saved thanks to my long writing sessions, similar to prayer or census, that I impose on myself in my room every day. My notebooks are swollen by the torrent of a single narrative, with neither head nor tail, which carries within its violent lessons walls, porticoes, odors of ground coffee or mysteries of female armpits, colors of dresses, gleaming almond trees in spurts of petrified water, it mixes birthdates, names, and hands in a total and devastating flood. The story is essential to lift up a dying person, but rescuing the village from futility requires a Herculean narrative. It's a vast enterprise: a meticulous description of the place, of the sign announcing Aboukir on the road which leads to the city all the way to the first Barbary fig trees in the south. The world owes its perpetuity only to the necessity of its description by someone, somewhere—that's a fact. Sometimes my stomach is in knots at the idea of forgetting a detail and thus participating in a death, or accelerating it. When I forget, death remembers. This important mission* has changed my body, hunched my shoulders, cultivated discipline. Yes, the lack of a library in Aboukir forced me to transform every possible notebook into solid, full books. Whom can I explain this to? Hadjer? The imam of the village, my former schoolmaster whom I still see, now old but still sharp and skipping? Whom can I tell about my Zabor? The ancient sigh of my ancestors turned into a proverb that asks, "Who will believe you when you speak as a prophet?," a proverb that the young hardly know. I'm reminded of the story of Daoud, David in the other Book, the prophet to whom God gave a single voice and the ability to sing a song for which the mountains would serve as a choir. Why did the mountains answer and not the men, the singers and the believers? Did God choose that metaphor in an attempt at gratuitous elegance? No. It was to say that language is a transcendent order. When it's perfect and precise, it provokes the response of mountains, of the mute. The Zabor, the psalms as the others say, are a song and a book, a writing of all kingdoms at once, and that's why even stone has a language within it.

I shout, "Yes, I'll be quick!" God had six days and I have only three hours. I don't know what Hadjer is saying, sitting in front of the bedroom door, to keep the tribe at a distance, but she is succeeding as a storyteller. "She postpones your decapitation," says my dog, with his improvised Thousand and One Nights, his eloquence, and his craftiness.) I was missing the dream, the mystery of the tale, I realized later. We were a country recently liberated from colonization and words acted as soldiers, imitating the uniform through their rigor and striving to sing the earth, the blood of martyrs, the water. In the courtyard, they were chanting hymns of the revolution; during the hours of drawing, they drew the flag or the severe face of our president. I found the same words on the banners of national festivals, on coins, on the classroom chalkboard, in the repetitive prayers. A prodigy, I was soon bored, exhausting one of the most beautiful languages of the world that had been offered to me without its arousing, bushy genitalia.

When I was around eight years old, I lost hope, with no playmates or possibility of naming things precisely. Even more strangely, I lost the last features of my father's face, which Hadjer's story had once patiently helped me to reconstruct. There was nothing left of it. No pain, no precision. During the weekend siestas, I observed my aunt's brown body, which she still took great care to bring to the baths at the time, her armpits accouncing her breasts, I inhaled the wood in the fire of the hearth, I placed my cheek against the cold tiles of our house, but all of it escaped the language of school. Written on paper, it stayed there without moving, powerless, when I returned home, to live once more among the objects of the house or to name things, paralyzed like my grandfather Hbib. It would die like a fish out of water when outside of books and school because, in our home, no one used it to control the scattering and the invisible. I discovered much later that it was eminently rich, capable of designating the nuances of water and sand impossible to find anywhere else, but I believe that its sickness, to my eyes, came from its incapacity to provoke mystery and pleasure. I never succeeded in turning it into a rite; it's not the language's fault, or mine, but the fault of those who presented it to me like a baton and not like a voyage, like a language of God barely permitted to men, which deterred me from a young age. The truth is that the language was poorly taught by frustrated people with harsh stares. Nothing that might open the path to desire.

I liked calligraphy, which contorted itself around objects to envelop them in ancestry, surrounded them like a wise old serpent and then flowed like a dress, like women's hair, ivy, or trails. I loved writing in Arabic, but my words sometimes looked like heresy to Mr. Safi, who didn't understand this extravagance in my notebook, next to writing that was quite diligent and obedient.

Today (*Steps scrape the ground. A chair. A child whines until his demand is met. In the distance, a eucalyptus tree being sawed?*), I sum up this evil from my childhood but I believe that I experienced it in disorder and confusion. As a child experiences his parents' divorce. But learning to write in school gave me a glimpse of the gap that exists between the object and the sound. Before Indian films. The texture of my universe was not yet the ink of my writing, it didn't correspond, and remained unruly, distant, as if on the other bank of a river I couldn't cross, not knowing how to swim. Suddenly, because they could be named in two languages *(including the language of Hadjer, who is still unleashing her stream of words on the other side of the door)*, the trees of the house, the walls, the vineyard, the spoons, and even fire take on a strange face.

That was the beginning of my sickness and my first screams.

17

I like to go down the hill as quickly as possible. I feel—and have since childhood—like I'm taking giant footsteps, seven-league leaps. The village below spreads its roofs, its TV antennae, and will peter out in the south, at the first fields. Where I faint, always, when I try to get away from Aboukir. I glimpse the giant eucalyptus trees, below, which turn their back to the village and leave in pairs, at the edge of the road. The whole valley is green and yellow because of the harvests and the inevitable summer droughts. Hadjer follows me, speaking again to imaginary crowds. *(When did I start recounting a story that will lead me to the end of the world? Where does this verbiage in my head come from, that nothing can stop? Anger and clenched teeth. Behind the verbose gift, a sober certitude, sometimes masked, sometimes tenacious, that repeats to me what my father has always said: I am a freak.)* It's like the flight of mother and son through the desert. I have my notebooks in my bag and I walk quickly. I have to evade Hadj Brahim's son, but also the disappointment that weighs in my stomach. Did I save the old man or did I condemn him? I don't know. Hadjer pitted herself against everyone for several hours and I wrote without stopping. In the end, she opened the door and told me to make a run for it—"The dogs are coming!" Harsh words, as always. The story ended with a strategic retreat. His own was a long delirium about our history, the debts, the money, the number of sheep. My aunt deployed the talents of a lawyer or a storyteller, or both at once. Like an excerpt from *The Thousand and One Nights* meant to distance the inhabitants of the palace from Scheherazade, immobilize them before they could alert the evil king. As for my story, it was also long, torrential.

The old man was perceptive to it and his story resumed in his head, I think. He didn't awaken entirely but his body changed color, the noise around him was that of sleep, not of insects. I don't know what came over me, I almost broke my golden rule never to touch the dying person. I gently arranged the sheet that covered him and felt the urge to speak. With the cold voice that I have always used to speak to him. Why? I don't know. As if his agony signaled a truce. I was struck by a sort of lucidity, beyond my writing, and I thought of grazing his face, feeling his body (*"The father's body doesn't exist, we feel nothing but the weight and the hollow, in turn,"* my dog *tells me, mindful of my unprecedented gestures*). We had never had physical contact, a caress or squeeze of the hand, an embrace of protection and tenderness. I had always kept the same distance from him, one and a half yards, ever since I was four years old. In fact, I had never seem him touch anyone, only his sheep, which he groped before purchasing and when he slit their throats—eyes closed, concentrating on his art, feeling the tendon or the fat to deduce the price or the origin, to imagine the taste of the meat. I brought my hand to his forehead and remained there, like an idiot, with no language able to describe my sentiment. I was afraid he would wake up and smile at me, victorious. So I sat back down. Another two or three hours of vigorous writing and he could open his eyes and get back to counting his flock.

I had a title for the notebook of his salvation: *To the Lighthouse*. I plunged in and that was the beginning of the miracle. The blood was ink black, the body was a calligraphy that I could wind and unwind to set a rhythm according to the mysterious art of correspondence: each time I found a good formula, its blessing spread to the dying man and restored a cadence to him, the breathing of a slow awakening. My father came back to life, I knew it without even lifting my head, because of my power, because of this mystery within me that comes from far away: when we tell a story around a fire, the night recedes and grows attentive. Why do we write and read books? To amuse ourselves, responds the crowd, uncritically. Wrong: the need is more ancient, more vital. Because there is death, there is an end, and thus a beginning that it is up to us to restore in ourselves, a first and final explanation. To write or recount is the only way to turn back time, counter it, restore it, or control it. There's a link between conjugation and metaphysics, I'm sure of it. It's the first law to decipher. As soon as I lift my head, I suffer from fragmentation, guilt knots my heart when I stop and everything flees from me like sand through my fingers. So I come back and feel close to discovering, at the end of each lovely phrase, a sort of ultimate explanation. It gives me courage, grandeur, self-confidence. That's when the breath returns to the other's body, as if I had managed to plug an invisible leak. There you have it. My life would have had a simple beauty if the old man had kept me instead of swapping me for sheep fallen from the sky of his superstitions. He was there, dying, and I was at his bedside, diligent. Another two or three hours and he would have emerged, thanks to the details in my notebook. But Hadjer opened the door to shout at me to leave. Her ranting couldn't hold back time any longer, already my stepmother was slapping her thighs, crying that I was a demon that had to be chased away. "Before he kills his father like he tried to kill his brother!" she yelled, forcing her indignation.

The sun sets and the sky leans to the west. Gravity, perhaps, or the dimmed brightness will elevate the stars to the east. The end of the day is always fragrant because of the numerous shrubs. The island of desolation is desolate no longer. I know its outline, I bred words there, a language of order and inventory, I pushed back the savage world through work and tillage, in a way. A title: *The Sleep of the Just.* Because of the image of a giant sleeping under a tree so big that it requires the wild race of a horse launched at a gallop for one hundred days to cross it. I like this title as the expression of the right to sleep, the possibility of deep sleep after acquittal, a possible return to innocence. I lower my eyes so as not to meet the stares of others. I already have enough lives to save. We hurry back home, like foreigners *(but my writing slows down, my hand lifts, and I search. The house seems like a calm island, the moment between day and night when every kingdom goes quiet. I allow myself a moment of laziness. I lie on the back of the whale).*

18

I'm lying down. And I feel the old book with the dog-eared pages. The same for years now, every time I need to consider my story from a different angle. On the cover is a man dressed like a bush, holding a long rifle, speaking to a parrot striped with all the colors of the world. The longtime scarcity of books in the village has forced me to cultivate a habit: rereading. Without exhausting myself. I read differently: I start with the first word or I hold the book like a closed box, to force myself to dream it, to imagine it in its enclosure, or I stop right at its title to transform it into a kite. Or I read a part to provoke the mesmerizing digression of the dog that speaks within me. Rereading doesn't kill the mystery because the book is a body, not a straight line between a beginning and an end. I turn it around or enhance it or caress it or charge in, word by word. I discovered one day that the word for "page" was derived from the word for "country." Thus, when we open a book, we enter a world. But my link with the word is carnal, and I decipher in an attempt at fulfillment, at stripping a body bare.

Robinson Crusoe is the most fascinating of my found books. I fell in love with that story a long time ago, and it has since become something of a holy book for me. Ah, the hours I've spent following in the footsteps of that man who was in search of the footsteps of another! I went down all the bifurcating paths, all the possible combinations. I remember the encounter with Friday, the discovery of his footprints in the sand, the emotion of the first harvests, and Robinson's attitude, ceremonious and unnatural, when he speaks to the person kneeling opposite him. Friday's beautiful response about his religion and the first name of his god: *"the country of O,"* which he pronounces solemnly, designating the vastness. Indicating through his exaltation that the gods are born of our unanswered interpellation, their names will come later, with books or preachers and wars. Which goes to show that I'm wrong every time I think I've exhausted this book.

My long adolescent years spurred my interest in the third character that is almost never mentioned: the parrot, the symbol of hidden meaning discovered only with time or meditation in this book, as mysterious as a cave. Robinson himself tells of how, for lack of any people to converse with, he tamed a parrot. And I swear that I was a disciple of that bird, whom I consider the pearl of that insular space: a being that was commanded, on an island with no way out, to reinvent the entire language with five words: "Poor Robin, where are you?" It was the bird's only phrase, its entire dictionary, counted on one hand. During my illness, I felt so close to the bird that I dreamed of telling the world about its martyrdom and its crucifixion on a palm tree. A secret narcissist, Robinson taught it first to say the name he had given it, Poll, as if to stave off menacing oblivion and revive his own ship-wrecked name that the island had threatened to engulf, for lack of conversation with anyone else. If the parrot had a name, Robinson must have said to himself, the castaway couldn't forget his own!

That was my first discovery, during my illness. The second was the limits of language. The bird soon embodied my terrible fate and that of the entire village. To have to recount, fix, exchange, perpetuate, and speak with only a few words, or even millions! Yes, there were thousands in Hadjer's language and hundreds of thousands in the language of school, but that didn't change the fact that those languages had an end, a threshold of powerlessness; sooner or later, we would reach the limit of five words or five million words. Beyond the last shore(line) stretched the void.

I spent many years meditating on this fate but also on this legendary story written by someone I had never met. And, at each free and uncertain hour, I found myself rereading this story. With delight. Like a Bible that imposes its law on you when you lack even clothing. And today *(I remember, I don't know why, that the old man stirred when I rushed out of his bedroom. His hand hinted at a gesture, which was perhaps only a nervous twitch. His last)*, I return, fascinated by another mystery that I skimmed years ago: the fate of the island after salvation, which is to say the fate of the parrot after Robinson's rescue. *(Hadjer calls me to have our end-of-day tea. It's served with cakes. It's the last sugar I'll eat for the day and, ever since my childhood, the taste of sugar has been associated with dusk.)* I think it's the most enigmatic passage, the most metaphysical, the confession of the castaway turned educator. I reread it endlessly and sink into it imagining the blare of what comes next, the cosmic uproar around a god who's left the place forevermore. Oh, the great mystery! The man raised a parrot and lived with him no less than twenty-six years. "How many years did the parrot live after that? I don't know," he recounts. He would have heard that in Brazil those animals could live to be a hundred. As a teenager, I reread the same passage: "Perhaps some of my parrots still exist and are still calling for poor Robin Crusoe right now." I was obsessed with imagining that island populated with hundreds of parrots repeating the same phrase, deafening the other kingdoms, jabbering endlessly and crashing, in the insular enclosure, into the intransigent glass limits of their fate. Perhaps in the village, we were no better than these birds. Perhaps our languages, in the eyes of the deserter god, possessed nothing but the meaning of a single phrase, reiterated endlessly for millennia, infinitely recomposed. Perhaps the village where I lived was nothing but a contained, deaf island that I had to liberate through long stories and through learning a vaster and more vigorous language, closer to that of the castaway than that of those parrots that spun in circles, obliged to invent a grammar, religions, books, meals and fruits, names and passions with only five words and a mysterious, deserted name.

I was Poll. And faced with a rare reflection of our house down below, I didn't see a young puny man, exhausted by masturbation and writing, already a widower and cursed with a goat's voice, but a bird, incapable of flying for very long, of course, but skilled in inventorying, in labeling, in language, in writing, and in dueling with death. I was the bird that perpetuates a phrase, reproduces it until the arrival of rich language. Guardian of the island that would have sunken into the silence of a tomb if I hadn't kept it above the waves through my conjugations. There you have it. Vibrant colors in the mirror, red, green, or yellow, blazing with plumed fire, effusive blood, and the twitching of a neck searching for the source of a noise. The eye kept its harshness despite the fantasies of fashion and the nose had a certain noblesse in its profile. There was nothing left of the sheep that my father had sacrificed to save his fortune. Writing gave me wings, islands to name and prestige that I wouldn't have obtained by walking through the streets of Aboukir. So I kept returning to that excerpt, which sent me dreaming for hours and hours: "POOR ROBIN CRUSOE. I wish no Englishman the ill luck to come there and hear them; but if he did, he would certainly believe it was the devil." Or God.

19

The rest of the day was calm. I didn't see anyone except for my aunt. A recluse in Hadjer's universe with her brief monologues. I almost didn't come out of my room. I examined the plate that Hadjer had served me, in case she had forgotten a piece of meat. Our house is still preserved, an enclosed space beyond the false sorrow of the hill. My aunt had procured me a second opportunity for grace at my father's bedside. Is it because she believes in my gift? Age-old question. I hear her busying herself behind the door. She is my living clock, eternal hour, endless hair. Now all I'll find out about the old man will depend on her and her informants. Even to her I can't promise that with three more hours I would have been able to bring Brahim back from the sky to his shoes. Half of what we live sometimes cannot be expressed in language and, for the other half, you'd need millions of books. *(Or a body against your own. A woman we save with our hand. My affair with Djemila is thus hanging by my father's breath. The very idea that I could marry a spurned woman with two children scandalized him. Even Hadjer didn't know how to defend me when he found out.)* I wake up with an obsessive idea: What is the world of Brahim like, struck by the imminence of his death? The sound of a book leafed through too rapidly by the wind? A dry page that's dissolving? An uproar in the voice of a cosmic crier? What thought came to mind, as he suddenly understood that the void would move through him? When I started all this, I often asked myself a question with no answer: Why did that person have to die and not someone else? And, if there was no reason or order to death, why should we search for reason or order in life? The truth is that I felt a sort of sorrow, a doubt about my gift, a suspicion that it might be an illusion, that I always kept outside of my notebooks. But the books were there, around me, serious and light, chaotic, conquerors of my bedroom. They are the proof of a perpetuation, of a possible salvation. Leaning against each other, on the shelves, secretly attentive to each other's universes. They surrounded me, preserved me, I knew it. I had no reason to doubt it. No one in our tribe knew how to read or write, and so if this gift had fallen to me, I had to bestow meaning, perpetuate, consecrate my family and save them from complete, idiotic death. Hadj Brahim could mock me, I had saved dozens and dozens of dying people over the years. Not to mention the lives I was maintaining on a razor's edge, the people I was responsible for solely because my gaze had met theirs, all connected, united by my care, protected from the wolf and secluded ravines. He could doubt me, but he had never been responsible for anything other than his sheep.

I wrote a lot today: hopeless letters to Djemila who doesn't know how to read, or write, or revive (excerpts from poetry about stone, suggestions of imaginary encounters at the exit of the bath or in a cemetery); the fabulous, meticulous description, spanning a notebook and a half, of a window; or the account—in multiple synonyms—of the sounds of the village behind the curtain and the surrounding wall. Poll exploits an unprecedented, rapacious language that reduces distances through metaphor or allusions to other books. "Every metaphor contains a folded page," says the bird, perched on the coconut tree, testing out his unique role as savior after the departure of his hairy instructor. The notebook and a half will be added to the collection of

this gigantic book that I've been writing for years, *Zabor*.
A life-saving story, slid under the armpit of the world,
bearing the sacred mission of keeping alive as many of
the people I meet as possible. When did this torrent
start? To be exact, you would have to reverse the image:
speak not of the flood, but of the ark. The flood is the
swept-away debris of the world, the frayed floorboards
and animals in children's books, the trees uprooted by
the rain, pushed toward the sea, the screaming nonbelievers, carved-up sidewalks, twisted tree trunks, empty oil
cans, mismatched shoes and bushes. And the ark is my
writing, the order facing off against the deluge. Yes, my
God, every day I postpone the end of the world. When
did this story begin? When did I start erecting my ark? I
spent years searching for the traces of the first scream. It
goes back to the day of Eid, when my father slaughtered a
sheep before my eyes, happy and proud, as though standing on the peak of a holy mountain. There were droplets
of blood on my shoes and a red river in the courtyard,
and everyone was laughing crudely like ogres. Yes, yes,
creation is a book, and it's mine. Always the inverse: the
book is the world, entirely, it is what will remain when
the sun rises in the west, at the Last Judgment. Oh yes,
eternity is a "forthcoming" book and mine is the only
possibility before the end. I write. I write.

Although the date shifts by twelve days each year, the end of the world has an exact hour and a wretched voice. Its bleating started to spread through the village the night before, an echo, like a rumble of displaced lands. It grows louder as I try to block my ears. At first the night is the deaf trampling of beasts, the anger of truck engines, men panting with effort, then it settles in, reaches the summer moon, wards off the dogs in the fields, erases the friction of the tree branches or the clinking of dishes. It's not the sun that rises to the west or the cry of the Angel with gigantic lungs, armed with deafening instruments, but the bleating beasts, shut in their enclosures, who speak to each other through the partitions before the moment of their slaughter, just before the Eid prayer.

My grandfather was still alive but had already blended into our objects and didn't speak to anyone, for lack of words. Hadjer took care of him as best she could and sometimes I sat near him, with my notebooks, to keep watch. In the beginning, I showed him my alphabet, then I understood that his world was reducing to a single infinite syllable. At the time, my father Brahim was already playing the tightrope walker between the surveillance of his wife, my stepmother, who bore him as many children as he had sheep, and the guilt about his sister the spinster, his father who was now a tree, and me, the son brought here in a red balaclava, accused of attempting to murder his half brother. Two times per week, he would bring or send a basket full of vegetables, meat, and bread. And, at each celebration of Eid al-Adha, he would bring a sheep to our house. It was all of the captured sheep, promised for the sacrifice, that I could hear bleating in every house the whole night before the feast of the slaughter. That wildly excited my father, accelerated his gait, threw him into a quasi frenzy: he had to be everywhere at once to carry out the sacrificial kill. Hidden under my covers, I tried all night to decipher the desperate language of those about to be sacrificed, tied up or shackled in each house. A chorus that seemed ancient, magnificent in its sadness, and which continued, softly, between beast and God. What encouragements or memories were these sheep unleashing? Why should they be sacrificed to save the very people who were about to eat them? Proof that the feast of Eid al-Adha was the end of the world replayed on a large scale in our village, in a sort of redemptive repetition. Each family had bought its sheep the day before and, after the morning prayer, every sheep would have its throat slit to save a man, a child, someone among us. That extermination thrilled the children and flattered the elderly. An odor of hay, manure, and sharpened blades replaced that of mint and eucalyptus. Aboukir sullied itself in a crude celebration of devouring.

That day, out of fear of my father and his murderous mockery, I witnessed the terrible agony in our courtyard. Brahim had decided to slit the throat of the sheep offered to his sister himself. The beast, which arrived that very morning, on an empty stomach "so as not to affect the taste of its meat," as my father said, thrashed its horns in the other direction, writhing like a child. My father's helper knocked it onto the ground and bound one of its hind legs to the leg in front. On its back, the beast then offered its bare, white neck, my father recited a prayer, turned the sacrifice toward the east, the direction of all our prayers, and examined his favorite knife a final time. Death uttered a hoarse and foamy word that no one understood. The blood splattered on the cement in clots, it reached my pants and shoes even though I was several yards away, sitting paralyzed at the doorway of our kitchen that opened onto the courtyard with the lemon tree. The same raspy bleating rang out from every house, the same beast writhed on the floor, staining its wool with pink, trying to pick up its twisted neck, its eye addled beneath the sun. The entire village had gone insane, in my imagination, echoing the cries of the dying, already stirring the charcoal and embers, while the children rushed to hang the slain beast on a tree and skin it over basins to collect the blood, the offal. In the red pool, I saw my father's wet boots and realized he was speaking to me, barricaded behind his vanity and his throat-slitter know-how. They explain to the youngest how to preserve the meat by making a clean cut through the gallbladder. The sun gives the force and breadth of a season to the stench. I wasn't sad, I was wretched, my entire body on the alert. The blood turned into a dryness in my mouth and I saw the large courtyard rock gently like a tray. As if they wanted to throw the lemon tree and the surrounding walls overboard. The bleating rang out from everywhere, chaotic, loud, sometimes muffled by hands, dissonant but unanimous in their calls, and the end of the world was a beautiful day, with a blue light, bright like a revelation. The universal indifference struck me as a disdainful betrayal. I understood that no language in my village, not that of the Holy Book, nor that of Hadjer, nor the others to come, could translate the essential. Everything remained forbidden, short of the limit marked by the knife and the blood. The jubilation around the sacrificial animal didn't conceal the most important thing from my eyes: it was a suspended sentence for us all, a way of making our procession forget death. I saw an abyss, barely concealed by the ritual. Everyone threw themselves on the beast to carve it up, sharing the task as they did in ancient tribes.

Even Hadjer was smiling again and enjoying the company. She served coffee for the throat-slitter and his helper. My grandfather had been brought into the sun but he was still contemplating us as if we were a flock of birds on the horizon. No one paid me any attention. Except for a fixed, bulging, glassy eye. Dyed with henna, placed in a basin, hanging over the hooves arranged haphazardly, the head of the sheep was grimacing, and its giant horns were curled up in shadows twisting toward the sky, in a perfect capital letter. The slaughtered animal seemed to be the guardian of a new secret. It was staring at us all with compassion. It loved me with an affection that almost made me cry over my fate and the fate of my whole family in Aboukir. I became aware of the silence of the village, suddenly deserted like an altar, without the bleating of the day before and the morning prayers. The head of the sheep, crooked in the green basin, became the smiling and perilous disguise of another presence, so tender, that taunted the knives, the ropes, the display of blood and the barbaric gestures of the butchers. As though it had been placed on the threshold of something. I stood up too abruptly and lost consciousness. But not only that.

20

I started to scream when I woke up, around dawn. My eye revolted at the sight of a monster that had taken the shape of all the objects in the darkness around me, which had turned hard, horned, piercing my skin, screaming their strangeness. Squeezed against Hadjer's breasts, I was sweating and trembling, invaded by a pillaging spirit. "Struck by the evil eye!" Hadjer concluded, before giving up on any explanation for my fits, which became more serious and kept me from pursuing my studies. For her the performance must have seemed like a possession, I would salivate with my odious bleating voice, point at things with a trembling finger, mangle the words, mix the language from school with her own deformed language. Ah, such a beautiful spectacle! She must have cried with disappointment and rage over the rumors that spread, recalling the fate of her father Hbib.

Mr. Safi, my schoolmaster, came to see me after a week but declared that the situation was beyond him. He advised my father, who accompanied him, to consult the imam, who was more equipped for this kind of problem. They washed me, covered me, and courteously invited Hadj Senoussi to come see me at our house. Young at the time but already amused by the spectacle of the world, he kindly answered the request and came to have tea in the very room where I was lying. He caressed my hair, recited entire verses, and concluded, without saying so, that I was more likely suffering from being abandoned than from being possessed. My family history was as well known in the village as a film. He examined me with affinity and intelligence, smiled at me, then whispered that the Prophet, before receiving the revelation, had experienced something very similar, and thus I must have been chosen by God. With a wink he slid some sweets under my pillow. I was reassured, to be honest, and I might have had the motivation to overcome my fears, but I understood instinctively that my fits guaranteed me an audience and affection. Cunning in the way intelligent children can be,

I resolved to take advantage of the show and the cycles. Suddenly, the fragility that emptied my arms and gave me an awkward gait in the street took on meaning, a dreaded meaning.

I was seven at the time, I was in my third year of school and my unusual childhood, my defects, and my disorders had become an unfortunate legend that led to me being quarantined, sometimes happily. Suddenly, I was the center of the world, and a groan was enough to attract the attention of the neighbors, the relatives of my tribe, and distant aunts who came both out of compassion and to savor their poorly concealed vengeance. The house was filled for a short time with incense, gifted eggs, honey, names of marabouts, and the coins they stacked under my pillows. Of course, I enjoyed that fake convalescence, even if I was ashamed of it, as when I found my bed wet in the morning. Except that, when night came, I went to sleep and always woke up faced with the snickering of countless angular objects. I had always spoken very little, and only Hadjer understood that I was suffering when I started to mix my words, relapsing into ancient gibberish.

Oh, of course I lied about my condition a little, but my panic attacks were real even if I often exaggerated their effect! Deep down, I didn't want to go back to school, I preferred to withdraw to the shadow of my aunt's brown body and never move again, wrapped under my red cosmonaut hat that had become too small for my head but that I kept anyway. I could no longer tolerate the order of the letters in the alphabet, nor that of the rows of tables in our classroom, nor the battles in the playground and the prolonged mockery, nor the law of our village. The other children didn't play with me and were content to yell my name, "Zabor!" as they mimicked convulsions, lying on the sidewalk, encouraged by the enormous laughter of the other schoolchildren. I experienced that period of my childhood as a waste, it slowed me down when I think I had already sensed my obscure gift. I secretly hoped to punish my father, push him into his entrenchments and force him to abandon his poses, stock phrases, and bawdy bragging. I renounced him in my own way, with my entire body.

What was I suffering from, really? From worry—objects were becoming threatening—from fear—the darkness was spreading and hollowing my bedroom until it was a vague, nocturnal terrain. I had no more confidence in myself or in daily life. I had vertigo, headaches, and hallucinations: I heard unknown words, but above all, things had begun whispering names, acting as the accomplices of a threat that was hovering behind them, at once mother and ogress. I tried to describe my fear but no one paid attention to my notebook at that age. Scribbles piled up next to calligraphic letters like jaws. I felt isolated and disconnected from my family, despite their concern. That affected my solidity, erosion became a permanent sensation. I felt in my bones that I was wandering in a sort of weightlessness. I lost my appetite, of course, but also the desire to leave my bed, to cut my hair or speak to my cousins who had been brought to distract me and who remained there, torn between the fear of being contaminated and suppressing their hysterical laughter. My secret occupation was to search for rhymes with my first name, Zabor, and to turn them into the meager rebuses of my days. There you have it. *(I'm getting a bit lost in description, but fear has no image, in my memory it is above all oppression, breathlessness, and panic, as above a well. In my chronology, it's when I was crawling on the sand, just after the shipwreck, when the island was still nameless. Swallows fly through the sky in the window. They are the sign that dusk is complete and that the night is now possible.)*

The path of the gift is old as the world and always sows disorder before revealing its flower. That helps to explain my first attack. Sometimes, in the past, they confused the Prophet's ecstatic trembling with the fevers that, according to Tradition, afflicted him during his business in Syria. For me, astonishingly, fear wasn't caused by an angel ordering me to read in a cave, but by my incapacity to bear the sight of indecent things, the flaky paint on the walls, the stone distorted by the invisible, without the serene and orderly mediation of a rich language, capable of outlining the contours and keeping the distance between me and surfaces. All tongues are mother tongues, and mine was dead before the awakening of my memory, turning me into a panicked orphan. Oh yes! That's it, my first sickness: the death of a mother and the desertion of an Angel with a book. *(I was bleating every morning like a badly slaughtered sheep, at the sight of the invisible blood of my universe.)* This lasted months.

At a certain point, tired, Hadj Brahim settled for sending money and asking Hadjer about me, awkwardly, on the doorstep of the house he no longer entered. The entire tribe and my cousins concluded it was the evil eye or, more discreetly, God's vengeance on my father, guilty of abandoning my mother in a desert. I remember his gloomy, extinguished voice in front of the door (my stepmother had forbidden him from entering our home), asking how I was doing, while my ears were ringing and my head was wrapped in a scarf soaked in orange flower water. I had an irrepressible desire to groan, to cry or throw stones at him. It was impossible for me to explain my fears. The words were on the ground, powerless like empty gloves. The language of Hadjer, my aunt who had never gone to school, was old and half blind, impoverished for centuries, it didn't have nuance except for hunger, jealousy, or the fabrics of the Aboukir seamstresses.

Those around me didn't give in right away, although they kept their distance. The second phase resulted in a wave of advice and the addresses of powerful occult places. My "crying sickness" meant long treks with my aunt, sometimes accompanied by an old, idle relative, to seek healing: I visited all the green-and-white mausoleums of the saints of our region, I was asphyxiated with eau de cologne, my forehead was tattooed with juniper oil drawings supposed to ward off the evil eye, wrapped in veils and surrounded by the dismayed murmurs of curious women with no compassion. That went on for a long time. I also remember that one day, they made me eat, unbeknownst to me, bread drenched with the blood of meat cooked in bitter herbs, they made me drink tasteless liquids, and we searched for the root of my illness by interrogating wrinkled women and throwing lead on embers. Which didn't reveal anything more than the routines of my universe: jealousies, jinxes, or curses from imaginary neighbors. Useless diagnostics for my word sickness.

Suddenly babbling with worry, Hadjer showed signs of an inner fever. She started to speak without stopping, as if to fill the void or distance the beast that had devoured her father's mind, she was rambling, she who normally kept a distance from the village women, she squeezed me in her arms ten thousand times for no reason and stopped watching television. Her low voice stumbled over the reasons for my illness and, this time, she couldn't come up with a nice story to tell me, she was incapable of interpreting the universe in my favor as she had always done up to that point. If I screamed at night, it was because I was an only child, she said, not quite convinced. She reminded me that I was born with a mark on my arm, like a prophet, that she had seen our house inundated with white feathers falling from the sky while I was sitting in the middle of it all, smiling. She cried. I knew that I was suffering from not possessing a language that was vibrant, powerful, and rich.

At exactly eight years old, I discovered the horror of the inexpressible. God had ninety-nine names but my world had none. A name is a talisman, a clause, which is to say an enclosure in the former sense of the word. Something that separates property from the wild forest. Everyone needs enclosures to keep from going insane, colliding with others and dying in the scramble. My childhood fits stemmed from a serious and ancient affair: language. I had a duty to discover a language that was cutting as a judgment, with the precision of a claw but also the patience of condensation. An intelligent language with the ambition of spreading from east to west and filling the tiniest hole, the tiniest bump, the tiniest cracks and crevices in my village, invisible to the naked eye. A language that would be my flock, multiplying with the blessing of a god, which I would watch over with tenderness, vigilance, and love while searching for rhythms like a shepherd in former times. I dreamed of it, with panic and without understanding, of course, but that gave rise to a quest that would lead me to my gift. There you have it, but the path was not easy, because I had no guide.

I had been placed in a public school but was profoundly bored. It's not that I wanted to retreat or was afraid of others, it was the slowness of their minds and their mouselike memories that the teachers tried to rectify by rapping sticks on their palms and buttocks. That's what astonished me most about my classmates: their incapacity to remember. How could they, when their universe was nothing but trepidation? I could memorize a text by reading it a single time, an entire surah just by glancing at it. I'm not even talking about the names of the Prophet, or of his companions, dead male children, wives, adversaries. I remembered everything, as if caught in a spiderweb, and as soon as I moved even a little bit, my movement rattled all the rest. In class, I recited my lessons with disinterest, brilliant but switched off, as if sleepwalking. I didn't think my memory was anything exceptional; it was their childish amnesia that appeared to be a handicap. How could they forget? I was surprised to see them hesitate over the names of the Prophet's companions, which had been imposed on us like constellations, the names of the rivers, or the total sum of equations tall as minarets. How could I forget, when everything I heard, understood, or deciphered in French or Arabic was so incredible and new that I couldn't imagine ridding myself of any of it?

It wasn't a question of trying to remember, I was in fact in the immediate presence of all the things I learned, at the very moment of their spawning, and writing was like a swarm of bees multiplying vigorously and set-tling on the surface of things like vibrant fur. Today my memory, trampled by my comings and goings and falsi-fications, does not have the same loyalty. My present lan-guage is rich and comes to me from the sea, preserved by the dog in my mind and a savage dictionary, but I suffer somewhat from the repercussions of good harvests: my words are more numerous than the objects, the metaphor has become an ivy plant, a devouring, and I find myself weaving a thousand stories just from looking at the back of a chair, for example. This accentuates my mutism in the eyes of others, while on the inside I experience an ear-splitting racket that will never cease, and pauses only when I sleep.

I experienced many troubling and stifling years. Sometimes I went back to school, slightly better, mocked by others, saddled with new jeering names. It was hell when school let out. I ran toward the house inhaling the smells of coffee from the roasters on the main street with delight and anguish. The fragrance meant that school was over but also evoked the memory of the schoolchildren waiting for me outside to mock or chase me as they screamed. I can still see myself running until I was out of breath to escape the others, wishing I had wings or magical invisibility. Every day, or nearly, my stomach was in knots by the end of the day, troubling numbers and the letters of alphabets, plunging me into the distress of an orphan without a big and strong older brother. My only moment of happiness was when I saw the shadow of the house where my grandfather was growing old and where Hadjer with her brown skin was waiting for me with an explanation of the world that centered me as its pearl. My aunt's ferocity and strong voice could distance the aggressors, the cockroaches, the night, and the nameless objects. Hadjer didn't read the future, she wrote

it: she told me about her gift that allowed her to see
omens everywhere, describing for me one of her favorite
dreams in which she saw the entire house invaded by flag
bearers searching for me to carry me on their shoulders.
I particularly liked this dream because it sounded like
an anonymous benediction. I was a sick child, suffocated
as though in an egg, in love with Hadjer's breasts that I
sized up by leaning against them, her body coated with
healing and fragrant substances, smeared with juniper oil.
I was surrounded by a land of various signs and rituals: I
was forbidden to approach standing water, extinguished
candles, salt on thresholds, keys, and scissors, or to go
alone to the bathroom or to be naked at the baths without
having first recited the names of God or a few prayers.
Hadjer explained to me that the body is God's window,
but also the devil's door. She examined my body carefully
each night, like a notebook that had to stay blank. I wasn't
skinny because I was sick or malnourished, but because I
hadn't yet fully descended from the sky, she claimed. The
stakes were immense, and I felt guilty when I skinned my
knees as if I had torn pants that cost months of savings. I
was treated like a jewelry box, and Hadjer presided over my
temple, confusing her bitterness toward the hesitant men
of the village and my fate as a child rejected by his father

and left in the wild with the name of a sheep. After Ishmael, my first name, I chose Zabor, then there was a third, Sidna Daoud, which my teacher at the Koranic school gave me, after the prophet of Israel.

At that time, I lived in the company of a series of miniature books, troubling, powerful, inviolable: hanging from my neck, they fascinated the schoolchildren and neighbors who touched them with respect. There were seven, fastened with threads and knots to my neck, under my armpits, in my schoolbag, in the pocket of my black apron, and under my pillow. I think they are what instilled in me the certitude that writing is not merely transcription but also the inauguration of power. In the village, it was well known that writing could cast spells, stop marriages, or heal illnesses. An implicit law, in the degraded religious beliefs of my family, decreed that if the world was a book, the body was its ink. And that idea echoed strangely within me, made it possible to redeem my story, and then, eventually, to save everyone. If writing passed through me, it could vanquish fever, sterility, the evil eye, and the passage of time. *("But then why not death itself, the ultimate battle?" my dog asks me one day. "Remember the Hadith of the Prophet, which says that life is the writing of a pencil in a notebook, except for children, sleepers, and the insane.")*

According to our village's reciters of the Holy Book, the very composition of the ink contributed to the creation of meaning, as did the paper pulp, the writing style, the choice of words, and the state of mind of the expert talib. The Holy Book spoke of itself as a text written on a celestial tablet, protected by the sky, the perfect version that pilgrims and writings were striving for. *(Where am I? The sound of a truck engine. My palms go rigid in the contortion of writing. I think of Djemila. I feel guilty, as if I'd forgotten to finish something essential, every time she creeps into my memory. What are the days like for a decapitated woman? I can't imagine. A kind of darkness, with no language or writing. Something of what I feel for her escapes me. For months now, I've been sending her letters that she keeps, and I write others that I don't send, intended to preserve her, to save her from old age, from wear and tear or suicide. Her daughter Nebbia acts as courier with a discretion and gravity that clashes with her impish age. Between the two of them, I think I glimpse the solidarity of a woman with her equal, not a daughter with her mother. I address Djemila as though through glass. "Love at the window does lead to meetings," they say in our country. I speak to her as if my head were an empty street where I might cross her, in the middle of a summer day, with no worry or slander. In a floral dress, shoulders bare to make the sky shine, hair in the wind like a memory. On the street, there's a benevolent dog, trees that keep watch to gently calculate the weather and the shadows, and signs all over the walls, tattoos intended to preserve this world from crumbling when I wake up. The only way to save the decapitated women of* The Thousand and One Nights *is to give them back their own bodies.)*

21

The first time Hadjer brought me to a talib, we took the morning bus, between the eucalyptus trees and the fields, which led us to a small hamlet on the southern border, near the forest of Barbary figs. "Your mother's village is on the other side of the thorns," Hadjer explained before plunging back into silence. I had stared at the countryside for a while before I slept, head on my aunt's thighs, face covered by a swath of her haik. A spring sky, luminous and cool, lifted up the crops and foliage. From time to time, I looked for my aunt's eyes, barely visible, which gaze valiantly harsh and steady, as if to shun curiosity and keep men at a distance. It was her way of imposing respect through a mask of false anger, deliberately expressed through her features. No one dared speak to her. The truth is that such things weren't done in our country. She had carefully calculated the duration of our wait on the side of the highway, at the exit of the village, asking what time the bus came. And when the door of the old coach contorted itself open in front of us, she dragged me like a bag, pulling my arm firmly down the aisle between the seats, then sat and didn't move again. It was an ordeal for a woman, a spinster, to go out in the streets alone and take the bus to the rest of the world, I understood that even then. Hadjer was an old maid but she wasn't old. She could be easily coveted or slandered and she knew it. But we traveled rapidly toward the Seven Mausoleums, without incident or murmurs as we descended in silence.

We walked between the bushes through the yellow, fragrant flowers while I watched over the dogs in the distance. There were poor houses, tiled roofs, the ruins of old farms behind the fig trees. I had the marvelous impression that I was at the end of the world, because there was no more road, only a path through uncharted land. The green-and-white mausoleum was astonishingly small, modest, with an immaculate flag raised on its roof, a small courtyard, and low walls repainted with lime wash. The entrance was blocked by the other white haiks of women who were waiting, seated in a group or already inside a sort of antechamber. They had taken off their shoes and piled them in a jumble, as at the entrance of a mosque before the prayer. That's where they had us wait, each of us inhabited by our own evil. The contrast between the light of day and the darkness inside blinded me like a faint. Little by little, I distinguished shadows and giant candles that gave life to the rugs and the dark green paint on the walls. There was a pervasive odor of must and incense; no one spoke. Which worried me because, outside, only a few yards away, there were animated conversations and the bushes in the fields rustled in the gentle wind. The women were quiet here, out of fear or respect, while outside people competed within the hierarchy of pain or of the "evil eye" and told long stories about jealous rivals. They spoke of desperate treks before being shown the right way to the mausoleum. Some mentioned miracles.

Once more I placed my head, crushed by a migraine, on Hadjer's thighs and the darkness withdrew into the room, transformed into gray nuances and then into sad faces and dresses. There were women of all ages but no children, I was the only one. I was taboo, searching for something to attach my curiosity to, while my aunt nodded her head in response to an intimate soliloquy. At the end of a sort of alcove, the face of an old woman was floating in the halo of a white veil. Her eyes stared at me for a long time when I noticed her with unease. They were minuscule and harsh, through the interlaced, tightly squeezed tattoos that devoured her like a book or a scribble. Suddenly, she started to chew, exaggerating the movement of her dry lips, scrutinizing me avidly. That frightened me and I started to groan, squeezing my aunt's knees until she noticed and hid me under her veil. I followed their duel, eyelids shut tight, between my aunt invoking the names of God recited on loop and the sound of the old woman's chewing. It wasn't the first time I had seen tattoos but there, in the shadows, they seemed alive, feeding on the flesh of their hostage, strong as tree branches and capable of spreading to other bodies, binding them in a grip to impose the indecipherable. It was at once monstrous and alluring. Suddenly, the old woman yelled as if they had stolen something from her and they quickly dragged her away while she tried to resist with her skinny uncovered legs. I heard the sound of a struggle and then the silence returned, as though summoned to erase the incident. I almost cried with fear in the stifling stench, under the black, faded rugs of my squeezed eyelids. The wait seemed to drag on even longer amid Hadjer's strict silence; she seemed in a hurry to leave this place, but they summoned us before the end of the day.

22

An old woman, slightly haughty, brought us into a dark room that reeked strongly of the old dead smell of confinement and the specific odor of soaking clay, and she stayed there, planted and immobile like an abandoned tool. Then I saw a young man, sitting cross-legged, smiling in the darkness—seductive in his excess of benevolence. I had grown up in a house where faces were harsh, bountiful smiles hadn't been anything but deceptive masks. I was wary as a result. The talib, wearing a tidy, golden turban and a white djellaba, presided over his kingdom in the shadow of God. He didn't even look at me, but was intensely interested in my aunt, whose curves he examined rapidly. Hadjer's eyes possessed a strange gleam of respect but also a merchant's vigilance, fearful of being tricked. The consultation cost money, and Hadj Brahim gave us only a little, at least in cash.

My aunt didn't wait to be invited to speak, she threw herself at the reciter, kissed his hand, and whispered the list of my ills and the signs proving that I was possessed. I had never seen her so loquacious, describing my fits in detail and everything else that, according to her, proved the adversity of fate, the evil eye, or the harassment of evil spirits that lived in the wastewater, according to my family's beliefs. Her story stretched on, strayed into my birth and the death of my mother, went back to the time of the colonizers, then stopped in the vast sea of the evils of all creation. As she spoke, I scrutinized the dark room tinged with green, decorated with verses sewn onto various fabrics. Next to the talib, I saw a bowl of ink, the tablets for the recitations of disciples, and wet clay, as well as sharpened reeds to write the word. It was the scent of burnt hair perhaps, or wool reduced to cinders to make the ink, that worried me for a moment. Hadjer was still whispering, narrating my caprices as a strict vegetarian, the slaughters of sheep I had witnessed, and how the sight of blood always made me faint. The beauty of the fabrics that hung on the walls, depicting verses I couldn't comprehend despite my mastery of the alphabet, enthralled me; I touched them with my fingertips and followed them to the end of the room where I almost bumped into the woman who had brought us in. The man listened with the necessary care to justify his fees, signaled for me to approach, and when he bent toward me, his face made me even more uneasy.

It was a face that hesitated between genders, smooth and hairless like that of a woman but with a male grin exuding lechery from behind a fake cheerfulness. He had the fine mustache of his age, but rosy cheeks that were embarrassingly sensual. Today I can decipher, through memory, the sensual upstrokes and downstrokes of his ink on his plump body and the rigidity of the stylus stemming from the virility he concealed behind his gift. The look he gave my aunt was not innocent, but he had understood that any attempt in that direction would be in vain. I curled up next to her as she waited, silent now and seemingly paralyzed. A hand touched my hair—I closed my tired eyes—then the slow, low voice of the talib brought me back, reciting the Holy Book at an insane speed, monotone, repeating the verses and animating them with enchanting vocal effects. The art of the reciter, which I had loved since childhood when I'd witnessed it during burials or other important rituals.

I decided to half open my eyes and I saw this person
who was neither woman nor man, honeyed and cunning,
grasp a few sheets of paper and a reed pen. He scribbled
for a long time, in the chiaroscuro that made his laughing eyes shine, before folding several small talismans,
hermetic "books" I was forbidden to read, that we had
to use according to strict instructions given to my aunt.
I had to keep seven books on my body, stuck to my skin,
in my bag, and under my pillow. The other three had to
be steeped in a combination of oil, honey, and thyme, so
that the ink would dissolve in a mixture I was to drink
on an empty stomach, Friday morning, facing east. "He's
been struck by the evil eye and bitten by the spirit of a
night dog!" he concluded. His smile made me even more
afraid when he looked at me for the final time, as if he'd
guessed the origin of my terror of waking to the world.
Still today, I remember his strange knowing gaze and
I struggle to interpret its meaning. Had he guessed the
source of my misfortune? That asexual being, who was
like a skilled juggler between two reigns or two genders,
obsessed me like a stolen key. My aunt took the "books"
in one hand and her nephew with the trembling knees
in the other and never again did we return to that place,
which had been as disconcerting for her as it had been
for me. (*I turn another page of the blue notebook and I continue.*

When I lift my eyes, it takes me a few seconds to find my bearings and the name of this place. As when we wake up in a strange house. It's already night. I'm on guard duty. I don't know whether to take a walk to bury my notebooks, or smoke in the courtyard. That very indecision is a joy in itself. I decide to head for the hill, walk among the eucalyptus trees.)

23

The book talismans fascinated me, hanging from my neck like silent bells, keeping watch from under my pillow to ward off nightmares and imaginary animals, hidden in my schoolbag or shirt pockets, like spies. I wasn't ever supposed to take them off except for a rare bath or to go to the toilet because it's forbidden to bring the word of God in there. Hadjer made me drink the mixture three times, following the talib's instructions—a broken key had also been slid under the sole of my foot while I swallowed the liquid, as he had advised. My grandfather, lying on his favorite lambskin in the kitchen, watched this ritual. He had lost his appetite weeks ago and spent his time undoing the seams on his mattress or trying to hurt his face. Hadjer's gestures caught his attention for a moment before he turned his back to her. The beverage was sweet and heavy. After I swallowed the mixture, I let myself fall into a long reverie. I was trying to understand the link between the talib's writing and the power he invoked, his way of penetrating deep into the body to affect even the dark blood inside.

How could writing command spirits? That belief was profoundly instilled in the village, where calligraphy wasn't considered merely a game of curves and inflection of form, it also depended on a choice of scents, tastes, touch. Writing was legible but not only that: it had an odor, a material, a sound under its reed pen. People believed this with certitude, decomposing and recomposing the finished Holy Book, with its 6,236 verses and its 323,670 character count, so that it could respond to singular cases, to daily life and every time period. A sort of combinatorial art that neutralized the finitude of the book through the art of recomposing each letter, word, or verse, depending on the circumstances. The reciters, the sorcerers, or the heretics were like jugglers of the invisible, specialists of the interpretation that prolonged the book beyond its last impossible page.

Alone in my room, the next day, I set about writing letters in a false disorder, sticking them together absurdly to study them attentively like the cries of unknown animals. I searched for a copy of the Holy Book in our house but couldn't find one, and God saved me from blasphemy. I had wanted to compare the Book's verses to mine. As a child I understood perfectly that the chaos of letters it created could lead to a meaning it would be incapable of emanating. Did the "books" attached to my life change something about my panic attacks and chase off the threats of the night? I'm not sure. Perhaps simply by provoking my curiosity, they diverted my attention. I woke up without night terrors but with the sensation of wearing a necklace of stones that I carefully caressed each morning. The books didn't escape the mean attention of the other schoolchildren, they spared me the stone throwing and the usual insults. In the village, the children knew the legends evoking the power of the reciters and the punishment reserved for skeptics or the insolent.

The idea germinated in my head, fantastic and dangerous, like a reverie: I saw myself crossing the threshold of the forbidden, unfolding the little "books" hanging from my body, and being immediately set ablaze by God or one of his angels, devoured by tattooed old women or thrown into the world with a shout that would never end. I decided to abstain, but bad ideas have the power to linger, until the moment you find yourself alone in a room, on a Friday, at the hour of the siesta. So I took one of those "books," sewn into a small green fabric sachet, a little dirty from the dust and my sweat, and, hands trembling, I opened it to try to read it, to see how such tiny words written with a special reed pen dipped in a mixture of water, gum arabic, and the charcoal of kindling or burnt wool could heal. "Nūn! By the pen and what they write," says the Holy Book. The reed shaped like a stylus, plunged into the ink of the oldest ocean, Nūn. The image fascinated me when I learned the stylus surah years later, but at that age I didn't know. I just wanted to unfold one page of this first book, the quarto which, according to Tradition, contained the entire Book. To understand the link between power, sovereignty, and the upstroke. To discover how God had filled the void between things and me and why the fear had disappeared, turned to shadow then a vague gray sigh. And all I could read of it was a wild writing, chaotic, dense like a secret fleece, tangled with signs, numbers, and exclamations, punctuated with crude stars and celestial bodies, incomprehensible like a constellated sky. A deceptive trick? Years later, I would come upon the same script and understand that, to express the essential, writing couldn't be restricted to a finite alphabet and had to utilize the blanks between words and in the margins of the page.

24

Did Brahim half open his eyes? Did he groan, with no words in his well? It obsesses me. The night I fled—it was only the day before yesterday—is still chaotic and painful in my memory. I'm sure I missed a detail of the ritual, violated an ancient rule. But which one? Of course, I hesitated, my writing stumbled, spun in circles, and searched, muzzle to the floor, for the trace of a path. But that doesn't explain my powerlessness. There, near the switched-off TV, I brusquely remember that, on the threshold of Hadj Brahim's house, as I was fleeing, distraught, that first night, someone threw a fistful of coins at my back yelling at me to pick them up and never return because that was all the inheritance I'd ever get.

Then I walked quickly, head lowered, but calmly, on
the path that leads back down to the village; I crossed
the priors rushing to the mosque, who avoided my gaze
as if I were a Christian loitering on their land. No one
greeted me and I filled my lungs with air. The night had
penetrated my chest like cold water and I felt cleansed.
"By the star when it wanes," swears the Holy Book in my
head. I adore the descriptions in the Book, when it speaks
of stars like a calendar of eternity. It's always a marvelous
tête-à-tête between disbelief and infinity. A god declares
his laws and a man tries to sleep in the desert. *("Imagine
a name for each month and each month represented by a star, which
would give an endless account and a time without interruption," my
dog whispers to try to distract me.)* Dawn is sometimes lacerated
by shooting stars lambasting the spirits who listen at the
doors of God. Tradition says that this is how divination
is explained. I know it almost by heart, the Book, but
those verses about the night sky are my favorite. The
private moments of a god, perhaps.

The clarity of stars and their constancy consoled me
after I was hit and humiliated in front of my cousins—a
catastrophic night without glory. But nothing explains
my gift's hesitation this time. I like to be precise. I was,
during my long years of investigating death. I thought
like a clockmaker so that I could study death like a

piece of machinery, a set of cogs, and I was searching for the original spring. Because, as a teenager, the funereal routines piqued my curiosity. Starting from the funeral for my grandfather, who died in front of me on a Friday after nearly regaining his speech. When that happens, when someone dies, mourning takes on two faces. On one side, the women slap their thighs, throw themselves into each other's arms, shout their heads off recalling the virtues of the dead person and their generosity, interrogate the Sky about who will be able to replace them; on the other, the men, serious, heads lowered under the will of God, organize the meal, erect the tent, decide the number of sheep to slaughter, and summon the reciters of the Holy Book. A curious reversal: the women become visible, audible in the streets, exuberant as though faced with an adversary *("Death is feminine, like birth," concludes the dog)*, while the men are discreet, contradicting their virile force, their ambition to guarantee security.

Fascinated by this question during puberty, and a bit disoriented—for I hadn't read much on the subject—I started to visit the surrounding douars, hurriedly, to watch the dead leave and study their final gestures, to witness the long ritual of funerals or follow the processions to the Bounouila cemetery. They got used to my presence. Blinded by the memory of local saints and the great sermons of imam Senoussi, the villagers wanted to interpret it as the beginning of a profound faith, but then they realized it was an inhuman curiosity, even though my gaze and gestures showed the indubitable traces of compassion. For me, death was not a matter of religion but of laws that I had to decipher, mind clear and soul cold, and the village inhabitants came to understand that. Today I realize I wasn't convincing. I didn't recite the correct verses, I didn't have the serious, customary body language that one adopts in the face of divine will, and I spoke little of God to the family of the deceased, only asking questions about the concrete details of their last hour, the color of their skin and the temperature of their feet and hands. At the cemetery, I didn't pray with the others standing around the hole, I jostled to see the final burial and scrutinize their faces from up close. The peasants weren't literate but they had a reliable and perspicacious instinct. So in the end they chased me away from the burials and barred my access to the families in mourning.

I noted everything in my first notebooks, refining the details and the still unanswered questions. I don't know how, by intuition perhaps, or because of the buzzing in my head and my alimentary discipline, I knew I was putting my finger on the crux of the matter, and with

patience I could resolve the enigma of death or postpone the end of the world that the Holy Book declared
was imminent. People tolerated me for a while, then the
eldest protested to my father who explained that he had
no authority over a crazy person he hadn't raised himself.
One night, after the prayer, they knocked on our door,
and Hadjer solved the problem by screaming, scratching her cheeks, and slapping her thighs to make me feel
guilty. It was the first manifestation of the devil. Or the
angel. Or of death, who had accomplices. What could I
say? I had already, by the time I reached my magical and
tormented teenage years, discovered that ritual is a line
of protection people draw between themselves and the
abyss. For lack of a powerful, defiant language, they rack
up customs, tattoos, talismans to protect themselves,
they dig deep into the earth to bury proof of the end.
Ritual is the antecedent of language, a cadence against
anguish. And the people of the village, normally peace-
ful, didn't want to upset the equilibrium and attract a
dreaded anger. The country was new, finally free after
more than twenty years, though buttressed on its new
certitudes, wary and paranoid. Dissent was regarded with
an evil eye.

They negotiated my status for a long time with my
father, who succeeded, I have to admit, in calming the

believers and quieting the hysteria. They agreed that
I wouldn't go into the village during the day, that I
wouldn't attend any burials, and that, if I wanted to
continue to describe the village, its walls, its deaths,
and its trees, I had to do it alone, in my house, without
involving anyone else. They parleyed for days before
reaching something like a pact that left an opening for
my gift: they would not speak of my madness anymore,
and would simply ignore me. That judgment gave me a
sort of aura and authorized me to live without school,
without work, and without accountability. Secluded
in my aunt's house, sleeping during the day and visible
in the streets only at night, I gained an unprecedented
status: neither man (I didn't work, I didn't pray, I didn't
visit my family) nor woman (obviously). My body was
invisible like women's bodies, I didn't walk in the street,
I didn't go to cafés, I didn't leave the house and its walls
except to visit the ill; all my information about the world
came from Hadjer and her visitors—slander, murmurs,
metaphors about sex, the sounds of weddings and sorcery, conversations about fabrics and baths. But, unlike
women, I could go out at night, visit the cemeteries,
speak out loud, walk without hiding under a haik, pray
alone, or sit facing the café, to the east, near the main
road, next to the gas station at dawn. Before I discovered

my gift, in those years of learning, I felt like a third gender, a wandering, a cautious grazing of things. I rejected my body and it showed in how I dressed with scandalously bad taste, but, until I had the perfect language, I could only live in chaos.

25

My bedroom is like a cave. They forced it on me as a teenager, when it became unseemly to nestle against my aunt's brown breasts. I pile up books haphazardly, sometimes half read, suspended like conversations, faces turned toward the wall. Some don't even have covers, like ancient tombs or voyagers with impossible languages. My library wasn't big but it was implausible and incoherent, which bestowed it with a richness to my eyes. It was made up of old books people had given me, what I could gather myself by knocking on doors, and works that my relatives brought me back from their trips. A few years ago, after my time in the Koranic school, I heightened the chaos by ungluing the covers of some and sticking them to others, creating an inaudible racket, an amalgam that increases the possible combination of texts and, as a result, their meanings. A sort of unprecedented auto-da-fé, acting like a demiurge. As if I were throwing the novels in the air and they were falling back down rich with new plots from chance encounters and collusions between virgin titles and orphan stories. The tale became a thousand tales and the night a thousand and one nights. It was madness, I know, but what else could I do to combat the finitude of a meager library and the double threat of boredom and the last page? Fortunately, I also had hundreds of notebooks. Of all kinds: plain notebooks made in factories and others that were more delicate or more robust, that emigrants to France or their families gave to me as thanks for my secret aid. I also had many elsewhere, in the fields, under the carob trees and old gigantic trunks with enormous roots that people feared because they are said to house spirits and snakes. That's where I buried them. There you have it, it's been said. For when we aspire to save an entire village, describing it with the asperity of the stone down to the genealogy of first and last names creates a forest between the walls.

The archiving of all those notebooks became problematic when I was about twenty years old, forcing me to find a solution. I could have simply destroyed them, torn them up or burned them, but it proved imprudent to light fires in the house for fear it might bring on one of my fits. I could have thrown them in the trash, but our neighbors and their children were too curious, and I didn't want to find the pages of my works scattered, thrown to the winds, examined by everyone, used to clean windows or bottoms. Goodness no! Later, I found a solution that allowed me to camouflage my gift and avoid the mounting questions. For I was watched (the devil had ninety-nine forms and God ninety-nine names), and those notebooks could be used against me: they would accuse me of madness or heresy, they would set fire to our house or drag me to the gendarmes whose boredom makes them receptive to trivial suspicions.

The work of a sorcerer, healer, or miracle maker was risky, I should note. From time to time they would arrest a witch doctor or sorcerer, accused of manipulating the sacred verses, of writing the Holy Book in the wrong direction, or of making nefarious alliances with the spirits. Orthodoxy suffered from fits of jealousy and monopolized the invisible like its own property. I found these various facts fascinating, not because of the courage of charlatans, often tricksters, astute and manipulative men, but because of the law that allowed them to be arrested. How could one arrest a man in the name of a god and a book? I sunk into meditating on the destiny of this book that I knew almost by heart, that ate its own, the earth, that could kill men or heal them, that spoke in their place or claimed to know the weight of stars and the detailed account of the end of the world. A unique Book that had slowly hatched in the desert, devoured the other books, forbidden them entire swaths of the universe, then spread as the legendary catalogue of all things. Those charlatans seemed to me like heroes who didn't realize the profound impact of their actions and whose greed obscured their admirable rebellion. I told myself that the line between heresy and gift was fine and fragile, and that I had to be prudent, disappear after the success of a resurrection. *(I change position because my back is hurting. My body has always been painful and awkward, as if I had been born on a slant: face turned, desperate, toward the sky, legs agitated by the fear and chaos of whom to cling to so as not to fall. Hadjer is no longer here and her absence provokes worry, but also hope. Perhaps she's at our neighbors' house? Is she speaking to Djemila? Did she leave to negotiate now that death might have cleared the path? I hope to save that woman buried alive, this time with my entire flesh and not only my notebooks. Djemila doesn't need a story, but a man who can rediscover her body.)* Oh yes! I have to be discreet with the dog in my head, be humble, not move when he speaks

221

and I write, let the starry animal approach, place his head
in my hands and recount the oldest stories of the world,
the stories that heal and transport us, that give us several
lives and reverse our age, that heal sickness, sadness, help
us to understand bad harvests and decipher dreams. The
beautiful stories that live like eucalyptus trees. *(Tonight,
I'll go out to bury a stack of notebooks. The night will be clear and will
show the way to the best trees. I've made my decision.)*

26

At night, I'm free, there's no body or shadow hunting me. There's generally no one in the village streets. The streetlights keep watch, silent and absorbed. I like to look around the property. To the right, leaving our house, is the main road. It leads to the east exit, near the French cemetery, and to the west, to Bounouila, the Arab cemetery. It's bordered with trees whose names I don't know. In the center is the mosque, like a navel. A resting place for the storks, formerly a church but no one wants to talk about that. That's where the old men I've saved come to sit and speak about their bones or Mecca. The town installed benches, but most people prefer to sit on the steps. Some recognize me, but they never speak to me in public. Embarrassed, they smile at me, lower their heads, or look away. At night, the area seems more vast, hollow. It's my turn to sit down, chin in my hands, facing the street that leads to the south, down to the fig tree forest.

Sometimes, depending on the season, I cross paths with the wine enthusiasts on their way back from drinking in the fields, discreetly, a bit shamefully, stumbling but rigid in their effort to appear sober. I feel tenderness for them: it's not easy to drink in this country without being lambasted by eyes or stones. So they hide. The tavern of the fields was an amusing discovery: to avoid the gendarme raids, the dealers bury their merchandise under the trees, circulate among the groups of clients scattered in the countryside, and come back to unearth them after taking the orders. I'm precise in my inventory when I walk at those hours. Time is also precise in its cadence: the night is often inaugurated by the dogs, in packs, trash lovers in heat, it settles in with the arrival of the moon in summer or the looming dark clouds in winter, becomes infinite when cars pass in the distance and hollow it, then fades into sounds. It begins with coughs behind certain windows, the first people awake who drive their cars to the city, the priors, then those who work in bakeries, and the owners of the village cafés, automatons with the same gestures, cleaning the terraces, rearranging the chairs, drawing the blinds. Then the garbage collectors come last to bring the night to a close and herald the day.

So I walked aimlessly, serene, calm, confident. Walking at night is exalting because we're absolved of our bodies, indistinct and thus free. Gravity comes from the sun, from the harsh light. My bag under my armpit, heavy, secret. At dawn, I went east. This time I chose a carob tree larger than the others, distant, twisted toward the sun like a hand trying to grab a big fistful of earth. I crossed through fields, happy as though I were caressing a desired body. I was crazed but I liked to move this way, like a pilgrim, light as if I had just accomplished a task. Because that's how I see it. Burying notebooks means that I've saved people from dying, maintained the equilibrium of the village, and postponed the end of our world. The notebooks are proof and there they were, in my bag, and this splendid secret would not be hidden but entrusted to its source, the loose soil, where the roots find their purpose. In the beginning I feared dogs or snakes but I soon gained confidence. The night is an illusion, a mirage protected by the desert of our head. When we confront it, it reverses and turns to brightness, luminescence, pearly and fragrant. It's a Milky Way for pedestrians; I swim through its haze. I arrived at the foot of the black tree and sat down, short of breath but full of a rare happiness, as if I were reuniting with a relative or a foundation.

I invented this ritual years ago, when Hadjer told me to find a solution for my overflowing papers. And still today, on this night, I consider the meanings of my gesture, its amplitude, as if I were entrusting my lineage to my ancestors. Oh yes! I make slow progress. Silently removing the earth with a tiny shovel, mumbling, mindful of the barking dogs that might approach, the sounds of cars, or the footsteps of farmers surveilling their crops because they're wary, those insomniacs, but also cowardly when it comes to rumors of jinns. I tear out the weeds, I grope along the roots, then I dig farther down until I reach the right depth and there I place my inventory, my notebooks. I feel no pain burying them for I know I'm not muffling a secret: I'm giving it breadth. I'm restoring a gift to its source. I protect myself from questions by entrusting myself to the earth, which is silent. Those fields that spread to the east are not very interesting, with their few almond trees, their tall grass and their carob trees around whose trunks sterile women used to tie ribbons and leave sugar to attract the spirits' goodwill. That's where I first began to dig the holes to bury my notebooks. And that's where I return. I operate at night, alone of course, once a month. To declutter the shelves and floor of my room. I keep a secret map of the burials, but that doesn't stop monstrous dreams from visiting me in my sleep: ground soaked with words, roots mixed with writing, bad fruit amalgamated with alphabets. I dream of a forest where each tree—the carob tree, the olive tree, or even those fig trees knotted in former times and the eucalyptus trees taciturn without the winds—served as my witness and guardian. It's amusing, to restore paper to the tree, which it dissolves to nourish the vast project of fighting against the end of our world. The fields in the east have become gigantic margins, a sort of extension of my own body or of the image I make of it. Thus spreading the deciphering to those immobile beings, sending me farther and farther to the east, toward the apparition of the sun itself. The exact location of its hatching. Madness of my magnitude.

The truth is that these burials preserved me. My notebooks didn't question the simple cosmogony of my family and the hierarchy of their crude beliefs: God, his Prophet sent for the world, us, then the rest of the world of nonbelievers. The hierarchy has been strictly established for centuries: Allah at the very top, then his favorite Prophet and the Prophet's companions, then the great believers, the imams and the reciters, and finally us, the mortals. Centuries ago, God dictated a book for twenty years straight to his Prophet Mohammed. The book is as important as a final word, a gravestone, or a verdict. Everything is said in it, according to Tradition.

The most fervent believers in the village didn't really like me but struggled to interpret my strange compassion: it helped others to live, a sign that it was granted by a god, I didn't earn a living from it, or very little, which spoke to my innocence, and finally, I didn't murmur any forbidden prayer, proof that the devil played no part in it. The imam, who had been asked for his opinion, had opted to cite a verse: "To Daoud we gave the Psalms." He was clever: he knew that I might be useful one day, and he'd spent too much time around men to believe in certitudes. Imam Senoussi had a beautiful smile, he called me "the soldier of God," I don't know why, and he knew my father, his harshness, and my true story perhaps even better than me. That was probably the reason for his distant but cheery affection. Hadj Senoussi was cunning, almost mischievous, a bon vivant but prudent: he was careful with his sermons in the mosque. I think he liked me deep down, because I embodied the proof that the mystery of life was more complex than the recitations, prayers, and verses he lived through. His peasant ruse had kept jealous metaphysics at a distance.

I was between two worlds: on one side the pious who suspected me of devilry, on the other the people of the village who realized I could prolong lives. They approached me, but on tiptoe, at night, secretively, not knowing if it was licit from a religious or black magic point of view. I benefited perhaps from the distant memory of numerous saints of the region, who shared their blessings with sterile women, crops, and feasts. More modestly, the green-and-white mausoleums served as meeting places for the women who, according to a tired rule, shouldn't, for all their lives, leave the hearth except for the baths, their wedding, and their own burial. My visits to the mausoleums were included in the catalogue of my childhood perfumes. I liked their shade, the chiaroscuro—I remember the murmur, the sudden sobs or choked laughter of visitors distressed by their stomachs or by the future. There was one at the top of the village, not far from Hadj Brahim's house, and another right at the entrance of the village from the road to town, Sidi Bend'hiba, veiled guardian of our houses, a white dome that the passing drivers would throw coins at, turning down their car music out of respectful fear. There were many of those saints, their names were still given to newborns and scattered throughout the region on their decorated tombs. A lasting impact of their blessing, the villagers tolerated my gift but preferred it to be discreet: it wasn't mentioned unless every other recourse had been exhausted.

I too dreamed of living under a sort of dome, instead of in my bedroom with its high ceiling and flaking paint. Our house already seemed like a strange mausoleum because of the stench of cold tobacco, candles, and stacks of notebooks piling up on collapsing staircases. Hadjer often bought them for me, and some black pens, when she sensed I was agitated or caught me rocking like a reciter when I sat with a sad look in my eyes under our lemon tree. The sounds of others—schoolchildren let out of classes, scattering and yelling, merchants, teenagers talking about a match—was sometimes painful for me. An unfathomable sadness ripped through my gut, contorted me, and I suffocated under the weight of my destiny, caught between the desire to write an exhaustive inventory of creation, my goatlike voice that made a fool of me, and the profound compassion I had for our people, every one of them, despite their pettiness. Sometimes I refused the notebooks, imagining I was healed or stripped of my mission, and I would sink back, like my cousins, into that absurd bodily sluggishness, settling for a beautiful armoire for my wedding, sipping a coffee at dusk, and going to see Indian films in the big city every Friday.

The night still resists but there's already a breeze hinting at its retreat. I walk to the village with my bag empty, light, happy as if I'd just visited a friend and unloaded a secret. No one saw me (I've been startled one or two times, long ago, by night owls who preferred not to see or conclude anything). The village, at first distant, reduced to shadows and silhouettes, reassembles its houses behind the black trees, and when I reach it, through detours, I find it intact and firmly planted in our soil. It's almost dawn, the sky concentrates for the fire. The call to prayer rings out, slow, subdued, and sleepy. Old neighbors cross my path but settle for nodding their heads. I do the same. When I get back, I try to make as little noise as possible, but my aunt is already awake. She comes out of her bedroom, her long mane undone, searches my face for traces of violence (or stolen and secret kisses?). "Go sleep," she says, categorical. It's the inverse hour of my nap. When I sleep, God keeps watch. A total of 5,436 notebooks. That's my count since the beginning. That's dozens, hundreds of trees, figs, carobs, eucalyptuses, and giant vines.

27

The Hamza affair was a strange incident, like a fever. It caught me off guard. I was distracted by my fight against the mocking laughter of my father, the ridicule of my cousins who were my age, the start of the slander about my celibacy. My gift was ripe at that age, I defended it and imposed it on death. I was in that powerful period when I could write fabulous things about a vine, an intersection, a facial feature. The story had reached its plenitude and possessed me. A juncture formed in my mind, which seemed absolute and definitive, joining my compassion, my beliefs, the metaphysical, and the grammar of a language I now mastered like breathing. I was saving lives with ease and the ridicule of my body had been nearly eclipsed by a sort of aura enshrouding my goat voice with a sublime language. Oh yes! Everything was going well, heading for happiness. That's when the devil (or the jealous angel) returned in the form of a young man with a bulky body, a bushy red beard, and a sharp eye. Hamza. I had known him as a child, he was a felon, a bird hunter, raised by his grandparents after the death of his diviner father. Unlike me, the liberty of being an orphan launched him into the streets, with no fear or hesitation. He was the boss, the ringleader, he imposed his rules and his way of dressing.

I had run into him all over, at school before he dropped out and near our douar, on the hill. Except back then he wasn't called Hamza, he was still Aïssa. When he was eighteen he suddenly changed his name, refused to turn around when they called him by the old one, grew silent and started selling sardines to make a living. That contrasted sharply with his typical verve and joie de vivre. No one understood his renunciation: but Aïssa was the first name of the prophet Jesus, cited in the Koran, respected and venerated, but who died in a different manner according to the Holy Book, which explains that he was not crucified but hidden, kidnapped alive and taken to the sky, and a doppelgänger was killed in his place. He turned it into a crusade and waged war against the recollection of his old name in others' memories, through weak explanations and dubious historical facts. It was his first war, and he won it. Which gave him the idea to conquer the world, which is to say our village, proceeding in the same way: by erasing all evidence. I knew about his life, of course, his secret bitterness, and also the details of his face, and I had saved his life, several times, by writing *The Upward Roads, Light in August, Cities of Salt*. Pensive books on the fate of summers.

That didn't change when, more recently, he came back into my life with verses and Hadiths that he used to shout, threaten, and speak to God, as if He had sent him. It was a strange time and I felt it: the village smelled like must but also like exhaustion. On television, the songs and hymns rang slightly false and a new kind of preacher showed up to offer a new story that began with fire and blaze; or the sand of the desert that suddenly became an ally. Yes. Over the years, Hamza had gained disciples, cast judgment on everything, and one day mentioned me and my gift. Cunning as he was, he avoided evoking politics and the law of God in the village, for he knew the State was watching him, but he preached virulently and denounced me as the worst enemy of our religion: not the godless barbarian from an obscure land, but the traitor, the hypocrite, that age-old obsession of the religious, the ambiguous believer. I was the portrait of the man who wears both the mask of God and the body of the devil, walks in the sun with a slight limp reciting verses, proclaiming the sovereignty of God but perceptive to the whispers of Iblīs, the devil. Skillfully manipulating the Arabic language, he named me as the worst enemy of the religion of the Book and the Word. It was thus me, Zabor of the night, impostor Ishmael of our religion, born of infanticide. The clever man played on an ancient competition between the verse and the line, adversaries of an unsurpassable speech. In the Book, the poets are in fact mocked, suspected of rivalry and wandering.

.

As for the poets, they are followed by the lost.
Do you not see that they wander aimlessly through every valley...
And say what they themselves do not do?

A gloomy and withdrawn teenager, I used to recite those verses to try to find a reason for this accusation, other than jealousy. I found that divine hostility unjust when I had to memorize the Book and give it my voice, my body, my intimacy, my footsteps. That was when I intended to use it to make my bread and bolster my dignity. My rival with the henna-dyed beard and the magnificent voice knew how to utilize those verses and saw me as an enemy to denounce, but also as competition to the budding influence of his word. Hamza got to work, with a few fervent young devotees, distributing books of exegeses, collections of Hadiths, feverish quartos on the prayers and ablutions, and imposed them everywhere. He didn't know how to read or write very well, but he knew how to speak about his unique book.

Hamza sought me out, wanted to provoke me into an absurd duel, but I always managed to avoid him. How did I vanquish him? To be honest, it was his excess that was his downfall, not my cleverness. The village inhabitants were fascinated by him for a time and listened to his version of the world, but he infuriated them the day he tried to set fire to the Sidi Bend'hiba mausoleum. That was his fatal error. They found him hidden in the meager forest at the entrance to Aboukir, surrounded by a few companions, hairy, dirty as during the early days of his beliefs. He was arrested and imprisoned for two years. I have to admit, I was obsessed by the idea of him for a while. Like a monstrous twin gone astray, an evil version of the gift.

28

In the morning, Hadjer would see my clothes sullied by my nightly wanderings (and burials) but rarely asked me any questions. She would simply check my face to ensure I hadn't fallen into the hands of my thieving shepherd half brother in the surrounding fields. The rare times I came home hurt, it was from the stones thrown by the children lying in wait for me under the vines, who followed me and shouted. *"Zabor eddah el babor!"* they would yell before scattering like wasps. "Zabor was carried off by a boat!" I was angry, but often what went through me was a wave of pity and sincere compassion for the miniature sleeping universe of the village and its hamlets, unaware of its fate as a child that

was mute and deaf to the world, with no books to save
it from oblivion, with no language other than my own,
constructing its illusions and its lives in a small crevasse
between the distant sea and the hill that sealed off the
horizon like a tombstone. Were those people aware that I
was saving them not only from death but also from futility and oblivion? Could they understand that my notebooks were the only rampart shielding them from erasure
and that if one day I might reach absolute description,
I could render them eternal or save them from the end
of the world? Two books competed for their salvation,
the one that descends from the sky and the one I write
endlessly. Except that mine didn't impose a Last Judgment or death and preserved the earth and its pebbles
and shadows.

PSALM

... The great stories imperceptibly govern the world
like mountains. They divide up the earth as soon as
they flush it out. Sometimes they wage war and it's
horrible and bloody, as the newspapers and histori-
ans testify. The reason is that no Story, no history
of creation wants to accept another as a relative
or kin or as being born of the same womb around

the same ancient fire. Nothing, except a ferocious jealousy and an irrevocable desire to be the first to recount things, in a singular version, and without ever pausing to let others speak and let people enjoy the difference. Nothing. In my books, I respect them, these Stories, I was afraid of them and they could have devoured me like whales. At one point, I asked myself which one was the most sincere or correct about the origin and value of the sun, the steps of the sleeping man, the troubling reason for the animal skins and the feelings and especially death and its way of walking in a zigzag. Sprawled on the earth that they crush, these first Histories terrified me and seduced me with their power—like sullen or spoiled children who only want to hear their own name and possess every golden object in the house. Children of Gargantua as they were drawn in one of my books, with men hidden under giant lettuce leaves and ewes reduced to olives or grains of flour. I think it's because of this childish side that the stories kill and shout their heads off at each other to fight over the prophets, the poets, and the tales of tribes. It's an assembly of jealous divinities but with the mentality of children who don't want to grow up and accept that the world can settle for silence and light.

From time to time, these stories come back in force and provoke wars, beginning with the readers, the copyists, then the interpreters and finally the preachers and the stories of the end of the world. Sometimes, tired and somnolent, these stories about the world calm down, and then they become books, novels, or amusing explanations about the night sky and the birth of constellations.

That's how I explained to myself, gently, over time, the power of holy books and the reproaches from my family when I started to speak about the Greek gods or other divinities in our small unknown and tenacious village. The suspicious Story of our own earth slowly lifted its eyelid and began to search for who, in its stables, was starting to doubt its version, its sovereignty, or was surreptitiously sowing doubt into the tree trunk of great truths. The dissonant voice is always perceptible within ovations, I think. But who recounts these stories first and gives them life? The gods or the blind? No, I don't think so, for the gods themselves are unstable characters, constantly dragged around. I think the Story is earlier, older, I came with age to understand that it's our gift to ourselves. We can find the vague outline of a god in a stone and lichen

and explain the world with a tree and an animal
that tries to climb it and falls back down. It's in us,
and we are in the story. Plunged into ourselves every
time we try to look outside of our universe, trapped
in our sleep. I think that was, in those years, my
most profound intuition, the most distant place
I ventured thinking about the books I had read,
countless in my imagination, and the books still to
be written, which are constantly reborn and repro-
ducing even once we're dead. At night, I imagined
giant faces, and I asked myself what was the greatest
importance of things. I dreamed of my father, too.

    That immense vision made me cry with com-
passion, because I realized I was truly the only one
of my people at that altitude.

29

The sun rises. The light comes back as though to confirm the order of things, their number. At first soft and golden, it mixes with the paint on the walls, then turns harsh and reaches the corners, the books, the notebooks, my bed. I shiver. For me, the world is a sort of indirect incandescence, eclipsed by the horizon. A book we burn but that is never reduced to cinders, that lights up for a long time with an entire story inside and then slowly darkens when the sun, the eye of the universal reader, shuts. At nightfall, the novel is scattered into luminous points, into the Milky Way, and becomes infinity and chaos before coming back together the next morning. It goes from starry table of contents to solitary eye. I will sleep in this fire, curled up until Hadjer comes to shake me awake to eat sardines, which I love. Who would I be if I were to marry one day? I could be the other bank of the same river for the woman lying next to me. It intrigues me, this sudden need. How would I be able to write, stay up until dawn, recount the world to keep it from crumbling, to a woman who doesn't know how to read or write? My gift's ultimate challenge: to go further than language, make it collide with its impossibility. *("Opposite challenge," says the dog in my head: "the man who recounts, night after night, a story to a dead woman and, little by little, she comes back to life, to her senses, the palace rises from its ruins like the donkey of the Prophet who asked God to prove resurrection.")* That's what I keep thinking about: Brahim's suffering also brings a strange celebration. I am ashamed.

30

My screaming came back with even greater intensity when I was about ten. Nothing worked: not the unctions, not the imam summoned by my father, not even the sheep slaughtered in the mausoleums. I was becoming fragile like a tibia and my father's heart was crushed with shame whenever he passed me with his friends. Even hidden at my aunt Hadjer's house, I was an abomination to him and his reputation.

My body, the resemblance to my mother, my dietary preference and my bleating voice, all represented the reversal of his fortune that swelled like a hill at the top of the village. Even only glimpsed on the floor, drunk off the ground after the slaughter, blood still evoked a warm and ferrous taste in my mouth, lowered a black veil under my eyelids. As for food, I couldn't touch anything but vegetables or cold fish that no one had slaughtered. Anything else meant vomiting and wretchedness for my stomach. A limp finger flipped at Hadj Brahim and his role as sacrificer. He felt profoundly insulted: why was God, who had given him sons and sheep, mocking him like this? I imagine he rifled through his past for a long time trying to find an explanation for my abomination, but he never seemed to find a satisfying answer. He firmly believed in God, because of tradition, by default, but his faith permitted a sort of secret irritation in the face of divine desires. He was reminded that he was guilty of infanticide every time he passed me and knew I had a solid recollection of his first fatherly act: abandoning us in a land of sandstorms and ruins with a few sheep and some change. Everything was arranged in circles in his house to conceal this first murder and his cowardice faced with his wife: his burnoose, his fortune, his prayers, his lavish generosity with the poor, his lofty phrases and the stories of his destitute childhood. For lack of courage, he had opted for an imaginary saga.

He declared one day that perhaps God had chosen me to serve Him with my voice, because its quavering grief, its plaintive, irritating tone, and the guilt it provoked were perfectly suited to recite the Holy Book. And so at ten years old, on a Monday in June, around the time of the siesta that emptied the village of men and allowed women to venture a few steps outside, I was brought to the house of the reciters, behind the mosque in the center of town, and handed over to the master of the old Koranic school packed with noisy children. They had decided that the modern school was no longer enough to protect me from being possessed by the devil and that learning the Holy Book could only heal me in the long term. Absent from public school for months because of my panic attacks and migraines, I had been excluded gently, politely, for my own benefit even. Since I couldn't hope for the prestige of medicine or teaching, it was conceivable that I might earn my living and respect by reciting the Holy Book over the tombs, during weddings or burials, to soften hearts and consecrate nuptials.

A sweet and docile child, I followed my aunt to the door of the madrassa before I realized they were throwing me into the mouth of a whale that shook the entire village with its discordant voices. The master caressed my hair in front of my aunt who had slid a bill into his hand, looked me in the eyes with the false tenderness his profession requires, then declared that I must have been sent by God to honor the Book, to be its guardian until the Last Judgment. "Those who uphold the Holy Book cannot be touched by the fire of hell, said the Prophet," he concluded, solemn. Hadjer's suspicious faith and anger at destiny always left her skeptical about those who spoke in the name of the heavens and its justice, but she pretended to accept the sermon. After some hesitation, she let go of my hand and I joined the curious children, sitting in a circle on a halfa rug on the ground. The room was big, cool, and somber, and had a strange, subtle odor. Fermented clay, I learned later. The master didn't look at me even when my aunt left the room and reminded him that I was the son of Hadj Brahim. He told the eldest of the disciples to give me a tablet with the shortest surah clumsily scrawled on it. The object, heavy, smeared with brown, tenuous ink, was fascinating to me. Like a talking stone. I plunged into contemplation, while around me children's voices recited the words of God to embed them in their memories. The master dozed off all the time, half asleep, only seeming to wake up when the cadence dropped slightly, indicating a lack of attention, an absence, or cheaters reciting poorly. He was vigilant, his ear susceptible to the tiniest slip in tone or syllable. The Book was so holy that it couldn't suffer a single erasure or voice crack without jeopardizing the miracle. Did I hate those summers in the village, stuck in the backyard

of the mosque? Sometimes, yes. Especially when I had
to hold in my pee and flatulence so as not to pollute my
ablutions, when I had to complete my prayers without
bursting out laughing or scratching an itch. I hated the
constraint imposed on the laws of the body, and the
conviction of the imam and our master, who served as
the caller to the five prayers, that the body was something
filthy, an obstacle to meeting God, to understanding the
Book and accessing its meaning. We couldn't recite or
touch the Book unless we had been purified with water
and intense cleansing.

Even so, I had happy friendships. Like with Noureddine, who gave me my first cigarettes, and Hadji, a sneaky
child who had already had his first sexual encounter, who
showed us his penis and told us about sperm and the sorcery used by girls. But, beyond those insignificant memories, those times introduced me to the disappointing
mysteries of the Book. A child unsettled by silence and
by waking up in the morning, I plunged into my studies
with a force sometimes inspired by fear. It astonished my
master: I memorized the surahs with a worrying speed
that delighted Hadjer and my father, surprised by my
rapid recovery. I slept better, always glued to my aunt, but
my panic attacks were rarer and rarer, objects had started
to recede into the darkness, my attention now absorbed

by my studies. The cycles of recitations synced with the rites: we had to erase our tablet at the end of each month, reciting the memorized surah in front of the master who either certified our proficiency, and thus our right to erase the tablet and copy a new surah, or condemned the apprentice to another month of recitation. The Book was never explained, discussed, or recounted, we simply had to be its guardians, uphold it until the next generation. The exam session ended either in baton strikes on the soles of our feet, our hands restrained by two zealous members of the group who laughed at the cries of the boy being tortured, or by the rare ceremonious rite of replacing the master during one of his absences. I did that quite often, prolonging the delight of seeing the words of a god recede under the sponge soaked in water, plunging back into the primal silence like fish.

I loved inhaling the smell of the clay we used to coat and whiten the wood to better accommodate new verses. And, above all, I liked to watch the elders make the ink by burning sheep's wool and mixing the residue with water and pouring it carefully into the *douaya* to make the *smagh*, the holy ink. This task was the privilege of the elders but I was very quickly authorized to perform it alone. The moldy odor of the *sansal*, the clay, and the smell of burnt wool were, for me, the perfume

of a mystery. And although the Holy Book had sometimes been boring for me as a child, with incomprehensible words, shouting, and narratives too scattered to
hook my imagination, I enjoyed meditating for a long
time on the first mysteries. Man had been created from
clay, proclaimed the surah of The Heifer, the longest in
the Book, just like the writing before my eyes, and that
had to mean something.

Little by little, as the master watched with great
interest, I surpassed my colleagues, memorizing chapters
at wild speed, discovering the rhythm that engraved the
verses in my head, transforming my plaintive sheep's
voice into a gentle melody, agreeable to the ear of the
mosque's imam. We learned the Book starting with the
last chapter, the shortest surahs, progressing toward
those that awaited us like tall mute mountains, the
chapter names revealing an unsolved mystery: The Cave,
The Heifer, The Poets, etc. Strangely, the surah titles
evoked powerful images for me and I daydreamed about
their shape, as when we try to glimpse the footprints of
a mythical animal in the scattering of the stars. I liked
the Book's descriptions of the night sky, its fascination
for celestial bodies and shooting stars, and its cadences
as strong as clashes around a watering hole. And I hated

the long laws, the threats to quell any disobedience or rebellion with fire. But I especially loved the obscure chapter heads that sometimes started the recitation with strange onomatopoeias. Alif/Lâm/Mîm. ALM. Or Nūn, whose Arabic outline looked like a pot of ink, a moon above a valley, or a black sea with a fisherman coming back from the horizon. I loved God's habit of selecting only certain objects from the bag of the world to turn into fetishes of his vows: broken moon, shooting or immobile star, pilgrim sandals, bunches, bracelets, eyelids and raids, burning bush and tunic. In the surah titles, I found a soothing alphabet.

I came back at night slightly reassured, armed with new verses capable of stopping the unfurling of the unsayable and maintaining the strange breath behind the wall of the words of God himself. I didn't really have a religious conscience, to tell the truth, and the rite of the prayers, the various invocations of God's generosity, his magnanimity and his anger, irritated me as much as sweet talk, but I appreciated that universe of rituals and routines, the dawn prayers, the clock of rites. After the second year, I think the master of the madrassa was already starting to suspect my impiety, or my half-heartedness, but he never alluded to it around Hadj

Brahim, who inundated him with generosity. I have an untainted memory of those fabulous seasons of recitations, the sound of cypresses in the mosque courtyard, the moldy odor of the rugs I buried my nose in during prayers, the stridence of insects or the tender rain, while we shouted our heads off, naughty children or young men anxious to grow a beard, to honor this sonorous Book that was trying to sum up the world.

At home, the change was very visible for my aunt Hadjer, who smiled at me more often as if I were finally healed. At night, I lay awake thinking of God and the mystery of his Book, I repeated verses in different tones to gauge the effect of each, then I fell asleep dreaming of paradise and its idle greenery, waiting for the end of the world. This period lasted about three years: I learned nearly all of the Holy Book and already the elder reciters showed me off in the surrounding douars like a miracle, despite my bleating voice. I read the Holy Book with them around the dead or the couscous, during a circumcision or to celebrate the return of a pilgrim who was exhausted but delighted to have been at the center of the world and to be a part of it from then on for his people in the village. Memories of rising temperatures and fig trees, dark and gnarled, standing up to heat waves, meat heavy with fat that I discreetly avoided, and long, tiring discussions about God, his names, and his generosity toward men. That could have led me to lasting virtue and the glory of a religious life devoted to the Book of God. Except that everything came to an end one day, in the most comical way. It was inexplicably banal.

31

One Wednesday (I was born on a Wednesday), I woke up late, Hadjer was already on her way to the hammam, a monthly ritual after her period, I believe. The abrupt and perfect silence of the house made me uneasy. My grandfather was sleeping and I made sure the burners, the sinks, the doors and windows were off or closed before I dressed in a hurry. On my way out, I grabbed a fat bunch of white grapes for breakfast. On my way to the madrassa, my world split in two: tripping over a pebble, I sprawled over the dusty ground and arrived at school with skinned knees, the bunch of grapes reduced to a memory. The schoolmaster, Sidi Khloufi, examined me, slightly surprised, and asked me what had happened.

I don't know what came over me but I pointed at the other latecomer who had just arrived quietly behind me and I accused him of pushing me from behind. He was then taken, whipped, and banished to the corner of the room. In protest, he stared at me with big teary eyes, without understanding why I, the most respected and inoffensive kid in school, would have committed such an abomination. That night, at the end of the recitations, he spat on me and took off running. Why had I lied? Perhaps out of fear of being ridiculed. Or a desire to break my own image in the eyes of others. Or a deeper sickness. Today, I think that my Koranic studies, deaf and mute to meaning, would have been the death of my gift, and so my gift, trapped in the basement, had simply harnessed ferocity to push me toward shame and, as a result, flight. The truth is that I had grown tired, without realizing it, of those recitations that certainly kept the devils on the other side of the wall of verses and allowed me to believe in something more powerful than terror, but didn't feed my desire for another body, cracks, and mysteries bigger than descriptions of hell, of paradise, and of a god that seemed more verbose than the world he had created.

One week earlier, I had gone with my elders to close a burial ceremony. We had been invited to sit at the back of an immense tent. The night was dark, dusty because of the paths leading to this douar and dirtied by the gas lamps that had been scattered everywhere. We smelled the heavy odor of couscous even before we'd arrived. Cars were parked haphazardly and half-naked children were running under patient trees. A sort of muffled conversation filled the silence and I struggled to find a spot under the rug to hide my shoes, because I didn't want to lose them in the scramble to leave after the meal was over. It was a funeral for an old man who had been repatriated from France that very night; we would wait for daybreak to bury him in the earth. I was dozing off and one of my neighbors pinched my thigh to wake me.

Immediately, we began the long surah of The Most Merciful, Ar-Rahman, a favorite among the people because of its rhythm and its detailed descriptions of paradise and its treasures. Distracted and a little tired, I stared at the coffin covered with a green sheet that was embellished with verses stitched in gold, knotted like chicken wire. The dead man was inside, useless, almost forgotten. I didn't know his name, only that of his tribe. Suddenly, in the middle of the recitations that were starting to heat things up, I fell into a sort of air pocket, a slow silence. I saw myself as though through a window, mouth open over the syllables, in concert with my people while the dead man was there, heavy, futile, and indifferent, in the obtuse gravitas of the cadaver. We were merely a band of public criers, invited to shake our pots and distance death and fill the silence it provokes with the rumors of a god. The verses did nothing and the deceased was deaf as a stone to the prayers. I felt ridiculous: something was missing, the words weren't powerful enough to rouse the cadaver or even to invest it with meaning. A guest had dared to hide his shoes under the coffin and children approached it, curious and insolent. I was struck by the uselessness of the box, which would soon be double-locked so that the hostage wouldn't escape. Realizing the deception, I suddenly felt the urge to vomit. Were my thoughts really that clear? I don't think so, but I still remember the unprecedented emotion I felt at thirteen years old, the feeling of being cheated and my resulting anger. Death had the same moves and the same ruses as Brahim. It used crude artifice to hide the essential. Were we the touters of faith? That evening, deep in the night, they led me back to our house, arms loaded with couscous and meat that I threw out and scattered before entering. Hadjer had fallen asleep waiting for me but didn't say a word when she saw me enter with that sinister look on my face. The sickness was back, like smoke, and she knew it. She called that night "the night of destiny" in my calendar: behind the Holy Book, I had come upon this stark territory.

The truth is that my first hairs were already growing on my lip and between my thighs; something deaf and blind was crawling through my body, provoking delicious frictions and troubling insomnia. Its opposite was this cadaver, mitigated death, and my unresolved anguish. I explained, simply, that I would not return to the Koranic school, thus initiating my reputation as a renegade and plunging my father—who, for a time, had believed his god had forgiven him—into even greater shame. They attempted every subterfuge to make me renounce my decision, but it was all in vain. I had lost that original faith, and never again would I manage to restore it within me. I hadn't turned into a nonbeliever, but I saw my religion as a worn-out textbook. The mystery was more honest when it wasn't explained by ablutions and prayers.

32

I often looked at my penis in the morning.
Pointed straight at the sky like a finger, long and
skinny, aimed at the virgins of paradise, perhaps, or the
lactation of the night. I was different, and only my father
and aunt knew it. I hadn't been circumcised when I was
little. At first because of my childhood trek, tossed between two or three homes, then because of my delirious
fits at the sight of blood. All my half brothers, cousins,
and other relatives had been grabbed one Friday morning by an adult who forced them to spread their legs in
front of a barber who cut off their foreskins, except me.
Hadj Brahim had been insisting sternly for a long time,
but my aunt had dissuaded him, gaining time year after

year until it became indecent to mention in public. But I couldn't fight the idea that my father thought about it every time he saw me. During my childhood and teenage years, Hadj Brahim and Hadjer's debates on the subject could get heated, provoking an anger in him that evoked God and tradition, but he could never make my aunt back down, she refused the sacrifice and argued with surprising theological reasons: nothing in the Holy Book required this mutilation, especially not for a sick and sensitive child. The power struggle turned violent but my aunt remained inflexible, using the force of her anger against fate, stubborn as though it were a question of slitting my throat. So I grew up with the impression that my penis was a battlefield whose stakes were the pride of my aunt and the pernicious desire of my father to exact revenge on me or my mother. Of course, with time, I understood that I shouldn't get naked in front of the other children, go to the baths after a certain age, or speak about my anatomy.

I only thought of that rejected pact of flesh when it came to the question of my marriage. What will Djemila think if one day I give her my body to restore her own? If we marry and she discovers that excess in me, that peculiarity worse than impiety? It might shock her. Or not. When we locked eyes for the first time, six months ago, I saw a pleading in her gaze, surprise but also subtle complicity. The body of a spurned woman is the proof of her impurity. Perhaps that will solder us. She knows, because of the rumor, that I am feared and mocked. Perhaps she understands that that leaves scars. What will I say to my wife and what will she say about me to her mother, which is to say to the whole tribe and the whole village? The public mystery of love collides with a story of locks and keys, in a way. Sex is a big deal for my people. We've devoted ninety-nine allusions to it in our language, long years of rumors and slander, and we see it as the final reason for creation. It's the real fruit of the fall and the ascension. It serves to measure habit, the force of the voice, the number, but also the honor, the reputation, and the savings for the costs of marriage, but it's invisible, unlike death: sex hides bodies, while the gravedigger exhibits them in mounds, hips, hillocks, and curves. Amusing, isn't it? We celebrate weddings or funerals with the same fury, the same verses sometimes. I digress, while the hour is critical and my father is at risk of dying, of being killed by my clumsy and incomplete tale.

I was writing that, in the village, my refusal to pursue the apprenticeship at the Koranic school caused a scandal. All the more so because there my voice had finally attained a promising dignity and my father a kind of reparation. No one understood my defection, especially not my friends at the madrassa, tricked by my serious demeanor, oblivious to what was taking place inside me. Above all, it was my disobedience to God and the interruption of my work that shocked people: I was the bearer of half of the Holy Book. Which was an anomaly in itself. I didn't care. For once, I felt free, I had an insolence stemming from both puberty and intelligence. That lasted a few weeks, my spirit mobilized to hold its own, to argue my dissidence or respond to Hadj Brahim's threats. But suddenly, one night, the horrible attack returned and I fell back into the mystery as I contorted, unconscious, on the floor of our house, biting my tongue and drooling as if I was possessed. I decided then and there to stop praying, doing my ablutions, and forcing myself to perform the rites. The bird was not an angel, but a parrot. That was my verdict. In sum, Zabor gained the upper hand over Ishmael, a rival twinship.

How did I discover the language of my gift? How did I liberate myself from the fate of my kin when I was abandoning their path, their formula for salvation? By accident, out of laziness perhaps. On the island of desolation, I found a bottle on the shore and, inside, my first French phrase: *"Elle s'avança vers moi nue."* But before mastering that language, I had to decipher it in ecstasy.

It was the language of sex and travel, those two sides that stretch the body to another, force it to be reborn. *(The old man isn't doing very well, according to my aunt. He's barely breathing anymore. Despite years of hatred, I feel his pain, a slight panic at the idea that his death and his illness might be real, irreversible. He's lied to me so much that the truth of what he now endures vanishes behind his life of artifice. Even his cadaver will not be authentic. A sheepskin will replace it at the burial, as in another legendary and odious tale, to replace that of his sheep fallen from the sky. Can he die even though I've been writing for such a long time? Why doesn't the miracle seem to be working this time, why does it refute me when this should have been the climax of my performance? I don't know what to do with my day, reduced to waiting. Write again to Djemila, or speak about her with Hadjer, this time without innuendos, without digressions? She doesn't like when I talk about her, I think, but that woman's story is clumsily linked to my father's, who scoffed at the idea that I speak about it to my neighbors. "Over my dead body!" he declared in front of a cup of coffee. Hadjer couldn't contradict him that time. It threw me into a terrible, ancient anger that encompassed all the quieted, underground anger like a storm. I was especially furious at myself for having gone through him, for having awaited his blessing and his action as custom requires. He restrains me with laws and I restrain him with my rebellion. As a reaction or a contradiction, I decided to make my story with Djemila the very core of my definitive liberation. Because, with the exception of two chance encounters, I had never been able to meet her or speak* to her. The young banished woman cannot make frequent visits to the Moorish bath, meet me at a wedding or on the street, or write to me. I don't know how lovers do it, or if they ever existed before marriage. The obsession with sex and the fixation on honor make such meetings impossible. Normally, we can call on mediators, vendors of new fabrics and jewels, or we station ourselves on the lookout at our windows. In our case, the only possible way, which we would have to plan, would be for me to see her at the cemetery. A strange place to profess vows, sealing the kiss with a tombstone.

I decided to go out, walk to the edge of the village, where I always faint when I try to go any farther. The walls of my world are in my head and sometimes I go there to test my role as sentinel. The book begins there where I stop.)

THREE

Ecstasy

33

(My father will die or is already half dead. This night is trampled by sounds on the roof, like scraping soles. Sometimes pebbles fall on the tiles, as if the house were a woman being stoned or a dog being kept at a distance.) As a general rule, I move slowly. As if I didn't want to collapse the pieces of my universe, pieces of porcelain from the height of the sky. I'm responsible for my people, the village, its possible end, its cycles of birth and death. I keep it balanced on my shoulders. That's how I walked east, once again, through the fields that were still warm because of the summer. It was that gentle hour before dusk. The sky was distant, intense, with hues of benevolent burns. "If the Sahara were an angel, that's what it would look like," whispered

my animal. I reached the French cemetery—ravaged, disorderly tombstones, as if that religion's resurrection had already taken place and its dead were between judgment and resettlement—and I passed it heading for the last carob trees and the fields of vineyards. Then to the most distant trees, the last ones identified on my map, which grow half in secret. I stopped there to keep from fainting. That's my law. I've tried so many times to go farther, in every direction, and I'm finally convinced. As a teenager, when I tried to escape to the city to see a movie or buy shoes, I fainted on the bus as soon as it started the descent down the hill. They brought me back home after calling my father. I also passed out in the south, as soon as I reached the first Barbary fig trees. And to the west, after the forest, in the high grass where they found me with my pants soiled, drooling and shaking with spasms. It happened every time, like a curse or a sign of the village's attachment to my footsteps. I'm sort of like Yunus, trapped by God this time to spare him from the flight from Nineveh, the whale, the sea, the shipwreck, and instead drown him in his own drool, in his village. I always feel the earth move like a rug that's been pulled out from under my shoes, nausea, then a swift night floods my eyelids and I spin. Then I wake up at Hadjer's house, sprinkled with orange flower water, squeezed in her arms, brought back by a murmur telling me that my exceptional life attracts the evil eye, and that a magnificent future awaits me, because she dreamed of a deluge of white feathers and I was there too, happy, in the middle of that snow of angels shaking their feathers.

My sickness became notorious, at a certain age, and they interpreted my fate as a sign, even though it was indecipherable. Our people have a strong belief in an equilibrium between gift and sacrifice. I knew I was a prisoner of my gift and of Aboukir, that I couldn't leave, nor remain there immobile and inactive. A voyager only through imagination, I had to stay there to save my people, the facades of walls, the old houses, the trees and the sick children and the poles and even the storks and various objects. If I didn't, God would rain down a deluge of fire on its inhabitants, as on Nineveh. I was the navel of the clock, I was walking slowly so nothing would fall, an invisible tightrope walker between the weight of language and the weight of objects, and I was scrutinizing every detail in case I needed long descriptions to fill my notebooks: the paint was flaking like the skin of a century, the pole was solitary like the finger of a believer, the street was paved like the future of a rich family's son, dirty black bags floated in the wind like orphans, the dusk air embalmed the implausible tenderness of a tree's

269

shadow, an old neighbor glanced at me rapidly and then greeted me with an apologetic smile, children stopped playing with their ball and looked at me without saying anything, wavering between respect and cheekiness, etc. This feeling of responsibility is painful, sometimes I reject it angrily but I always submit to it in the end: it's my destiny, I am the necessary table of contents of my people, the only place where they can allow themselves longevity, or eternity in the best of cases. I am the guardian against the wind that could erase them, the storyteller who feeds the fire in the void while the only possible path is a star. *(The best stories are the ones that captivate listeners in the darkness of the voyage and that, at the climax, nourish even the fire, which is also fully absorbed in the narrative.)* How many died definitively before I was born? How many ancestors have been lost because of the imperfection of a text or a writer?

I sat on the still-burning grass and tried to summarize my situation: my father is dying or maybe already dead. And when I said that to myself, I was struck by a feeling of immensity, as if my universe were becoming new. My heart skipped a beat, faced with an imaginary cliff. I felt like I needed a new first name. I know the truth: When your father dies, there's nothing left between you and death. It's your turn. I have no children, so I don't have to die. But that idea is a whimper. And now, I know, I have to write even more quickly, even more powerfully, without interruption. Because I'm saving my people but also my own skin *("And the skin of a woman, perhaps," I say to my starry dog. And he is still hesitant)*. Isn't it said that a prophet's salvation depends on how many people he's converted? That's how, at the end of time, of all time, he knows whether he's going to hell or paradise.

One of Hadjer's sisters came to visit us at the end of the day and she told us the rumors. Hadj Brahim hovers between life and death, and his children are already preparing to tear him apart, to divvy up his livestock and his riches. She elbowed Hadjer and tried to mobilize her for the coming war over the inheritance. It will be an ugly battle between the stepmother's clan and her numerous sons, and the sisters who have survived the patriarch. His possessions are numerous, but so are his descendants. First they will take his name and give it to the newborns. Then his herds, his knives, and his lands. For our people, there is no will, a vestige of nomadism perhaps. The legacy is not the land but the caravan. Hadjer didn't react but I saw her tense, I watched the dormant embers of her ancient anger flare up. The two women looked at me for a moment and then concluded, silently unanimous, that I would not be much help in the matter. I am the son of the dying man but I am sick, solitary, and afflicted with the evil of inconsistency brought on by books.

I drank tea in their silence and left. Why had my gift petered out this time, at the top of the hill? Why wasn't I able to save him when his story was easy, clear, honed? Birds moved through the dusk like twigs, black sparks in the fire of the sky. In the distance, cars came back from the village to the douars. Fathers returned home through the fields, arms loaded with groceries. I can draw the map of the village if I walk around it one more time. The island isn't huge, it's not mysterious. *("And its treasure is you," says Hadjer's voice.)* In the end, I never left Aboukir. Not even to find the tomb of my mother, of whom I have no memory. *(My mother is the sound of a body falling and violently colliding with the ground. She has no first name but a sort of long whimper. She was replaced, during the funeral, by dozens of women who passed my child's body between their arms to cry harder. I remember that I fell asleep and, after I woke, never saw her again.)* I watched the sky fade, open *(why is everything cyclical when we want to believe that the life of a man is half of a ring? One half in the sun and the other buried underground, rusting?)*, then I walked through the dry lands, following the slope of the hill that exhausts my chest.

I headed back down, an hour later, from the Bounouila cemetery. It took me two hours to arrive at our home, the house down below that was waiting for me. I know my brothers will chase me even farther away this time, that their ruse will be ferocious and mean. I am a legal heir and they will need to find the surest way to banish me. All of life is a book. The proof? The Prophet's Hadith that explains that the quill (the one that records our actions and our words and our thoughts) is suspended, inactive, for the lunatic, the sleeper, and the child until puberty. I am certainly in the first or second category. There was too much blood in the sky to the west. An omen of a bad wind. The entire horizon was a knife sharpened by the contrast with the dark earth. I glanced at Djemila's window but it was closed, blind. When I returned to our house, I found the spare set of Hadjer's keys on the ground. She had forgotten them on her way out. The house was empty, abandoned. In the kitchen, dirty dishes awaited.

34

Without stopping, electrified by a long surge of writing, I overflow my notebooks, it's urgent. The line isn't enough anymore, I almost need a fisherman's net. In the darkness of meaning, something enormous pulls on my line and hurts my hands. It's like there are waves in the phrases, sounds of heavy, billowing ink. I'm not exaggerating, I hear a breath. I wrote the whole night and Hadjer wasn't there. I found mismatched shoes near the entryway, an overturned bag, and her unmade bed. She must have left in a hurry. I hear the yipping of dogs, a muffled sound of things breaking, lowing in the slaughterhouse with zinc metal sheets that move like crumpled wings. The black-and-red sky seems ominous, mocking.

There was an electricity outage and a sandstorm invaded the village and the sky, dirtied the windows and the ground during the day. I haven't had any news of my father. A silence suspends the village, it resembles my grandfather *(immobile, head between his knees, arms wrapped around himself, at the entrance of our kitchen, where Hadjer still keeps the sheepskin she used as a flying carpet in her dreams)*. Nothing moves, despite the wind. Where is death right now? Sometimes I write just in case, as if to preserve an island, a tree, an unknown life, the steps of a man who arrives invigorated by the memory of an animal vanquished in his dreams. I reach a hand into the heart of hell, which has a thousand names in our tradition, and I try to find a burnt hand, to pull on a screaming arm or help someone trying to flee the well of the void, the hasty judgment of a god. I have to write, because there's always a life to save, at the end of the line, a man or a woman, someone spurned or elderly. I have a sort of faith.

I also feel a familiar anxiety: If I save lives by writing, who is the writer keeping me alive? The hidden voice that preserves me by telling another story in another palace that will be interrupted before dawn? Writing is speaking without breathing. I hold my breath and fuel my lines. When I write, there are two mismatched breaths: the breath of the dying person and the breath of my inspiration. I have to sync them. My gift is use-less against death by falling into a well, or death by car accident, for example. I've tried but in vain, because the accident rips the page, the book, and I have nothing left to write with. Writing must stand up to agony, which is its inverse. The story needs pages and notebooks, not ripped sheets.

The end, that's what I have to think about. Because what all stories have in common is the ending: it's the same for the hero and for the vanquished monster. One dies, slain, the other will die too, through perpetuation, paternity, the hollowing of his appeased world, a slow sinking into idle time. How does the victor die? We don't know. He gets married, finds happiness, experiences love, but he has no grave, while the monster has an altar, his memory is perpetuated by the tale or by the fear he inspires. So we have to lead the dying person back in time, to the moment when he encountered the monster of his own life (a father, an ogress, a talking animal, a toothache, a river, a memory of a colonizer, hunger, or humiliation), then make him travel backward down the path of his journey, to the moment when he's faced with the decision to leave, the question of whether or not to embark on his quest. The lives saved and returned are then able to continue for a long time to search, and thus to live, to reach a hundred years old by misleading the ancient order of the quest, sit at the edge of the path, on the stairs of our mosque, take pleasure in slander or in the shadow of a tree, settle for joining the gods with no disputes or feelings of incompleteness, no prayers or rebellion. We have to begin and begin again at the conclusion. Every story has one. In *The Thousand and One Nights*, it has to be pushed back, postponed. Here, before my eyes, in my notebooks *(while the troubling noises travel down the dark side streets and while men's voices try to reanimate the village)*, it has to be neutralized: I won't tell a story that will be interrupted with each dawn, instead I'll tell several, restarting them each time to overthrow the order of death and the false victory of the hero.

I have to write a great novel against the current of the Holy Book. I've dreamed of this notebook since I started mastering this sensual language. *(I've always hated the wind. It's my first memory. Me, sitting in the house of my maternal grandparents, almost in ruins. I remember the adults crying, their lamentations after the repudiation. No one was paying attention to me, the wind was my father's back as he left again, the trace of his abandonment, and nothing had an end. I was cold, I remember, but there was no wall to block the breath of the void. I was maybe three years old but I remember, because time always begins with an image and ends with an image.)* In sum, to save a person through writing, you have to salvage their story, make them drink it like holy water, gently, tilting back their head so the memory doesn't choke them. *(Like a feeble voice of reason, an idea crosses my mind: Hadjer hasn't come back, and it's not like her to run out the door, nor to leave the house in such a state. Nor to leave me alone. But it was just the devil, or his ruse to distract me, because this notebook is definitive, important.)*

Back to my reflection: Writing is the opposite of wind, because it's the opposite of dispersal. A recording in the manual of salvation. But I can't manage to maintain the thread of the story. Within me is the furious desire both to get up and to write. To write everywhere, on every surface. Perfect the miracle of my gift in a universal tattoo. It's summer, but suddenly the temperature drops, as if the world were retreating, fearful, into a hole. Something is afoot. Without me. I feel as if the end of the world has already happened and I simply didn't notice. Sitting, consumed by my task, while everything was folded and tidied under the Angel's armpit: the sun, the moon, the horizon, time and the tombs and the trees, all the monuments and roads and all the people who've been born and who've died.

35

(My father is dying. I've never done this before: write away from the dying person. Through the crowd and the walls and the trees. The distance that transforms this writing into prayer. It weakens the effect.) Before assuming the role of Hamza/Aïssa the antagonist, his beard dyed with henna, his mouth mid-scream, the devil had another form. I had stopped studying the Holy Book at about thirteen, despite my talent and the improvement in my panic attacks. That surprised quite a few people, and spurred animosity and cries of indignation throughout Aboukir. I lost the esteem of my cousins, and imam Senoussi (who was discreet about his disappointment), and a sort of immunity. Not praying was the worst form of disobedience,

and now they saw me walking like an obscenity in the
streets during the call while everyone else was praying.
I was indecent and Hadj Brahim's smile, generosity,
and fortune had to become all the more compelling to
divert their gazes. Ah, my poor father. I was his tragedy,
but also a living insult in the shadow of his story of a
butcher blessed by God: on top of my thousand birth
defects, I added insolent impiety. Only my aunt treated
me the same, serious, firm in the face of adversity, eyes
full of a stubborn pride against fate. I wondered about
her religious beliefs for a time, before concluding that she
believed in God but that she also believed he was a rotten
intermediary between her and happiness. She respected
him but did not forgive him. However, that was when the
real adventure of my life began, which is ending now, in
this instant, in this room, time held in this hand.

I left the mosque with half a book in my memory,
which spread its voice over half the world, in a language
that was half alive, and its writing was able to ward off
half my fears. I also felt as naked and trembling as the
prophet Yunus whose story I adored: "And when he left
irritated…" He's the only prophet without a community,
without a tribe behind him. The only one who battled,
left his people, and confronted God, who appeared to
him in the form of an old boat, a hateful storm, sailors,

then a whale, then a tree that lends its shade to his naked body, a castaway in the end, according to the Holy Book. However, the true story is not the story of the prophet, but the story of the appearances his god assumed.

I was naked and trembling but proud, insolent. Of course, my panic attacks were back, sometimes difficult, and so were my chaotic reflections on writing. At the Koranic school, I learned to practice my handwriting, the taste of the material (the *sansal*) in the hollows of words, the smell of wet tablets, and the certitude that there's a link between pronunciation and health, or, to be precise, between rhythm and life. A secret of power and dependence. I asked myself, a little lost, about the meaning of writing, the letters always lined up from right to left, as though magnetized by a slope. Why did we have to write in this direction and not the other? Why not write as the ox toils, back and forth, or like the bird, low to high then high to low? Or in the chaos of caravan tracks in the sand?

I was at an age when I loved to play games, I went out often to try to join the other children *("Zabor eddah el babor!" "Zabor was carried off by a boat!")*, but I kept an eye on my anxiety and its black ink, shiny as a star. It was a beautiful time, lazy, a vacation free from all constraints. Hadjer hoped for suitors, the Hindi films were rich with

blather and my father, Hadj Brahim, had not yet completely ceded to the pressures of my stepmother and her
dirty tricks. The only black cloud was my night terrors,
my screams, the frequently poor sleep that stunted my
growth. I tried playing soccer with the other teenagers in
the neighborhood before realizing that I was the object
of their mockery. I gathered lost balls and tried smoking
cigarettes with Noureddine, who maintained his friendship with me, the friendship of an elder, even though he
was younger than me, like a form of protection, because
he was muscular and feared.

I was hyper-aware of the rift between my solitary,
unconscious quest for a language capable of appeasing
and restoring the world, and my appearance as a common, puny child, tempted by the games of kids his age
and their ritual maliciousness. In my head, I had no age;
on the outside, I was the age required to join the groups
in the neighborhood of our house down below. I tried to
make up with others, with smiles and submission, until I
understood I would never be accepted *(Hadjer said that what
kept me from being good at soccer was my wings that no one could
see, not my legs)*. So I told myself that the essential thing
was the possibility of a language: if I wrote mine from
right to left, that alluded to the existence of another,
invisible language, written in the opposite direction, or

another still that went around the earth and came back to the phrase written at the start. Of course, my time in school left me with the persistent memory and the faltering mastery of a French alphabet, its spikes and its paunches, its uneven slenderness, but I remembered only a few phrases, excerpts from novels and poems. Arabic writing seemed even more fascinating to me but it wore itself out spinning in circles in a single book, between my schoolmaster, the verses, and my reveries about the stories of the prophets and their hardships or wanderings. *(I liked the beginning of the prophets' stories, the birth of the vocation, but the details of their laws bored me. I thought they were flawed: at the end, they died. A perfect prophet doesn't die, because of his proximity to his god but also because he has to save the people who have not yet been born. Why does each prophet dream of being the last? To perpetuate the belief in his presence for all time.)* I desired and sensed another solution to my fear. Sometimes, lying in the courtyard of our house, while the world was eternity and summer, I would contemplate a random object at length, a pebble or an unripe orange. Like a book I could read in two directions, three, turn it around, crisscrossed not with light like a backlit page, but with all possible words, the heavy knot of their encounter, the blind and exposed core of writing. I lost myself in strange depictions, calligraphic monstrosities, veins of ink. Idleness and fear led me to imagine, already, the possibility of an absolute glyph, the prospect of all of history in a single word *("or five," specifies Poll; "or more," encourages the dog).* I dreamed of a sacred writing: one that would embrace the object, constituting its bark and its vanished essence, half revealed through calligraphy, ink, the smell of the ink, the material of the ink. Something almost alive, a writing like an extended hand.

In those years, the fear came back at night, but also after naps. I remember I would always wake up late, slightly emptied, with the panic of the traveler who opens his eyes in an unknown place, feels his pockets, tries to find his horse and his own name. I feel my world, I try to overcome the brusque worry provoked by foreignness, very quickly I grant things their names again, like a ritual. I say "curtain," "window," "door," "lemon tree," my own name (Zabor, not Ishmael), the details of my body, the birthmark on my arm or the name of the headache medication placed next to me. I say Hadjer, Hadjer, Hadjer. The inventory is necessary to imbue order into the chaos of the world. I mumble my verses every time I wake up, I recite my mantras so the objects come back down to earth like sprigs of tea, settle in and resume their fluttering familiarity. The roughness of objects, that whistling of foliage in the courtyard, the footsteps of the invisible, and especially the apprehension provoked by domestic animals with their sly slowness, all that chaos boring into my flesh.

At that time, during my adolescence, despite my gentle happiness, waking up from a nap was nearly always followed by silent screams or the whimpers of the vanquished. My aunt, who kept her vigorous af- fection for me, would take me in her arms, invoke the names of saints, and have me sniff incense or pieces of onion. The truth is that I was terrified by the horror of unnamed objects, but I was also using my attacks as vengeance against my father. I knew in some way that it was his fault. *(I see him now, as yesterday and for so many years, the dangling arms, a yard from the doorway of our house, incapable of advancing or fleeing. Poor man, who thought he was running faster than time, whom time has caught with the consequence of his own acts and secret fears. "Ishmael's doing well?" he would yell. No one would answer and then, as always, he would turn back toward the street, look for any witnesses, then lower his head and leave.)* You need a father to give things names, without one they scatter, surge, and overflow belligerently, suffocate you and make you lose weight and then your sense of direction. I recited verses but they had less and less of an effect on the devil's face, which stuck its red tongue out at me through its tattoos. The truth is that this second language, the language of the schoolmaster and the verses, after the language of Hadjer and her painful powerlessness, was also exhausted in my mouth. I could have learned more of it, revived it or imbued it with strength, but the motivation was gone: I didn't desire it anymore. It had the face of the master, the imam, my father's adult friends, my father when he bowed for the prayer, Friday and its shouted sermons. Studying the Holy Book had allowed me to sense possibilities, but there were no other books to feed my curiosity.

That's when the world tried to speak to me in a different way.

36

It was the revelation, the click, the whirling angel whose wings created a squall of 250 to 400 pages, the fierce possibility of a solution. It was a banal, accidental discovery, but I think they called out to me, in the secret order of my universe. I was thirteen years old when other writings emerged, foreign, with dog-eared pages, numbered and faded. Novels written in French that I found piled up in the house down below, in a random room off the back courtyard *("When they are not read, books travel slowly, from one house to another, from one basement to another, from one box to another. When they are read, it's the reader who travels," says the dog, serious)*. An accident? A coincidence? I think not. My whole universe was crying out for a new language, an instrument for the essential secret of my people, for me. The devil could be successfully thwarted if I could stand up to him, but I was missing a book, an instrument. On top of my irrepressible fears, there was a vacuum, an emptiness where things, the balancing of the village land, the trees, everything was suspended, at the end of another language, hovering and fragile without the consolidation of ink. I felt my body buzz, it was changing with puberty, and all around me was a new silence sensitive as skin. My entire universe was like a bush electrified by the movement of an animal hidden within it, passing through it, unknown. Nothing precise in the house down below, but a coming melody. An unprecedented bliss promised by the third part of my life: ecstasy.

It was quite an adventure to learn, alone, surreptitiously, the angel's third language, the missing piece of the Law of Necessity that would save so many lives, add a thousand and one days to every encounter, in secret, humbly, through the art of writing. No, the books of that language did not come to me by coincidence, they were sent. Perhaps by my dead ancestors without memories, without books or names, who wanted to learn through me, speak and take back their stories which had been interrupted for lack of language and sheets of paper. Every book title I read from that moment on had in fact appeared at exactly the right moment in my life, like a wave of the hand. An immense bookstore was already conversing through me at that time and took me under its protection, as I would have to protect my people years later. *(My father is going to die and I am unmoved. As if incapable of feeling any sentiment at all. Pernicious, my vanity has already imagined the condolences of kin and villagers. Because, yes, his death will consecrate me as his son, forevermore! I don't need an inheritance, I need recognition from everyone, a vengeance that will prove he didn't win, he didn't crush me——he is the one who will be crushed by all that earth on his chest. The island will be mine, my language will be proclaimed victorious and richer than the flocks of his land. But it will also provoke vertigo that will twist my heart like a rag. He abandoned me in the desert, slit my throat with his eyes and his long story on the hill of his betrayal, and I'm the one who feels guilty, distraught. Hadjer didn't run out for no reason. I think she's gone to watch over him, or to have her say in the inheritance. The house is empty and resists the persistent assaults of the wind, still quiet. The image of a wolf pounding on the door. It bangs with a steel snout. This notebook will serve as proof, the great surah of my life. It's August, I had forgotten, a month that likes to play with fire.)* I will perhaps never be able to recount with precision and talent the curious nature of that time, the meaning of the wait that came to a brusque end with new verbs. The appearance of exactly twelve books, in a language with no guardian, was the critical event of my life. A thousand and one days, each time.

37

At that moment, that language, this one, was definitively marked by my body, my penis, the birth of my desire. It bears the trace, the weight, the marks of wakefulness and sleepiness, the shameful fold of the crotch and the erection of the first drop cap. It taught me lucidity, like an exercise in acuity, of trial and error, too. "Squaring off" is the fitting phrase. At thirteen, I left the closed universe of studying the Holy Book and wound up on a vague terrain scattered with new stones. That phase of availability concluded with a major vice that turned me into a chronicler of my people. That's how I describe that chaotic time, shameful and splendid like the nocturnal embrace of infidelity. I don't know how it happened but I remember the event itself, the anecdote.

On a rainy and mild Monday, while Hadjer was still in the bath, I wandered around the empty house, secretly spurred by the need to touch something new, a tactile curiosity that had been obsessing me for days. My voice was broken and so was my entire body. My grandfather was there, sitting with his head between his knees, as though in a personal winter, he wasn't moving (never has a cadaver been left in the sun for such a long time) and I was tired of speaking about the rain and the harvests, as old people do. I had spoon-fed him his meal, with difficulty, nearly forcing his lips open. He swallowed in the end, but always with his eyes staring at a final word that was perhaps on the tip of his tongue, the black hole of his memory that was turning its back on him. This was my part of the care we provided for our elder. Hadjer handled his hygiene, washed him, lovingly shaved his head, dressed him, and spoke to him about everything under the sun as if he could still answer. I watched over him often, when she wasn't there, and gave him food and drink (almost always couscous with milk because he refused all other food).

There were no engine noises in the village and no cries because the children were at school. It was the most beautiful hour of autumn, the oldest book in the world. I was walking around alone, opening cabinet doors, touching objects, and then, suddenly, I remembered the storage room in the back courtyard piled up with old things, the winter bedding, empty crates and provisions. I entered with a feeling that something was waiting for me there (burning bush, white stones, crumbs), and I scoured the darkness of the little room. I saw a stack of yellowed books, dog-eared and tied like criminals with their hands behind their backs. I advanced, curious, I opened the bundle, sitting on the ground, and started to leaf through one of the books, not expecting much, merely curious, as when we glimpse the faces of unknown visitors. An army of characters spilled out, an anthill, organized and strict, tiny feet in procession, indented paragraphs and quotation marks animated by exclamations. A dead butterfly fell out from another book, as well as a small braid of hair that frightened me when I mistook it for a spider. I diligently deciphered just a few words, remembering my persistent schoolchild's alphabet, and was about to shut the book.

But, dwelling in my slight disappointment, the images on the covers enticed me like windows. I leaned through them and sank, abandoning myself to the heat provoked in my body by what I'd seen. I suddenly felt a sort of link of cause and effect between my unexpected shiver and the image of the woman with the perky breasts, pointing out from behind a striped T-shirt, smiling with her whole face tilted toward mine, so close, within reach of the old paper's dry breath, happy because she was staring at me but she was also staring at something beyond me. Someone else that I could be? For once, the prescience of desire had a body to behold, a tangible release, and I seized it ardently, by intuition. Time stopped and the woman wasn't moving, allowing me to remain near her. She was not reabsorbed into a stream like the images on the television, but persisted, constant, full, complete in her immobile gift, waiting for me to come take her body, to come touch her, now that she'd offered herself. I caressed her skin that was both eternally young and already cracked because of the paper's age, lips of red ice, slightly open onto a fire, laughing eyes deciding the reality of the person they provoked. Breasts with hard nipples whose shape I couldn't fully determine, as sensitive as I was to their sadness sharpened in me, to their skilled evasion under the fabric of the striped T-shirt she was wearing behind the paper pane. I understood suddenly, instantly, that the thousands of characters, from the first page, were in a way the sound of her own life, her flesh, the explanation of her smile and the promise of her secret, her revelation, the frightening possibility of her nudity. I made a direct link between the story and the body both exposed and hidden, toying with my desire and my ignorance. The way to wrest the clothes from this woman wasn't to tear the pages but to read them. That coincided, shamefully, with a heat in my groin, an accelerated pulse, and the desire to touch my uncircumcised penis.

I knew, secretly, that I was on a life-changing threshold that would establish a new order, a hierarchy in which the bottom of the ladder was the pebble and the top that woman's lips, the enigma of a bite. Hadjer never spoke about sex and all the films we had seen together on television cut off at the embrace and the kiss. I remember the bodies of two lovers approaching each other, desiring each other, staring at each other, lips extending, then, brusquely, a messy separation, a sort of mechanical rejection that cheated passion. The censored sex was implicit, assumed, left to the imagination, crude in its absence. A rift, a blank that rendered inexplicable the next part of the story, the birth of children and the driving force of so many actions for the heroes and the women. The carnal side of the world was a confused silence and an embarrassment between me and my aunt. But with this book I could dream of the final revelation, indistinct, exalting and reserved for my use in the darkness of the storage room.

I guessed, I think, from the first glance, the solitude of sex, but it took me years to understand it. The promised desire was from the start clandestine, hidden, even shameful, it was condemned to be a contradiction: a cold body in the throes of an inner fire that never left me. I could only approach with closed eyes, only embrace through the implausible angle of absence. I deciphered the title, laboriously: *The Flesh of the Orchid*. That was the woman's name, or the name of a part of her body, or a sweltering heat, a lip, or something murkier. Forever. Both shaft and vulva, thorn and peat. Evasion and expansion. These words didn't have any immediate meaning in my mind or in my universe but were already shining like stars under my finger. My studies had taught me the essential, the alphabet, the possibility of writing, but also phrases, compositions, songs, poems from the end of the textbook and excerpts from books. But this was the first time I had encountered a liberated, wild text that was not meant to teach a moral or a lesson, but existed as an infraction of order, free and radical. It showed a way, a new path that my people hadn't seen. My body could have a hidden side, be the site of a doubling that would spare me from being exposed to questions or ridicule. Zabor and Ishmael. They could slit the throat of one but never catch the other because he was invisible, unknown.

I had two bodies, as I waited to have dozens and dozens of lives. *The Flesh of the Orchid*, when I was about thirteen, was an object in itself, a carnal thickness that was half illuminated, a secret, a shadow tattooed on a body. Or the inverse: a body that was slowly emerging through the interlacing of a tattoo, as if it were pushing aside the branches of the first tree. I grazed it, touching the frozen paper, leaning toward the proffered lip, I kissed its dust, I tried to lift the T-shirt to understand why the angle of the nipple threw me into a panic, and with the other hand, I touched myself. Clumsy, violent with my private flesh, I searched pleadingly, rumpling the cover, the word of the title that refused to give me its language when I kissed it, the eyes that lit up with a sort of mockery, then there was the wet fire, an electricity that made me moan, struck by a delicious disarticulation. I felt dirty, ashamed, but I also sensed the beginning of a magnificent vice. I knew that now I could go further if the words yielded or were illuminated, I could enter the hidden realm of sex, that perpetual room of encounter.

For days I contemplated the photo of the woman, suddenly reassured in the panic of desire by the certainty of deciphering, and already fabricating the ruse that allowed me to conceal this new debauchery from my family (Hadj Brahim and his mocking eyes) by hiding the image on the cover with paper. My aunt walked in on me once when I was holding a book between my hands, the sign of a gift or a vocation or, at worst, the desire to go back to school, which I angrily refuted. I conceived and compelled my disgrace and my liberty starting in that moment. I was obsessed with that woman. The old book was a dress, but devoid of contents because I didn't know how to read.

What can I say? I set about reading the book starting that first week. It was difficult, laborious, but motivated by the shameful, sublime desire to discover nudity, skin, the body that the letters written from left to right, tenuous and magnetized by a slope, designated unanimously and rigorously, in the veiled precision of the symbol. Straight lines of ants headed for a delicious spring, a revelation, an undressing. Memories of chaos and rage, because I didn't often succeed. The words, sometimes half of them, were illuminated within the line, but very quickly fell back into a twisting conjugation I couldn't fully grasp. Time was my hell in a way, back then, I was sliding without a handrail, without direction, deciphering a permanent present, deformed and impossible because it impeded the unfurling of the story. In the Holy Book, time was an illusion, God spoke in the present even in the future of the Last Judgment or before creation. He was prisoner of his eternity and that extended to his verses. Here, the hero traveled when he spoke. Conjugating tense was my first challenge. Without the right grammar, I was spinning in circles, lost in a gridlock, a simultaneity that made no sense except in the order of religion. Time was not the same in Arabic and in French, it was divided differently according to the way the future was understood and the present was possessed.

Then I decided to try something else to learn the woman's story: I reread a chapter skipping over the words I didn't know, only reading the ones I could decipher. The phases of my excitement became my conjugation. It was the beginning of a miracle: the paragraphs slowly became illuminated, populated with heavy shadows and whispers, revealing a breach, a possibility of nuance, of nudity. Then I searched for the phrases beginning with *elle*, the first name of a woman, roaming the pages to find her, like in a crowd or in a train station, running, stopping, then starting up again endlessly when I confused her with others. I turned my back on the village and on all my people in these moments. I wasn't the abandoned Ishmael with the goat voice, afflicted with fainting spells at the sight of blood or when trying to leave the village, but an Englishman (what was the nationality that the seas often spoke of?), a hand touching hair to calm a heart.

Hadjer, at first intrigued, decided that this was my own way of completing my studies or occupying my infinite time at that age. I have to say that the book was still descending from the sky in our world, guarding the prestige of a voice of God or a commentary on his verses. Destiny was "written," ink had the power to heal and must be drunk on an empty stomach (mixed with oil, honey, and thyme), facing east, and writing was still a sovereign order, a mandate. Seeing me read all the time, leaning as though over a well, calm and without yelling, she decided this was a better remedy than movies on TV, her caresses in my hair, or her fragile explanations about my mother's death and my father's abandonment. I stopped time, my games with the neighborhood children, and my idle wandering through the house down below. But my aunt wasn't duped for very long, because, through a strange intuition, she surmised that it was as much a fascination for the language of the former colonizers as it was about the troubles linked to this body that she saw taking on new angles and bones, and she noticed my goat voice change into the voice of a lamb with lowered eyes. Her femininity, exacerbated by the wait, sensed my transformation but decided not to worry about it.

The wild orchid resisted me for a long time, then, gradually, worn down by my persistence, she yielded, opened her mouth, her lips onto her tongue. I will always remember that moment of unexpected melody when I realized that I had mastered the language, that it had turned to music after having been carved stone, noise in my head, silent palm trees and flavorless coconut trees. Suddenly the book took on a voice and told me its story like a confession after the crime. Of course, I didn't understand all the words, but the language, which was flesh, became a knotted muscle and started to move with the conjugated tenses. All discovery is music, melody, vibration. Even today, when I write to keep the village out of the well, inspiration comes to me like the buzzing of a bee. And the music inhabited me for years, it heralded an erection but also voyages. I ate little, reading everywhere, rereading (for lack of books), by the light of the television, by the flame of the candle in the courtyard, seated near my grandfather who was still alive at the time like an ellipsis. My eyes gleamed with obsession but I was also tired as a traveler's back. A marvelous initiation— my panic attacks stopped and this language appeared to me in all its splendor and freedom with my first dozen books. It was of course a revelation about sex, but also about unexplored territories that were foreign to me, or almost: the sea, the valley, the tropics, the deadly fever, the sand and the shrouds, the island most of all, were revealed to me from the inside, touching my senses other than sight, in the rampant intimacy the reader feels faced with a world. Reading a book was like moving through a giant tree, climbing under its bark up to its fruit, inside its branches.

Learning how to read introduced me to the wonderful coincidence of the interior with appearance, it gave sound to the silence and allowed me to measure the exact expanse of the world on the other side of my fainting spells. It started that day, at the beginning of October, and culminated in my strange scars of a man hunched over his notebooks to keep the village healthy and safe in the face of epidemics, ailments, and the grief of mourning. The books, without illustrations and without images, were as dense as the tropics, and at first I spent hours staring at the covers, imagining the meaning of the titles, their shadows, their contrast with my hands made of flesh, their ink I was reheating. Each title was a universe in itself, a world. Even now as an adult, every time I read I sink with pleasure into a title's universe. For lack of books, I found a way to make my library infinite. The end of a novel (so dreaded in Aboukir, where Elsewhere was a bus that passed twice over the highway) was neutralized by a list of "forthcoming" books, with titles offered up to my reverie. I imagined their contents, their characters, their plots and roads, and I could spend hours reading in my head, gamboling through the outlines of beginnings. Perhaps my grandfather did the same thing within his silence? That's how I wrote *The Lord of the Rings*, *The Sailor Who Fell from Grace with the Sea*, *Confessions of a Mask*, *2010: Odyssey Two*, *The Plague*, *To a God Unknown*, *The Book of Sand*, *The Dreaming Jewels* (O beauty), and dozens of others.

Even when I hadn't yet completely mastered that language, I had written a dozen novels in my head before I was even fourteen years old. The early stages of my gift, the announcement of my responsibility and my mission.

38

(*My aunt still has not come back. I am alone with this language, and my father might already be dead if I don't write even faster. An owl hoots, a caricature of the imminent mourning. The wind has its own favorite animals: the owl, the wolf, which is its essence, the crickets, they say, the bloodless insects, the dry spiders... Scratches on the glass of the windows, in my bedroom, and always the creaking of every door in the village as the wind trawls house by house. Searching for me, surely. Djemila is like a loose sheet of paper searching for a book to embed itself in, to have a story and participate in it.*) My method was simple and ingenious as seduction: I cross-checked. I remembered the alphabet and a few words, from when I was in school so long ago, and I used pieces of texts I already knew, evocative and waiting in my head. With these resources, I constructed that language, entirely, alone with my own savage dictionary. A glossary fabricated from the scraps of shipwrecked language, findings made on the island, words made of bark, pieces of patched fabric and texts eroded by salt and oblivion, the tools of the survivor who tries to reconstruct a civilization with a few scraps of wood and a Bible. Or the titanic work of his parrot, Poll, offering to repopulate the island with variations on its only acquired phrase: "Poor Robin, where are you?" The familiar words allowed me to guess the unfamiliar words, through cross-checking, neighboring lights, the contamination of meaning. Little by little, *The Flesh of the Orchid* became a story, and I clumsily grasped the logic of its rhythm, the pulmonary meaning of its paragraphs.

The words working together in this way told me a story, and the first phrase, which to me was epic, revealed the link between sense and the senses, multiplied ad infinitum, and led me to the universal orgasm years later. The woman advanced toward me, in a hazy nudity that gradually took shape, became movement, flow, her body taking on flesh and leaving me feverish. Frantically, I read the erotic passages, the descriptions of kisses, embraces, the proximity of genitals and their wetness, the passion galvanized me and mobilized every effort at initiation.

Still today I masturbate to certain books because there's an intense bodily intimacy in them, but I feel an emptiness that can only be filled by the supportive presence of another body from after the fall. Adam did not fall alone with a piece of fruit in his hand. Writing always has the texture of skin, and the somber word is a mane of hair, as in those years. I swear. That first phrase, deciphered laboriously from the first crime novel I read, was that era's revelation, a ripped dress.

Sex was half mysterious during those teenage years because children are violent and cunning: the insults, the aggression, the hierarchy, like the mystery, are always sexual. Boredom soon inspires children to show their penises, to measure their virility by the length of their stream of urine in the sand, to evoke sodomy or attack the weakest by miming it. There were no girls to strip naked, no bodies to glimpse on the TV or in magazines. Suddenly, because I had dared to go down a new path, I had discovered that books could lift the veil and show me nakedness without anyone suspecting a thing. I was stunned. That phrase, unique and overwhelming, set the stage for my future readings and haunted me in its precision: I still don't know what a woman's genitalia are like, but nudity was possible, palpable and evident. All I had to do was keep reading, delve deeper into my comprehension of the words to more intimately touch the body and feel not only its form, but also its emotion!

This new world was dangerous in its splendor because it translated into a universe with unprecedented geographical possibilities. I discovered new plot motivations, climates and habits, names and histories of other countries. But in a chaos that brought deformities to this language I had only just learned. How can I describe it? The nautical novels were the most difficult, with their descriptions of ships, rigging, knots, their words for storms. What to do with those words, how to translate them for my people, in a little close-minded neighborhood in the village of Aboukir? "Starboard" resisted for a long time. Other mysteries were circumvented through the compromise of images. For example, the term "the late André" to speak of a dead man. At the time, I didn't know anything about the ongoing ancient ritual of the *chapelle ardente*. So I decided to attribute to the expression the metaphor of the blue crown of fire in our kitchen, surrounding the name like a ring, a sort of halo. The *Zabor* as a glossary became a game of wild and domesticated lands, harvests and crops, absurd or precise definitions.

That language had three effects on my life: it healed my panic attacks, introduced me to sex and femininity, and gave me the means to circumvent the village and its narrowness. Those effects were the origins of my gift, which was the consequence. That language was born from a personal deciphering, it acquired the strength of sovereignty, it was royal and needed a king. It was precise, with words that I was endlessly discovering, that soon overflowed my universe and promised thousands of books to solidify its order. Its final virtue was that it was mine, secret, intimate, concealed from the rules of my father, from school, from my aunt's gaze, and from the idiotic and redundant universe of my fellow teenagers. That was the start of my digression, a shameful satisfaction of the senses and a desire to flee. There is, in the word "evasion," the word "vase," infinitely expanded. I didn't think of the imaginary as nonexistent, unlike my people, because, in our language, the word "imagination" is the same as "shadow"—the distant legacy of caravans and deserts, perhaps, there where shadow is merely the conceited opposite of the very real sun. My panic attacks were nothing but a memory. Sometimes I spent hours, finger raised, naming objects, nuances, colors, finding the right words for them, and synonyms, too. I quickly consumed the dozen novels, sometimes half ripped *(O the memory of* In Dubious Battle, *with no beginning or author, and* Night Flight, *which I imagined at first was the monologue of a traveler speaking to a star that had turned its back on him to swim into the distance)*, before rereading them in every direction, wringing as much from them as possible until there was nothing left. Every phrase was a world, deciphered but also appropriated. *Twenty Thousand Leagues Under the Sea* was the most fabulous, with etchings, immobilizing dark whales and diving suits in the ink, like a metaphor for the reader or the prophet.

So then I searched for other books, any books to quench my thirst. That was another adventure and another frustration. Which led me to discover secret mechanisms, vital for my vocation and for the survival of the village itself. Poll was flying. And my goat voice, when I was silent, transformed into a great song of life. Yes. I read everything I could find on the gods, equipment manuals, prescriptions for medications for the benefit of my attentive, illiterate family, my aunts and other cousins, I read rare newspapers and decrypted the old French plaques dating from the colonial period. I mention this now because it's essential: my study of the language was a battle won against the poverty of the world.

I settled into a margin that was both shameful and fantastic, because I started to travel all over, outside the village, I saw with a bird's view from the sky, barely identifiable by the meager greenery of its small

eucalyptus tree forests and its fields of vineyards. I was
swept up in whirlwinds, I read through, discovering
the words or filling the gaps with my own imagination.
Words that had little sense took on meaning through
my effort and, later, when a dictionary corrected the
meaning, my prayer book resisted like an old tribe faced
with the arrival of the colonizers, walls, and clocks. I
collided with terrible difficulties that I resolved through
arbitrariness: for example, I didn't understand why
parfum was a masculine word; when the capital letter
was necessary, as if one had to stand up to speak; what
the purpose of the cedilla was, etc. An insane language,
rich, happy, a hodgepodge of wild roots, hybrid like a
mythological beast. I had the gift of being able to soften
the iron of a new barbaric language, oral and yet tightly
bound to the written, muffled like death. All kissing
happened in the silence of the language.

I lost weight, ate less and less and eventually became
even sicker, a sort of transparency riddled my skin and
lifted me off the ground. Things that formerly posed
a threat because of the deficiency of my mother tongue
became confused, afflicted with an alchemical duplicity,
hollowed by an endless polysemy. I felt myself sliding
infinitely, seized, as soon as I opened a book to begin
another story. The words illuminated one another, but

also the phrases, the titles, and I suddenly fell into the vast field of conversations between books that conversed in the imitation cemetery of their bindings, I got lost in them, as though I were hallucinating. But I believe that was what spurred the madness of sex, and then its convergence with the words on the page.

39

(Four in the morning? I'm reminded by the taste of dust left in my mouth by the squall, because the wind has turned ferocious on this late summer night. I hunch over even more. To make myself smaller. To be nothing but a word falling toward the blank page of my notebook. I curl up as small as possible to give less grip to the storm rumbling outside, sneering through its rotten teeth.)

My grandfather died without saying a single word during the last ten years of his life, or maybe more, I can't remember. Friday, August 8, 1984, he coughed the entire morning, spit up blood. I held him in my arms, I was alone, my aunt had left to go look for my father and my uncles, when he started to moan like a child. It was a strange moment: I was holding a body, his head on my knees, but I didn't know what to do for him or how to restrain him. I was captive, incapable of feelings. I said words to him, but I knew they were absurd. Should I recite one of the most powerful surahs of the Holy Book? I tried, but I stopped short, because it seemed ridiculous, in that moment, my nasally voice and that prelude to burial. So I waited for someone to come help me.

Hadj Hbib hadn't always been mute. To the contrary, I knew from Hadjer that he had been a lively man, dignified and stubborn to preserve his freedom to the point that he hadn't held any job under the colonizers for more than a week at a time. My memory is hazy, but I do remember him speaking quite a bit at a certain point. Hadjer explained to me, gradually, over the course of a story in a thousand and one pieces, that his state began to deteriorate the day he started to ask his sons, his wife, and his loved ones their names. His mind crumbled even more when, a few years later, he lost all memory of our universe on the hill, he became a stranger, an unknown visitor, then a passerby who sometimes interrupted a silence of several days to tell us he had just arrived from France and was disappointed not to have seen any of us at the door of the big city waiting for him to help carry his bags, heavy with a thousand presents. His way of inventing the infinite story of his return from a voyage was a wonderful moment for the children, who used it as an opportunity to mock him by asking what he'd brought back in his suitcases, where his car was, and what was the name of his French wife or the money over there. He listened to them patiently, then adopted a clever air and described France as you might describe a cloud, a swift and brilliant animal, a large garden you're forbidden to enter, or a tree defended by strict countryside policemen. He also had a habit, when they took him on walks around Aboukir, of pointing at remote and bare lands, recalling almond trees, sweet chestnut trees twisting in their very slow universes, vineyards that no longer existed. He knew the names of grapes, of vine varietals and diseases. His conversation was unique, for it was coherent, simple, guided by sincere emotions. As a child, I enjoyed watching him conduct his world, furnish it despite the black hole of his memory. His eyes were green, unlike mine, he had a determined face, a hard chin, as if confronting the invisible bust of someone threatening and terrible, whom he'd been standing up to courageously since his youth. Like Hadj Brahim, Hadj Hbib liked knives, but he kept them on his belt. He had an old pencil in his wallet, but no notebook, and he'd preferred to sew his things himself since my grandmother died of typhus. He liked to sleep in the kitchen, drink goat's milk, and eat nothing but homemade bread, not the bread from the bakery. I remember he was a snob about even the simplest of things, and that he long had a very haughty tone, powerful as a captivating river with eddies and silent swells when he couldn't find the words. In his ultimate struggle, the last months he spent at the top of the hill before being exiled by my stepmother, my father's father started to confuse names, he described dead people while looking at newborns and lost his temper with his wife, who couldn't answer his screams, fiercely insulting her even though she'd died long before.

His flood of words and his conversation constituted the background noise of my early childhood, the river that ran through our house up top, then down below, until it dried up for good. In his final years, he lost his speech in entire swaths, the silence inhabited him like gigantic avalanches of muffled snow from the top of a tall mountain. My grandfather could sometimes launch into a conversation with the same verve, like a novel he was leafing through wildly, and then go quiet, cut off, suddenly, staring with his beautiful eyes at a place where the words stopped and came loose. I tried hard, for a while, to grasp the thread of meaning in what he was dredging from the far reaches of his insanity. So I had the opportunity to rediscover former names, road signs from the colonial period, sometimes traces of lucidity that corresponded to recent events with him as the forgotten witness, scraps of dialogue between me and Hadjer and memories of his own childhood. A sort of surge, a swell where I could make out the outline of the former village, from one of its former lives or spectacular events like the flood he mentioned for months and which had nearly carried everything off in its wake, a snowfall at the beginning of the century or the theft of his shoes by nomads during harvest season. He sometimes called for Brahim, sometimes for his dead sons, gave imaginary punches to my uncle living in France, often mythic like a novel, a stream of words and calendars that today I can compare to the madness of a dictionary fighting against erasure.

So my grandfather spoke for ten years, nearly without interruption, exhausted everyone around him, stayed up at night, provoked insomnia and wore out his daughters who took turns at the top of the hill. That's Hadjer's version, at least. In the end, they brought him to our house, the house down below, so my aunt could take care of him. There too, his stream was occasionally fierce, but it was already perforated with stupor. He still recounted his return from France, he who had never left the perimeter of our region's vineyards, or detailed his encounters with nocturnal spirits seized by sadness or anger. In a final push he identified each object, described its details until he was dizzy, succeeded in the miracle of knotting the threads and links between events and objects by fighting against oblivion, and that struggle was burned into my memory like a heroic act never rivaled by anyone else among my people. It was tremendous to hear and to behold, but his river flowed in only one direction, toward definitive exhaustion, and everyone knew it.

Hbib lost his words one by one, twisted them, squeezed them, distorted them in an attempt to use them every possible way, then started to stammer, to salivate freely. I saw him, when I was still a child, suffocate like someone drowning, shake angrily against this new impossibility, sitting in our house's courtyard. And that lasted for a long time, turned my aunt's hair white as she stood vigil over her youth like a waning fire, then finally surrendered. At one point, his defeat proved undeniable: he had become slow, immobile, then started to stare at a point visible only in his universe and didn't move again for the rest of his days, head between his knees, hands on the back of his neck. That was the end of his life, difficult for us all. Hadj Brahim refused this fate, he didn't know how to handle it, then opted for courteous visits. Hadjer saw the ordeal as a sort of counterpart to the prayers she didn't practice, a way of reconciling herself with her god or paying for a future happiness. For me, it was a chance to learn reflection and silence. My grandfather had a pencil stub in his wallet and I imagined destiny was like that: a pencil held over the madman's book, as the Prophet said. "Held" meaning "suspended in the air"? Hesitating over the new language to find the words to describe losing one's mind? Without any words to describe such a state? How many styluses were thus suspended in the air, frozen army of the writer hovering over the heads of the world's insane, sleepers, and teenagers before their first ejaculation? I imagined that forest of pens in the sky, useless, writing nothing. And I was especially fascinated by the pages of blank lives, those of the sleepers, the teenagers, and the insane, flapping in the wind, immaculate, scattered or neglected notebooks, the swarms of storks on our minarets, with ink stains on the tips of their wings. A naked world, with no words, the first and last at the same time, united.

And I had a pencil over my head, I said to myself, worried. Which wrote on my skull as I slept. Perhaps my mission was to steal those blank notebooks and fill them. Or to steal the pencil of my own destiny to write what I wanted. Or to take, like a vigilante fighting for equilibrium, the immaculate notebooks from some to add them to the exhausted books of others, the old or the dying. Except at that time, my grandfather losing his mind worried me intensely, like a mute anguish. I had, before my eyes, the proof that disintegration was possible, despite the power of a language or the richness of a life, and the core became an abyss, testifying that nothing was stable, especially not words or their writing. Did that herald the threat of nudity that would floor me months later? Perhaps. The nature of my grandfather's agony was the most insidious part: it proved that life depends on the story we keep intact as much as on the possibility of telling it or writing it, which is even better. But the link was at once absolute and fragile, dictated by a necessity of correspondences but arbitrary to the point of desperation. The book could be sacred, but its binding was an artifice. Hadj Hbib, my grandfather, revealed to me the potential of madness and the urgency of maintaining a coherence in oneself, a powerful narrative and discipline that doesn't let any blank space settle or spread. It was a question of life and death under the guise of words and silences. My conclusion, even at that age, was that we might die if we stopped feeding the language inside of us, we might lose our minds. My grandfather came back to us only at the final moment and I was the sole person to witness it, like a swimmer surfacing from under the water for whom everything, all around, was a possible land, the lifeline swaying in the swell, the elusive beach, golden and untouched by any footprint.

I loved him, yes, but I had come around to the idea of his death a long time ago. Except that Friday, August 8, 1984, he was looking at me with his gray-blue eyes and waiting for something, with a pleading that almost made me angry because I didn't understand it. As if he were staring at me from behind a bus window, or wanted me to say something. Languages possess this terrifying quality that they reveal at essential moments, faced with fire, with ecstasy, with death or defeat. I was seized by panic, convinced that I was forgetting some specific ritual. Then I rested his head on the pillow and I did something unexpected, even surprising, futile but decisive in the order of the world: I grabbed a novel within reach, turned back toward him, and started to read aloud (with the voice of a goat threatened by the knife) a chapter to mask his death rattles. I wanted to cover up his choking with my voice, confuse it, erase it, or compel it. My act (irreverent, but let me explain) was spurred by the desire to make his agony more bearable, but also by a stupid idea: to make it tolerable through diversion, to prolong his brief attention to the world (to me). In films, at death's door, we say important and definitive things, we ask forgiveness or express regret. There, that Friday, alone faced with death in the house down below, while the imam was yelling his sermon through the speaker at the hour of the prayer, I chose a secret and sumptuous language to exorcise death, to attach myself to life, to divert my grandfather's attention or interpret his fate. What took over me? Arrogance, vanity, a whim of teenage panic? Or was I guided by the hand of an angel? My grandfather, crushed by a mountain on his chest, groaning like a sacrificed sheep, eyes watering, blood clots in his mouth, stared at me as I read, suddenly alert, stunned and nearly distraught. I read for a long time, and he came back to life for a moment *(I swear, Abdel!)*, scrutinized each object in the bedroom where he was lying on the floor, with a bowl for his spit, some water, and the stench of rot and urine. He turned his head toward me and tried to smile, to grimace with the upper part of his dentures, then returned to the objects, inventoried them one by one like an accountant or a child in a new home. Outside, the imam's voice tried to sync up with mine, waned in the ovation of the prayers, then was reabsorbed in a unanimous "amen." My own voice was powerful and calm like the sea in my imagination *(the sea, never glimpsed from up close, is a clock with ships marking the hours, the hands of the sun driving the wind, a sundial in the tropics, and islands that are, in my reader's dream, synonyms for the word "moment"*). I sensed that it might be helping him. Was there a link between the book and his life? A way of delaying the decapitation? I had guessed it from the first pages, when I had read the incomplete story, in French, of that woman who told stories every night. So I read and he followed me with his eyes, like a man saved from the ocean, begging me for a sequel to be forever postponed, with apprehension (but also surprise, because he didn't recognize me).

He died ten minutes before they knocked on the door, his head on my knees, listening to an unknown language. I didn't cry because I don't like pity, nor showing it to death. Death was there (the animal stares at you, vicious, while it rips apart its prey) and I looked away, full of another sky on the other side of the room's big window. My uncles entered, Hadjer screamed and collapsed in the hallway. Everything accelerated and they pushed me aside to take care of my grandfather's body. As for me, cloistered, elbowed out of the way by my tribe, I knew I had stumbled upon an important secret, that a law had been revealed. The first article of the Law of Necessity. There was a link. Either between my reading and death, or between writing and death, or between the book and death. My grandfather's pupils had stopped moving and lost their shine right as I had lost my breath at the end of a long paragraph describing the fall of the castaways from a hot-air balloon, at the beginning of *The Mysterious Island*.

"Are we descending?"

Which proves that the text is nothing but a pretext. An accident. The miracle is the possibility of the book. The power is in its coherence that stands firm. Its unity that prevails over death. Why? Because it proposes an alternative, resolute ending. It's a tombstone that we can move backward or forward on our paths as readers and writers.

40

("*The summer is beautiful, usually. But, sometimes, around August, the season of burning pebbles and the death of the elders, there's a war in the sky—the Smaïmes, we call it. A great spectacle of fire and wind. From the south, from the Sahara, reddish sand appears in the sky, it makes the clouds glimmer with a sickly auburn, a wind rises gently like a betrayal, then intensifies, gains power, and sullies the land of Aboukir. The walls can't do anything about it, and suddenly everyone—all those who know how to say it and those who can only feel it in the obscurity of a weak language—hide, can tell that the gap between their comfort and the desert is very slim, like the arc of an arrow in flight. The Smaïmes season lasts a dozen days around the end of the month. It carries off many sick people, hundred-year-olds, elderly women, it dries out the season's fruit, especially the bunches* of grapes, reduces the water to a murmur and coats our utensils, the groceries in the houses, and the greenery in dust. The sandstorm burns the entire sky for days and then attacks the earth, runs through the streets, extinguishes the streetlights that turn to embers, and abuses the doors, the windows, the hinges as if they were old bones. Even the night disappears: it becomes a long dusk.

That's what's happening tonight. The house moves like a rowboat, the world is its whale, and I am the prophet. I write rapidly. Everything depends on me. There's a link between the speed of my writing and the speed of the wind. If it moves faster than me, it might rip out all the walls, scatter my notebooks, force me to search for Hadjer or my mother under my eyelids. To moan. If I can outrace it, it will back off like a wolf, whine in its turn through the deserted streets, eat the empty wrappers, the village trash, and tear out its hair by tearing out tree branches. It's always an epic battle, but it will be even more intense this time. The night is not an anchor but a sort of ember in the sky behind a veil of ash.

It's almost five in the morning and dawn will not come. The wind is like an animal, a wolf. "They said to their father: We were racing, we left Yusuf with our things. That's how the wolf devoured him," said the Holy Book—half descended from the sky, because we reach the other half through meditation—about this Joseph and his exceptional destiny. It comes back to me. "Everything is in the Holy Book," Hamza the devil likes to scream. The wolf prowls through the village, the tree trunks droop, the roofs might be carried away tonight, there will be fires, I'm sure of it, in the fields. Strange, the Smaïmes this year: The wind no longer seeks its usual duel that sets the clouds ablaze for days, strips the bones and reminds them of the hierarchy. No. It's searching for someone in particular, going door to door. It will turn the houses upside down one by one, like shells or cans of food, to find them. It wants to devour. I think of my father and his agony, I write to keep both death and the wind at bay, I probe my desires and attempt the unprecedented by writing far from the dying person. And yet I exult. In my version, the wolf is the wind, I save my father, I foil my brothers, and I marry Djemila.

Suddenly there's a knock on the door and I'm snatched from my vision. I hesitate, then I decide not to let anything distract me from my notebook. I want my father to die so I can leave this village, or save a woman and marry her by restoring her body, but I want him to survive to bear witness to my strength and my gift, for him to recognize me. A window shatters, I hear a scream and the sounds of a car braking. Even the dogs, those pillaging kings, the first animals to walk on the moon, are nothing but whines. "Don't insult the wind, for it is sent from God," the Prophet advises. The wolf is searching for me and I make myself as small as possible. The Smaïmes have never been so vicious. Many of the elderly will die this week. I have to write, every year this season is my gift's great battle, but what's happening now is unprecedented. More hands rattle the door. Someone yells my name but I know it's a ruse. The wind has a thousand languages in its mouth. It can speak to you in Hindi if you want. It has keys to nearly every *place on earth and takes on new faces in the sky when it slips into the bodies of clouds. I hear someone yell "Smaïl! Smaïl!" I don't answer. "The world is a ruse," says the Prophet. This name becomes the sound of sheet metal ripped from houses. The wolf rages, tries to charm its way in.)*

The burial of my grandfather, Hadj El Hbib, threw Aboukir into chaos. I saw nothing, or almost nothing, from my spot secluded in the margin, silent, ignored by my half brothers. The Holy Book was everywhere, like a voice-over. I remained still the entire time, fascinated by a single detail: they had covered the mirror in our bedroom with a sheet. My father slaughtered dozens of sheep intended to accompany the dead man into the plains of his grave. I had seen him, I remember: Hadj Brahim seemed upset, but carried out the ritual with a pompous air that distorted his sadness. He tried to speak to me at one point, as if death could reconcile us, but I avoided his gaze. I ate couscous until I felt sick. With no meat.

41

(The sand tries to invade from everywhere. I check the
windows, the doors, the locks, then I plug up the bottom
of my bedroom door with a rolled-up sheet. But grains of sand are
already inside: between my teeth and in my notebook. The wolf rasps
through a thousand minuscule crystals. I see its grimace when I bite
my teeth together or swallow a sip of coffee. The sand represents the
great struggle between the desert and the Holy Book. The desert tries to
cover the book and the Holy Book tries to push the desert back toward
the constellations and the stars. The same pair, if we look from up close:
the wolf and me, the sand and the book, the god and the bush, the void
and the prayer, the temple and the road, the city and the assault. I write
down this idea, a match in the night. I get up just for a moment, rapid
and precise, I sweep a bit, make my bed, change my sheets, run a rag

over the surfaces. The sand is now piled in a small heap in the corner but I know it will return. Then I get back to writing just as quickly. A brief apnea to gather my strength. I remember, suddenly, that Hadjer has never been away from me for so long. Outside I can hear some of the raging din of the end of the world. Through the window, the sky seems even redder and grayer, twisted into aerial dunes. And still the wind, above all. It doesn't moan continuously but imitates whisperings. Sometimes it rises like anger, almost falls, and then scrapes the floor. It's a beast on the hunt, nostrils to the ground, claws out. Trees become distorted and I imagine all the land in our village keeling, pitching. And yet I feel secure, my notebooks are with me or buried in the distance, inaccessible among the roots. It all comes down to the speed of writing, or erasure, between me and the wolf. "The wolf ate him," the brothers said to the blind, tearful father. My father is dying and the end of the world exalts me, as if the death of one being could mean the liberty of another. What if I were writing to kill him, and not to save him? I stop, worried. The wind comes back with a surprising savagery, the whole house seems ready to give way and deliver me. Noises, still, of people gathered outside, but I know it's only the sand, the sounds are lost in the whistling and shrieks, the muffled blows of things falling or crashing in the darkness. The electricity is intermittent, goes out then comes back. And with an incredible vigor I write in signs, symbols, mixed alphabets, miniature drawings, tattoos. I know it's you, the wind, the god that has nowhere to go and who never knew how to write his Holy Book. Suddenly there are voices and I think I hear my first name and then my half brother's——"It's Abdel, open up!" But it's not words. Just a ruse. I'm not going to open the door. I have to write faster because one of us will give in, and the entire village has only me as its mooring. Since I learned to write, alone, in my head, I am its center. A vast canvas of my own creation that binds to me the entire description——meticulous like a miserly inventory——of this village [four notebooks entitled One Arm, filled during my walks with the help of the new names of anonymous trees], the lives saved, the slowness of hundred-year-olds who've become clever, the first names of children, nuances about the sweat of the sick, and the precise calculation of all the people I've met by accident who now depend on me. And the incomplete notebooks where I tried to describe the newborns, but never fully succeeded. I am a kind of watchman, the lighthouse keeper in the "sea of darkness" of Arab geographers for whom the earth wasn't round but saddle-shaped. I am responsible for order but also for equilibrium, a guarantor of gravity through the use of language. "Open up! Open up!" cries the wind, using Hadjer's voice this time, but I am no fool. I write faster. They knock on the door angrily but don't succeed. Sitting like a stone, I have with me the keys to the house and the spare set that Hadjer forgot when she left this morning. Trees run through the streets to escape the wind, which is now full of hate. There are no more stars, no borders, no cardinal points, the north is a bird with no nest, high and low are vertigoes. If I write faster maybe it will stop.)

42

When I was about sixteen years old, two years after my grandfather's death, when my mastery of the French language was admirable and vigorous, I came upon another book. At least a part of it. It was one of the rare books to clearly describe the Law of Necessity. It was *The Thousand and One Nights*. I read it patiently (volume one—I didn't have the others until years later—it had beautiful illustrations but was slow to unfurl, with lengthy preambles, stiff as an Egyptian saga), like a prolegomenon to my gift, an entryway, a possible explanation of secret laws at last. At the time, I had read dozens of novels, books written directly in French or that had come from other worlds, but it was the first time I had read a

major work, written by one of my people, translated into
the language of my gender. A retired teacher had given
me the book, slightly worn but voluminous, promising.
The story left me wanting more at the beginning, I was
fascinated by its technique but also by its ruse. Already
at that age I liked to discover the reasons behind books,
their source. The Holy Book hid its own, concealed the
evidence through threat or promise, but I knew that it
was a cry of solitude, a need. *("God is a treasure who likes to be*
sought and found," say the sufis. The mystic quest is a crime novel where
the dead person comes back to life at the end, or the murderer is time that
will become eternity and the woman is paradise.)

In *The Thousand and One Nights* (cut off without the two
remaining volumes), the plot was troubling: a woman tells
a story, keeping an idiotic and loathsome king like Hadj
Brahim in suspense by the power of the tale she invents
over time. Perhaps that was the clue. I don't know how
I inferred from this that it was possible to reverse the
equation and use it to save the greatest number of people. In the palace, Scheherazade tells stories to save her
life. It makes no sense. Or has another, more irreparable
meaning: she couldn't save the other women. I told myself,
even happy, married at the end to a monster, she would
have to live with the memory of the dead in the walls, the
wives murdered before she found her salvation. So, what I

imagined as a teenager was a woman who managed to save
her own life through her long story, but also revived the
decapitated, immortalized her contemporaries and those
who had not yet been born. No story as Herculean had
ever been written. Especially if we imagined a tale that was
even more absolute: a version where the power of the narrative, written or merely recounted, could keep people alive,
but also solder the stones of the palace, the surrounding
city, the houses cultivated by this reign, the country and its
creases. All of it kept intact, during the ascent, by a single
hand, one narrator who would save her own skin, bring
the dying back to life, and guarantee old age to those who
listened. That was impossible, but I liked to imagine that
kind of story, a holy book whose visible world was the back
cover, the binding. *(I know that I'm the storyteller who was able to
save the dying, the sick, the expired old men, the storyteller who maintains
the equilibrium of the village like a stork with the parapet of my writing,
but I also have my limits.)* My vocation was inspired by meditating on the act of storytelling, which is to say writing
with one's mouth and not yet by hand. The necessary link
between the book and the lives. A few years later, I understood the great wisdom of this book: *The Thousand and One
Nights* weren't told, but written! It's writing concealed by
oral diversion. In the first detective novel I read, there was
this essential phrase: "She walked toward me, naked." In

the second, the woman spoke while stripping her clothes off and stripping the monster to vanquish it.

I wasn't only a child of wonderment, I was also a child of fear and worry. My discovery of the French language was a major event because it came with a power over the objects and subjects around me. The possibility of a parapet right at the edge of the cliff. So I started to read furiously, populating the island, bumping up against a rare and unique language that, in my dreams, could be read from left to right, from right to left, and from bottom to top, in every direction, boustrophedon, as they used to say, strong and capable of grasping the essence. Hours walking in the streets, alone and subjected to their stares, silently listing in my head the names of trees, the nuances of stones, the angles and features of faces. Hours of trying new words on Aboukir's bodies and fauna. To enrich the imperfect conjugations through my voice: describe the future, the past, but also the gradations of the past, more distant, consummate, and closed than the still-ajar past of the perfect tense, and that present tense which was impossible (how can you chew and have the verb chew in your mouth? How can you look and not be blinded by the verb?). It was madness: Hadjer understood what was going on and tried to keep tabs on me, but I was already cheating.

I think my aunt suspected that I was in love with a girl. But the only available woman in the area would be, years later, a young divorced neighbor whom everyone regarded with suspicion and worry, like fruit fallen from a basket, tempting everyone. *(Djemila never looks at the world through her window. A head like Scheherazade's posed on a sill; we are forbidden from seeing the rest of her body.)* So Hadjer searched our surroundings, didn't find anyone, and concluded that it was a sign of the end of puberty or a consequence of my recovery, already in the past. And yet there I was, absolutely ashamed of my dissidence. Capable of fleeing, like a prisoner who still shares the fate of his fellows but who has already dug his hole in the wall around him. I could circumvent Aboukir inconspicuously. Work through digressions in the story of my people. I could, above all, see the women naked under their clothes, at fifteen years old, the age when my cousins and neighbors were describing women's genitals as realms of madness and ivy.

The new language was fighting the unsayable, imposing order but also undressing bodies. My creation was walking toward me, naked. Nudity was both that language and its impossibility. Sex led me to solitude, and so at twenty-eight years old, the child of a rich village butcher, possible inheritor of thousands of sheep, guided by the strength of my gift and by chance, I am neither circumcised nor married. Chaste and sensual at the same time. I searched the old houses in Aboukir for novels, every possible novel. Detective novels were my favorite, I skipped over the corpse, the mystery, the investigator, and the scene of the crime to get to the most important part: the widow with the wet lip, the lover with the warm shoulder under her coat, the temptress on the path to revelation, the lazy and lascivious woman, the hair whose exact weight I felt in my hand, the kiss, above all, described from the inside, from the point of view of the tongue, the sucking sound of saliva in the starry darkness. Imagine that freedom in the heart of a narrow-minded village, with no other revelation beyond a woman's knee or the story of the wedding night of a newly married imbecile. Imagine the explosion of senses inspired by this secret language, my interrogation of recalcitrant words, the violation of meaning through un-certain definitions. I could write simple, accessible words, scattered on a sheet of paper, and watch them assemble and describe the invisible and the hidden. Seen this way, they meant nothing, or almost nothing, but in my head, through my feverish dictionary, sometimes they turned into scenes of intense orgies, embraces or affairs resulting in orgasms, in new territories or triumphant returns.

A reader radicalized by potential nakedness, I became a voyeur, because that was the ultimate goal of language and books. I slept, an intruder, with the names of women from practically inconceivable geographies, in bed in situations where I mixed the cloak and dagger as deeply as possible in matters of the flesh, clumsy but posturing, confusing my body with the ink in monstrous, venomous curves. I gained an undetectable maturity even though I was barely an adult.

But, just after my wet return to the world (pants soiled, hands clammy), I came back to the stories and their ability to lend coherence. I became overwhelmed with a powerful feeling of guilt. I could only absolve myself by seeking a way to reduce the metaphysical misery of my people. Their absolute futility. I read, but already I felt myself hollowing with the need to do more. Solitary sex had to result, sooner or later, in either a book or a deranged paternity. I looked at my cousins, my aunts, and my father as though through a screen, at once compassionate to the point of tears and indifferent, for they were empty and prisoners of their fate, wandering in a world with no language or way out. I offered my arms and my new language to all my people, outside, in the douar, and one day I even tried, at the door of the butcher's, to shake my half brother's hand, who looked at me, suspicious, and then burst out laughing. Compassion had led to sentimentality, and I understood that this wasn't a real solution. I shouldn't be dreaming of love, but of secret self-sacrifice.

43

Oh, I swear I read everything in the village. Every single word. Every little paragraph. All the new or ripped books I could find: the manuals, the old journals, the notices, other people's letters, the old posters and signs, the schoolbooks with their magnificent "selected excerpts," the peanut wrappers or the newspapers that reached the village. Everything that transported this language, and that the language brought me in its proliferation. I even reread the few novels I had until I was dizzy, vaguely gauging their volume, their exhaustion, the dreaded intrusion of the last page. I dreamed of an infinity spent flipping through pages and not praying. Rereading was still enjoyable: stories returned to the stage for my pleasure alone, took on new forms, emphasized a line or a detail that had escaped me the first or third time. The island was never the same under my feet, and Poll the parrot knew that infinity was a way of seeing or reading.

I read everything, reread everything, reread it all again, and one day I wore myself out, exhausted by redundancy. As if the horrible emptiness, the face of the mute devil, would catch up to me if I didn't read enough new things, even faster and more broadly. I found myself once again threatened with solitude and reclusion if I couldn't find anything new. My language had become richer than the books and texts, it was overflowing the walls, my universe, demanding other bodies, a more immediate and more unpredictable incarnation than what I had gleaned from rereading. I paced in circles for days, worrying my aunt, before making up my mind.

44

(A sip of cold coffee. Sweetness on my tongue. My right shoulder like stone. My neck like a decapitated man's. I'm not sleepy or hungry. Like the first day, when I deciphered the first words. I use asterisks by the fistful when a phrase is obscure, I thicken the stroke, the calligraphy. No margin is possible on the blank page, for it would open a crack onto the void, the possibility of an interruption. I would have liked to reread all the words, like a sea, a series of waves harnessed to each other by the water and the swell, but the notebook was unreadable, a murmuring, like the ocean. No, I just have to hold my breath between words, leave no blanks or almost none, bring the stroke to the edge of the page, in every direction, all the cardinal points of my inventory. The writing must be small, dense, tied in knots and strict in its geometry. How can I simultaneously draw, murmur, describe, specify, and traverse the material of skins and objects with a universal writing? The wandering surface of an expanse of water, traversed by a single fish, can exhaust a dictionary on its own. I needed a greater and more powerful writing, a sonorous amalgamation of signs, letters, characters, periods, and indentations. The capital letter had to hoist itself to the height of a tree and the ellipses encapsulated a night horizon when a fire is lit to tell a story. I had hoped the word would be absolute, capable of recounting as well as a face, with a single surface, but that was impossible, distant, it would take me more than one lifetime. So I invented a way of writing and enriching the calligraphy of that language with no master. I compose novelties on the ostracon with an iron stylus. And when there isn't enough momentum, I add drawings, sketches, figures, or codes so that no detail of the dying person's life escapes. Everything plays a part in the resurrection, even erasure. The period is a pebble or a star, the grain is the indication of the distance.

My father will not die and I will prove it to him with twelve notebooks, returning to the house up top, proud, victorious, haloed. To the people in this village who treated me like a madman, with pity or scorn, I will finally reveal my law, the inexplicable miracle that links their survival to my skill. I'll liberate them and overturn their beliefs. Show them that there's another "sacred writing," the possibility of a gigantic final talisman hanging from the hill, around each person's neck, to protect them, even if they don't understand it. The Zabor will be folded, covered with a stitched cloth, mixed with the water of Aboukir, offered as a morning drink [facing east, a padlock under the sole of

my foot, seven times in a row, with oil, honey, and thyme]. Everything
outside must be mixed: livestock, verses, stars, people, half brothers, and
facades. The Smaïnes will take lives, I'm sure of it.

I jump when they knock on the door again, the voices of several
people this time. I hear Hamza, his treason. Oh, it's a clever move by
the eraser, the enemy of writing, the adversary of my law, the wind.
It uses everything, even the voices of my family, to drive me out of my
cave. I know the devil is clever, but sometimes his malice makes me
smile. It's almost predictable. Sand enters through a few cracks, but
feebly, mere grains. There's a total electricity outage this time, and I
light candles that make the shadows look immense, the ceiling recedes,
suddenly twisted with wicks, the walls retreat or move closer, noise-
lessly. I am the guardian of the flock, the brother of my brothers. I've
saved dozens of lives.)

There was a time when I was walking with something
like a smile on my lips to offer my services to the distant
neighbors: Would you like me to read a difficult letter
for you? To speak to a sick elder? To keep them company? Can I be useful to you? Where is Hadj Mohammed's bedroom? How is Hadja Ghania? They opened
their doors to me because I was the son of Hadj Brahim,
they gave me coffee and let me write at the bedside of the
sick because they thought I was fulfilling a duty (pre-
scribed by the Prophet) to visit the suffering. This was in
the early days, before mistrust devastated my reputation.

I had left the Koranic school, but my mastery of French had given me an aura, not as brilliant, but still commanding respect. French was the language of death, for those who remembered the war, but not a dead language. For others, those who watch movies, the families of immigrants, or the ambitious who dreamed of leaving the village or earning money without sweating under the sun, that language represented prestige, it was the proof that they had completed a grand voyage even if they had never left Aboukir.

I also visited cemeteries, already suspicious of their purpose, sitting near tombs and trying to meditate. It became more and more obvious to me that these places were false paths, a sort of ruse to disorient the crowd and their compassion. But I liked those falsely deserted surroundings, their trees, their roots, their stones, and their fragrant grasses. This was the essential decor of eternity: the cycle, the disrupted mineral, the plowed earth, and the sky, especially, overflowing the hill. Sometimes women came to cry over someone deceased, or men hurried to bury a family member in the scramble. The tombstones interested me almost mathematically: I calculated ages, played with birth and death dates, and was fascinated by the blank space of the hyphen between the two, that ravine of breath, irreducible because it was a life, but absolutely empty, because between birth and death the narrative of a story was missing. I dreamed about the possibility of a stone on which an entire life would be written, every detail, from the grain to the grandiose, the breath and the skin, every encounter and conversation with others or even in one's own head. But that wasn't enough. I had to dream of a tombstone that would be annotated in its entirety, surrounded, invaded, crisscrossed with the writing in its dry heart, which would be writing itself, the image composed of a thousand images in cells, hives, even the body. Of all the metaphors of the Holy Book, I most liked those in the surah titles, which gave each chapter the heading of a bestiary or a specific cosmos. The ark in the Book didn't carry away all the animals, only the bees, the elephant, the spider, the cow, the fig tree, the table, the loot, and the cavern and a few names of prophets. I dreamed for a long time about this table of contents, to be read all at once like a hidden text chosen by a god who, in his solitude, was especially fond of shepherds and stars.

I possessed a language that was now rich, nimble, almost obedient, slightly savage in the confines of the island, exciting in its blur of bodies and distances, usable. I had learned this language alone, granting it liberties that would have been denied by schools and teachers, and here it was, waning for lack of recurrence in the texts I knew by heart. The tombstone was my Rosetta Stone to imagine what revelation would come next.

When I was about eighteen years old, I knew the world was a book, that language was consumed in a kind of fire, that I could define every possible word, that writing traversed the body and objects, that time was a conjugation, that Hadjer was right in her dreams about me (a man carried on a sea of shoulders), that I could break my father's rules and extend my reign beyond his fortune, and that there was a link between the narration, the wind, and sovereignty in the village. I knew I was predestined to save lives because I had a language that knew how to reconcile precision, secret desire, and purity. It could bring about resurrection, because it was already a reconstitution. I just had to be clear and precise. Daring.

Then, I reached ecstasy.

45

There was another important night, when I was about seventeen years old. I prayed every day, but I had transformed prayer into interrogation. That night during Ramadan, the sky was vast and I was lost in it. Like the prophet Yusuf sitting at the bottom of the well where his brothers had pushed him, awaiting his glory. But unlike him, I was reveling in my fate, my head turned toward the sky. Where the wolf was immobilized in the form of a constellation (*"The night sky is a cave drawing,"* explains the dog). The Arabs gave beautiful names to the stars. They were masters of populating the deserts in general. They laid their best roads there, I think.

Outside, the village night was noisy, lively like every year during those weeks of fasting. The night prayers resounded with psalmodies that were almost beautiful. All the stars were close, like neighbors, and the night was populated with children, insomniac families. For some reason, I enjoyed that inversion of the typical order when people stayed up late in the village. I felt less alone, as though in the middle of an unspectacular, but pleasant, wedding. A calm day that would culminate in a sacred night, in a way. Rereading a novel, I stumbled on an ordinary, ancient metaphor, impossible in its essence but rendered banal through use: "The woolly forest extended to the top of the hill." Suddenly, somehow, because I had slept well, because I was alert and vigilant and my language was ripe, I lunged at the absolute miracle of metaphor and its infinite declensions. The forest, queen of the root and the peak, borrowed the form of the sheep's fleece, its meaning, amalgamating flock and conquest, ascension and scramble, density and deluge, to simultaneously evoke the ideas of the forest and the innumerable. That potential coursed through me like a strong wave, like electricity. I understood the combinatory potential of language, but this time under the possible authority of my writing. The violence of eruptions through language, the opportunity to take stock of everything, of each movement and condensation, of writing the definitive chronicle of every cycle. Since I had read all the books in our house, it was now imperative to write them, and the revelation of the mechanics of metaphor represented a path to liberation.

The world was fragmentation but writing was its Mass. Suddenly I understood that I could not only describe, save, and recount everything, but also imagine without disappearing, reconquer the land of fear and silence, be a master of nakedness. *("Writing is the temperature, time is the fire," concludes my inner animal.)* I could straddle the village and the curse of my fainting spells, and not only through reading the books of others. I felt able to save my life and the lives of my people through the vibrant and unprecedented metaphor. *The Flesh of the Orchid*, first name of the first woman, was a triggering accident, and I could prolong the wedding by imagining my own stories.

In the village, children were playing in the night, celebrating the upended hours. Meanwhile, sitting inside, between my coffee and the walls, I had just collided with the third and final revelation of my life. Through a logic that was simple, unexpected, and obvious: for lack of books, I would write them, and that language would be the instrument not only of my reverie but also of my purification, my redemption. If I had known how to write at the time, and if I had written without stopping, I would have saved my grandfather. I would have resumed my father's story starting at the moment when it had skewed toward confabulation and cowardice. I would have bestowed greater meaning upon each cousin, each person I saw in our village during my walks. The dying people I had visited could have been saved by a story, I was now sure of it. Except that I was also discovering the double imperative of speed and density: I had to write without stopping, quickly, about absolutely everything, about every encounter, every face, every name. I was realizing my power and my responsibility. Language had now become my entire being, and it was exhilarating. I was free!

At night, when the sky had descended over the earth, I felt ready to topple over the parapet and soar. Everything was suddenly connected: my years of anxiety faced with calligraphy, learning to write with the *sansal* and the tablet near the mosque, the blind recitations, and even the glimpsed nudity of the body and the traveler's tale. I could advance toward "her" and her nudity and no longer just await her, immobile. I could speak, continue other books, exorcise anguish through the legendary ellipsis and resume an ancient story. *(The three dots don't represent silence but the racket of books, of gods, and things reduced to the ellipsis. That's why I use it with caution and as a sort of illegible prologue in every notebook, at the start of every story. The ritual of writing in the notebooks is simple: the first phrase is half of another that will never be written. I have to unknot it, search for the end of the string and slowly unravel the ball of wool.)* Zabor would contain infinite possibilities from now on, not just a savage dictionary. I was already embodying the psalms. The call to prayer rang out behind me but I was high in the sky. My father couldn't slit my throat anymore because his knife was a minuscule pin, a splinter. The only person who might have understood me was Hadjer, but she was watching television while I was moving among the stars.

46

(The wind uses every trick, including my family's voices. Hadjer begs and pleads. I hear: "Your father wants to speak to you for the last time!" Her intonation is a moan, protracted on the ground like an abandoned hand. I even hear Abdel's voice. He yells, he yells. They try to force the door open and in the racket I can hear someone try a set of keys, then give up. We changed the locks a long time ago and reinforced our security, my aunt and I. They won't be able to enter. There aren't any keys or faces, it's only the wind. The wolf on the hunt, canines bared, come to bite me, to devour our house with dust, to scatter my notebooks in the fields, to kill me and kill my gift. I stand my ground, head bent over the writing that clamps down on its subject, protected by the red balaclava my aunt knitted, modeled on the hat I wore as a child. I know what to do. Every time since the first time, I've succeeded in adding almost a thousand and one days to every life saved. I prolong. I just have to write, give a story back to those who've lost theirs, and then they return to finish their narrative, alone in their lives. So I write, I don't pay attention to anything and I ignore the temptation to respond. The devil takes you by the heart, by emotion, by family, by blood, or by desire. It wants my body, the wolf wants to eat me, I laugh and I write and I know that I'm holding the thread that will save my father, I laugh at his surprise and continue our old duel between his blade and my language. Moving on. Yes, moving on. Because everything depends on me, from the plaque inscribed with the name of Aboukir in the north to the eucalyptus trees in the south. Everything is connected to my fist and I pull the cord toward the sky. I didn't take a wife, I have no family, I have no son—a horrible reflection—so that I could keep my promise and fulfill my duty. I would have dreamed of an even more powerful story, a monstrous caesarian, that could have brought my mother back, but that idea was suffocating, impossible. I have no memory of my mother. The wind wiped out any trace of her and her face is like the surface of a choppy body of water. I remember sitting in the house as a child while all around me they lamented the dishonor of my recluse mother's rejection and her face was removed and replaced by her two hands. I asked Hadjer about it but she answered me with cunning, concern, almost pettiness: I was her son and she didn't want me to climb back any further than her own stomach. My mother is a hollow, a feather, a dead weight when I think of possible women, a silence. I've never missed her because she never existed. I *tried one day to write her notebook, but it had no subject, just scribbles, the writing was tired, asleep. Let's move on, and quickly.*

The essential is that right now I know I have to write the most powerful talisman, the Zabor, *in several notebooks that I will place wherever necessary to save Aboukir, its hiding inhabitants, its beliefs, trees, storks, and cemeteries. I never thought everything would come at the same time: my father's potential death, the fire of the senses, the wind turned mute, a jaw, the Dajjal of the end of our world announced by the Holy Book, one-eyed and seductive, emperor of end times, the Christian Antichrist. In the burnt, gray sky, I predict the sun will come from the west this time, that there will be no cardinal points, no roads stuck to the lands, that everything will be caught in an immense whirlwind and I will be the essential crux of that confrontation. God is the wind, we mustn't insult him. But I'm not insulting him, I'm standing up to him, hidden in my blood-colored balaclava, absorbed in my writing.)* I had read absolutely everything in the village and I was waiting, a teenager, for that language to reappear in other books brought by the emigrants who returned for the summer, by teachers, buses, archives. The language came back to me sometimes loaded with novelty, sometimes it didn't come back, like lost storks. Those were vapid, boring times. Whenever I came out of a book I would stumble on my own body and fall back into gravity and the limits of meaning. With no book open on my knees or held up over my head when I was lying down, no wife, shiny lips, tides to separate with a staff, no foremast, breasts, or sweltering heat that made the refugee of the body groan. The island was a rock and the only story available was that of my father, who belabored his largesse, his lambs, and his misery under the colonizers.

Oh, how I hated his stories! The only one that escaped my grimace might have been the one about the bag of sand. According to legend, on a day of famine and typhus, during his early childhood under the colonizers, he didn't want to return home without anything in his knapsack. So he filled it with sand, went back to the house up top and went to lie down to avoid confrontation with my grandmother. At dawn, he smelled warm bread, ate some, and asked where the flour had come from. "From the bag you brought," answers the ancestor I never met, surprised. "Miracle of God!" he concluded each time, seeking pious approbation. A story that was surely stolen, I thought to myself, almost angry. But I, too, stole stories. Titles especially. Ah, how I loved those pearls with no strings attached! I had hundreds of them, then thousands. I could make a library from the back covers of books empty on the inside. Filled with sand. Like a Potemkin village for an indefatigable reader. The names of authors were details, guides, guardians at the gate. What they recounted wasn't theirs, but passed through them. "Finding is not stealing," says tradition. I had favorite stories, at the beginning. Which led to others, and so on. A thousand and one books. *Wind, Sand and Stars, Tropic of Capricorn,* which was an archipelago, *The Grapes of Wrath, The Flower Quay No Longer Answers, The Vulture Is a Patient Bird,* etc. I wandered.

And I started to write by stealing titles.

47

The night of ecstasy is important to understand. That was when I wrote my first metaphor. I was reversing the order of anxiety and night. I was illuminating as I went. Hadjer passed me in the courtyard smiling, exalted, light, bearing the most important news in the genealogy of my tribe, no branch of which really knew how to read or write. I couldn't sleep for days, I was so happy. I had just solved at once the problems of my lack of books, my bodily exhaustion from rereading the erotic passages of escapist stories, the weight of shame and guilt, and the feeling of indignity. I could bring order back to the world, write stories, escape my village and its pebble fate, encounter the invisible in its flesh, and reestablish the legend of my life from the beginning. The metaphor was like a verse that went from the body to the sky and not the other way around. It was a variation on incantation, a shortcut, a side road. I could gain time or add it to my stories.

The second night, still staggering with insomnia, I came to my final revelation: I could, through the order imposed by writing, and because I was respectful of the secret of the sacrifice, prolong lives, postpone death by writing stories. I understood that everything was connected, from writing to breathing, and that I was responsible for an immense discovery, which wasn't an accident but a revelation. My goat voice, my body, my uncircumcised penis, my orphaned status, my night terrors, everything was knotted and connected. The amulet of the storyteller who had tried to heal me, the horror of tattoos, all of it had been necessary to reach this mastery of language. I could not only prolong lives, but also give reprieve to my own, and that responsibility was universal, spread to everything I touched, everything I could see. Each detail of the village, the houses, the trees, and the names. All of it might disappear one day, slowly or abruptly, if someone didn't start to write in my tribe, in this village, in our house. This unjust fate contorts my heart with pity for every being, their ignorance, their naïveté faced with the void, their innocence. I embraced Hadjer and she squeezed me in her arms, she didn't understand but was happy like a mother, close and reliable.

A book is only sacred if it's the inventory of all things, the hand that holds and holds back, the necessary reminder before the oblivion of death. Books are pedestals, moorings. If a man stops speaking to himself in his own head, writing in his soul, he will stumble, fall ill, grow old quickly, and die. "We have told you the tales of the ancients," the Holy Book says. Because they maintain cohesion, cover the abyss of the beginning and push back the abyss of the end. I cried. *(And I'm crying now because if I stop writing my father will die, and he's completely unaware of this sacrifice of my youth, my body, my time.)*

I need a language that's even more precise, even stronger, but on the verge of ecstasy language is impossible and writing is nothing but a shiver. Have you seen how sufis describe ecstasy? With simple and almost old-fashioned words. As close as possible to the burning star, poetry is a croaking. I saw it on those three holy nights when I started to write the next day in my new notebooks bought that very morning. And since then I've filled an enormous number of notebooks that I've buried all over. I visited the sick, the dying, candidates for death, sweating children, and women ripped open by birth. My reputation grew and caught the attention of the devil and the wind. My father laughed mirthlessly, my aunt was proud, my half brothers were jealous of my kingdom, but the poor villagers continually turned to me as a last resort. I saved hundreds of them, adding a thousand and one days nearly every time, made the island habitable, and Poll was flamboyant in the night, phosphorescent when he read. My gift came with mockery but I didn't care. Why do I write? Because I witness, I am the guardian, I chase death away from my people because they are important and worthy of eternity. God writes, I do too. (*The wind is outraged and tries to make me shut my mouth. It attacked me with the knives of my father, my half brothers, Hamza and the odious story of his name, the gendarmes, and the slander. The same scattering wind. My father is dying but he's the only one who senses, perhaps, that I'm holding his hand and that without my sacrifice as a perpetual writer, sitting for hours in the same place in this bedroom, he will die and become a blank space between two dates. In the agony that lays him bare, forces him out of his bones one by one, makes him hold his breath until the Last Judgment, I see him and forgive him. He had no other story to tell but his own.*

And the door smashes to pieces because the wind couldn't let me win.)

48

(Writing is a tattoo and, behind the tattoo, there is a body waiting to be freed.)

They stopped me on the seventh day. I was brought to the gendarmerie, where they treated me kindly but firmly. The truth is that they ignored me for almost half a day because they didn't know what to do with me, then they put me in a cell and left me there for a night. From time to time, a gendarme would come to examine me, ask questions about my father, share his condolences or gravely shake his head. They asked imam Senoussi about me, who tried to calm their fervor and explained that sadness is a wind that can provoke insanity, but that there was nothing blasphemous in my scattered notebooks or the cramped handwriting I had scrawled on the walls, plaques, doorways, sidewalks, and every possible surface for days on end. Mysterious signs to a layperson, tall and radiant capital letters, incredible excerpts and fake novel titles, with dates, numbers, moons, and names. I had sprinkled them everywhere. In addition to this excess, I had left bags of my notebooks at the entrance of the village, to the south, to the east, to the west. I had put some under the prayer rugs at the mosque, on nearly every tomb at the Bounouila cemetery and in the Christian cemetery where covert drinkers had watched me with curiosity. I had given some to children outside the school, I had placed some in hair salons and in the village's administrative buildings. I had even managed to pile them up outside the hammams and in the mausoleum of Sidi Bend'hiba, the saint of Aboukir. They were absolutely everywhere, pages flapping in the early September breeze, used as wrappers by the peanut sellers, folded into planes by children, carried into the fields and stuck to tree trunks.

"Damage to public property" was the charge that would have been brought against me had imam Senoussi not intervened. He ordered them to let me go. I was stunned, smiling indecently, as though victorious.

It was a strange week for me, hallucinatory, free but joyous. Like the end of a season, an apotheosis for my writings as they commemorated the seventh day of Hadj Brahim's death, accompanied into the afterlife by a thousand sheep. I had spread my pages nearly one by one so that everything was touched, reached, or amalgamated. A sort of leafy deluge, strewn in lines. People had seen me all over, rushing around with a gray bag to scatter my writings, in silence, serious and rushed, trying to unite the outside of everything and to spread the virtue of my law to all. *"Zabor eddah el babor!"* yelled the laughing children who harassed me. But I smiled at them, finally free and exposed, relieved.

This undertaking humiliated my tribe even more, and my aunt cried as she did the day when the family that was supposed to ask for her hand hadn't come. Busy with condolences, they ignored me at the beginning, they tried to reason with me, my cousins tried to shut me in the house down below. But it was in vain, I knew what I had to do and I accomplished it with joy, gravity, seriousness, and happiness. To free Djemila, I needed a greater freedom to share with her, to offer her. Creation is a book, rendered page by page. My psalms had to be read everywhere, exposed. My father now nothing more than a stone, I was the transparent river that he lay in and quietly ballasted.

49

The wind on the night when they snatched me from my writing caused horrible damages: burned vineyards, destroyed houses, toppled streetlights. Three people died, buried under collapsed walls, and two people were electrocuted. Aboukir emerged with a lacerated face, wrinkled and gray. Everything is simultaneously familiar and as though suffering from an extreme drought. People still feel a species solidarity in the face of cataclysms, but gradually return to their routines. These have been the most violent and persistent Smaïmes for decades, blowing away their share of the elderly and the fruit. But this is not a dead place, it has merely been reduced. I feel unbalanced, as if on the verge of a birth. The sky is luminous again like joy, high and blue enough to fill your lungs, new. But it contrasts with the trace of everything else. The red sand still dulls the colors of things, but is starting to wane like a dying ember. They've piled it up everywhere with their constant sweeping, but we know that it'll just be blown somewhere else in a few days, little by little. It will come back from the south, over the clouds.

I don't know whether to recount what happened in detail. It's no longer important that I write now, in fact. I'm no longer responsible, neither witness nor guardian of any secret. I was delivered from my fate nonchalantly, almost negligently. My father is dead. I'm not responsible for anyone. Language won, it is everywhere, bark and ivy, nuance and condensation. It doesn't need me anymore. I wanted writing to embody a form of speech, which is to say a face, faces, of living beings standing together around a fire.

When they smashed my door, the wind rushed in, raging, and scattered everything with its teeth. Hadjer came in with it, face obliterated, along with a few of my half brothers and neighbors. They found me with numerous notebooks that the whirlwind started to mix into its current. They snatched me from my task and I found myself lost in a sort of red haze made of sand and cold, pushed from behind toward the hill, the house up top. They were yelling, Hadjer was crying. I don't know how, as in a bad dream, I found myself crashing into dogs sick with fear, tree trunks, then suddenly I was in my father's bedroom. I learned he had been asking for me for a long time before he passed away. They had sent family looking for me, cousins, then Abdel and my aunt, but I had refused to open the door. They had yelled, tried keys, then decided to break down the door.

The house up top was full of cries and plates and the smells of cooking meat. They grabbed hold of me to look me in the eye and hurl insults at me, women crying as though warning all of creation. Abdel was standing there, withdrawn, his eyes full of hate, like the day I pushed him into the well *(no, I never pushed him, he slipped and fell)*. There was a yellowish light, the body had shrunk, now a heap under the sheets. They were all pushing me to embrace him. He had asked to see me all night during his death throes, had wanted to say something to me up until the last moment. Everyone yelled the same thing at me, the same reproach. I fled trampling over bodies and shoes. The wind was still going and warped the funeral tent they had set up despite the inclement weather, in the small clearing between the eucalyptus trees. They tried to limit the sand's intrusions but it was everywhere. In my mouth, my lungs, my pockets, under my skin. When they had forced me out of our house, leaving the wind there, I had managed to grab my last notebook, the one that had delayed me, that had made me forget time and led me astray, perhaps.

I decided to scatter everything on my way down the hill, to repopulate the island with my pages, to make this the final revelation and transform the very flesh of Aboukir into a manuscript. Creation is a book? My village and its people are notebooks, talismans, prescriptions against oblivion. I made my decision as I left the funeral. Unshakable, letting loose a torrent within me. I felt my shoulders straighten and unknot. Then I ran through the streets and the fields to make my writings public, read by every possible wind. I went back to our house down below, I reflected, and then, at the end of the third day, while they were commemorating his death, I took the first bag and walked toward the entrances of the village and set down the few pages I had left, my talismans. Then toward the south. The west, the mosque, the schools. Everywhere, I scattered my secret. Unveiling my gift in the nakedness of daylight, revealing my entire story. Sometimes, children would follow me, yelling my name, *"Zabor eddah el babor!"* Other times curious people would bend down to collect the pages and try to read the dialect, at once so familiar and so foreign, free and like ivy, present but quiet. It contained drawings, alphabets distorted by two temptations of language, attempts to create masses of writing, whirlings of wind sculpted into capital letters. Memories of the Holy Book, warped by the interrogation of mediation and possible variations. Names of the dead, dates and numbers returned to their essence as gestures, fingers, and hands.

They had given me a book—"We made the mountains and birds his accomplices, who sing hymns with him," the Holy Book says—and now I'm returning it. Little by little I feel delivered, acquitted, free to keep quiet and shed the weight of my responsibility. Maybe I'm wrong. Like Yunus under the tree, body naked and trembling, I understand that Nineveh is saved without me, far from me. I don't know. The devil tried one last, feeble assault: Hamza (or Abdel?) alerted the gendarmerie about my blasphemous texts, my insane writings, and they arrested me to interrogate me. They let me leave the next day, at the hour of the Friday prayer, after imam Senoussi had seen to my fate. All the charges against me were dropped, but it will be enough, I think, for my half brothers to allege insanity and disinherit me. I had guessed their plan from the start. They forbade me to attend discussions about the inheritance. Hadjer is on her own this time, as when faced with her wrinkles. I went back home and, under my footsteps, in our neighborhood, pages dragged in my wake for days.

I'm not responsible for the village. But perhaps for something vaster. Will I still read and write? I don't know. I'm certain I've found the most effective ruse against death. The most efficient. But I have no more desire to save others, at least not everyone. I feel light, delivered from an immense responsibility. That language liberated me, but liberty doesn't mean anything in solitude.

Children still followed me to the entrance of our house with the smashed door. In the street, vigilant or compassionate, numerous women leaned out of their windows to watch me. Some in scarves, others, younger, hair in the wind and eyes squinting in the bright light unfamiliar to their pupils. I thought I could smell their perfumes. The majority didn't know what to do, how to express their condolences, they remained forbidden and mute. Others were there, curious to see the young man who had provoked the scandal with his scribblings and who had just been released by the gendarmes. Beautiful decapitated heads, bodies dislocated by the laws forcing them to be invisible, lands where language is still a murmur. That's where I have to find new stories. I picked up my pace, felt another gaze. Djemila was there, too, on the other side of the wall, watching me from her window. She signaled to me and her daughter Nebbia came out to find me, a basket in her hand. They knew I had nothing to eat in my aunt's absence. Djemila's face was beautiful, calm, and it was as though I recognized someone absent. The little girl handed me the basket and then stood there staring at me for a long time before running off. I thanked her mother with a smile: her gesture will not escape the rumors, because it was dared in front of other women. Like a sign. Suddenly I had an idiotic idea: I would no longer be afraid to sleep at night, if I could just sleep next to her! Her body that I had almost never seen would be my parapet above the void.

The door to our house down below was wobbly, broken. The sand was everywhere, like the cadaver of a monster, dead and vanquished. I wandered through the dirty rooms and my bedroom now empty of notebooks. In the courtyard, everything seemed buried and dried up except the lemon tree. A green-and-yellow bundle resembling a bud. I went out and sat on the doorstep, my body aching.

50

I wanted to show my father my perfect notebook, the final one, in which I achieved the
equilibrium of blood and senses, the site of my revelation, my body finally repaired by a precise and sovereign
language. I wanted to tell him that I was ready to heal
death itself. I wanted to swear to him that I had encountered nearly everyone in my writing who cursed night:
his father, his mother, his great-grandmother, but also
the first ancestor who was a midwife and a rug weaver,
all those who had preceded us. That I had reconstituted
the history of our tribe, that evil had been vanquished,
and famine too, that I could repair the hollows, the
blanks, the absences in our story, and that everything is

linked, dependent on me, on each person, on each word in my language, in my writing. I had imagined running to the top of the hill, but it was too late when they brought me, pushed me from behind.

They told me that he died asking for me, while I was sinking deeper into the abyss of my salvation, while I was trying to hold his hand in that nocturnal hell, while the wind separated us, erasing his footsteps and my words. They watched me enter, insults and lamentations already flying. Hadjer herself was cold as a lapidary stone, eyes red. My half brothers were there, lined up like tomb-stones, and I looked at his cadaver. I noted the droop of his jaw, the traces in his skin of the cold emptiness of the sky. They had closed his eyes, he seemed to be sleeping, but the way objects do, refusing all conversation. I kissed his forehead and was surprised by the cold of his skin. I cried, later. Out of anger. Because there was something unjust about it, someone cheated behind my back by speeding up the hands of the clock. It should have ended differently. Never ended. He should have at least read the notebook, had the opportunity. It's my best notebook, elegant, short, sober in style, refined until it looked like a dune. It tells some of my mother's story, and an even older story that was poorly written, formerly incomplete.

I wrote the most important parts of what I know and of the art that this language has given to me: the necessary equilibrium between evocation and life, the bond, so hard to break, between my writing and reparation. I don't understand how my apotheosis missed its date.

What error did I commit? Is it that I wasn't able to write fast enough at the crucial moment? I would have needed him to hold out just another two or three days, another few hours within the yellow, mocking wind, and I would have vanquished death, I swear. The wind would have stopped howling, pushed aside like an old wolf limping in the valley of the west, I would have succeeded and my father would have been able to read a beautiful story, well written, balanced and dense like verses. I should have written faster. He should have believed me, believed in my gift.

It's a nearly perfect story, especially because the goal of the quest and its final fulfillment are precise and glorious. A story in which my brother is my brother, my mother is still alive, my father returns after a lengthy absence and welcomes me with a rare smile that is not a blade. It's all written on the first page of the notebook.

"Good God, my brother!" my half brother says, "your tale is marvelous!"

"What comes next is even more surprising," I respond, "and you'll agree if death decides to let me live another day so I can tell you about the following night." Death, who had listened to Zabor with pleasure, thinks: "I'll wait until tomorrow; I'll kill him as soon as I've heard the end of his tale."

Oran, Perugia, Tunis

My thanks to Nedra and Karim Ben Smail, who've proved that Tunisia is the vastest country in Africa and their house the vastest in Tunisia.

To the people of the Civitella Ranieri Foundation for the interlude in paradise.